POSSESSED:

DELIVERANCE

BOOK I

The Tiger's Eye Demon

Sara McDowell

HORROR PUBLISHER

Beverly Hills Triangle, 9701 Wilshire Blvd, Suite 1000, Beverly Hills, CA 90212

horrorpublisher.com

POSSESSED: DELIVERANCE
Book I
The Tiger's Eye Demon
Sara McDowell

First published in the United States
in 2025 by Horror Publisher

POSSESSED:

DELIVERANCE

BOOK I

The Tiger's Eye Demon

Sara McDowell

CHAPTER 1

Siobhan couldn't stop thinking about it.

It had been on her mind since her wedding last month, but for some reason the thoughts were getting stronger and more persistent and she couldn't shake them off anymore.

She pulled up to her modest house, listening to the rain pelt on the soft top of her Jeep. The old black rig's door made a loud thud as she slammed it shut and made her way up the steps to her house.

The front door creaked its familiar creak; a balm to her ears, the sound of home. After shutting the door behind her, she made her way to the kitchen, where Adam busily prepared their dinner.

"I hope T-bones sound good. They were on sale today, and I couldn't pass them up," he said.

"I can't wait," Siobhan replied impatiently as she hung her purse on the hook near the pantry.

"How was your day?" Adam asked as Siobhan put her arm around his waist and pushed on her toes to kiss him.

"Okay. You?" she replied quickly. She bounded with a spring in her step. It whispered to her from upstairs. It called to her, and it embedded its image deep in her mind.

"It was just another day," he said. "We're making

progress."

Siobhan smiled and bit the inside of her cheek. She ran her clammy hands down her shorts.

"Do you like being at that place?" she asked, stepping backward toward the staircase, trying to hide her haste. She clenched and unclenched her fists, wringing out impatience with each clasp.

"Sure," Adam said as he shrugged. He closed the seasoning jar and washed his hands. "It's work. Derek told me I'll get a raise soon." He sent a wink Siobhan's way.

"I'm happy for you! That's great!" she exclaimed. She took a deep breath and blew it out audibly as she took one more step away from the small kitchen.

"I'm a mess. Would you mind if I took a shower while you do this?" she said, jerking her thumb backward toward the staircase leading to their bedroom.

It awaited her. It whispered to her. It called to her.

"Nope," he said. She took off upstairs barely hearing him say how great she looked. She took the stairs two at a time, her ponytail bouncing softly against her back.

It waited for her, upstairs.

Siobhan turned on the shower, keeping her eyes on it. She laser-focused her gaze on the box as she strode toward her nightstand. She picked up the strange wedding gift she'd gotten last month.

It hadn't included a card, and unlike the other gifts, it was not addressed to *The Kellers*.

Helen, Siobhan's best friend and maid of honor, insisted the necklace hadn't been from her. She hadn't seen anyone put the small package wrapped in a simple piece of white paper on the stack of gifts at their wedding reception.

The small package stood out like a sore thumb among the other gifts wrapped in silver and floral paper. Siobhan's name stood out written on the white wrapping paper with a black permanent marker. Inside the plain white box, a crystal rested on a bed of cotton. A quick Google search had told her it was a tiger's eye.

Intricately wrapped with gold wire in beautiful swirls and attached to a gold chain, the crystal stared back at her in its stunning nature. The first time Siobhan saw it, it took her breath away.

But today was different. She needed it. She wanted it. And it wanted her to have it, and she knew it.

She had been compelled to bring it home after the wedding and own it, but until today, she could always stop the nagging thoughts in her mind telling her to wear it.

It didn't even fit her simplistic style.

Siobhan picked up the necklace, pulled it out of the box, and put it on. Her entire being felt soothed—she'd needed this all day for some strange and inexplicable reason. She let out a deep breath.

The golden-colored crystal had warmed like it had its own heartbeat, maybe even its own soul. She lifted it off her chest and looked at it. It belonged to her now. While she'd given this necklace space in her mind over the past month, she'd never been consumed by this gift until today. She couldn't put her finger on why she hadn't put it on sooner.

As soon as she had the thought, she forgot she had put it on like it had been there forever.

It sat against her skin like it had found its home. Its perfect weight and size, resting on her chest, forced an attachment to form, sending vibrations throughout her body. The unexpected soothing nature seeped into her body.

Siobhan took a quick but steaming hot shower, constantly stealing downward glances at her necklace. When she finished, she wrung the water out of her blonde hair and stole a glance at herself in the mirror. She stared at the necklace and cocked her head to the side. She admired how it looked against her bronzed skin.

She put on some pajama shorts and a T-shirt and brushed her wet hair.

She flipped the light off and smiled as she glanced down at her necklace and made her way downstairs. Outside, Adam stood outside watching the steaks on the grill with his arms crossed over his broad chest.

"Long day?" he asked as she sat in a chair outside. The humid, rainy air smelled of dirt and the ozone of a hot summer day. The scorched grass in their backyard took a beating from the rain, causing it to churn into a pleasant, green scent that clung to the thick and muggy air.

"So long. I like owning the gym, but it's overwhelming most of the time. I need more employees, but this is all so new to me," Siobhan said, enjoying the time outside. It had been a record-hot summer and this rainstorm had taken the temperature down more than ten degrees.

"Yeah. Being a business owner is tough. But you can do it. Give it time to get used to it," Adam said

"It feels familiar since I managed it before we bought it," she said. "But it's different being the owner."

"You. You bought it. You don't have to give me credit," Adam said.

Siobhan smiled. "Well, technically, yes, but your name is on the loan, too." She sighed. "The workload is a lot, and speaking of loans, the debt is making me nervous and stressed. If I fail, we will lose everything—even this house," she said nervously. "I couldn't do it without you, you know?"

"It's still your gym. I'll give support where needed. And I'll do my best to keep money coming in so you can breathe a little bit.

Derek is the best, and he's happy with my work, so stop worrying and do what you know how to do," he said.

"Thanks, Adam. I have the one interview tomorrow, and I'm hoping it goes well," she said a little timidly. "Do you have any advice? I feel like I need you there with me," she continued.

"It's your first interview. It'll get easier," Adam said, trying to be supportive. Siobhan often needed reassurance on her business decisions. "You need to trust your judgment. You don't need me there, Siobhan."

She nodded as thunder rolled in the background. She spoke into its rumbling. "It's hot out here today for sprinkling rain," Siobhan said as the dark clouds continued to spit out droplets of musky-scented water.

"Sure is. But it is July. The rain will always remind me of our wedding," he said with a smile.

"Me too," she said with a flashback of her in her sleek satin wedding gown dotted with water droplets. She imagined she had been wearing the necklace at her wedding, even though she had worn no jewelry at the event. "Hopefully, it'll cool off some by September. That way, we can have a party here for your birthday." You still want to try to make that happen?"

"Sure!" Adam said. "I need to make sure I get this grass growing better before a party, though. I don't have a green thumb like you do. Maybe it needs fertilizer. Or I could mow it again."

Siobhan laughed. "Mowing it won't change it from brown to green. Let's water it more. Notice," Siobhan said as she motioned toward the rosemary bush, "this is still alive."

"Yeah, yeah," he said.

She stole a glance at the rosemary bush she admired so much.

"But you're probably right," Adam said as he picked up a large meat fork and flipped their steaks on the grill. "I should water the lawn more."

The steaks made a satisfying sizzling sound, and the smell started to make Siobhan hungry.

"You're wearing the mystery gift," Adam observed once they started eating.

"Yep. I decided it was time to try it on. I love it," she said as her lips curled into a wide grin.

"It looks great on you. You should keep wearing it," he said, lifting his gaze to her blue eyes.

"I will…"

BAM!

Siobhan jumped at the sudden sound.

Adam looked up, surprised, and furrowed his brow in confusion. "That's weird."

"What happened?" she asked, turning around.

"A bird." Adam set his fork and knife down. He stood and

made his way to the dead bird.

"Oh, poor thing. It landed in the rosemary bush," Siobhan said with a pout.

"Are you more upset about the dead bird or that it landed in your plant?" Adam asked playfully.

"I don't like either, to be honest. I always hate it when birds fly into windows."

"Well," Adam said, shrugging. "Memento mori."

"I know. It sucks he had to die by smashing into our house."

"It's a bird, Siobhan," Adam said as he returned to his seat.

"I know, but it—"

"*It's just a bird*!" he snapped.

Siobhan recoiled.

"I'm sorry," he said. "I shouldn't have snapped. I don't even… this…" He motioned toward the black bird and shook his head.

"It's okay," she said soothingly. Adam rarely lost his temper and snapped. "Let's finish eating."

He stabbed a big piece of meat with his fork and lifted it off the plate to look at it. "Now, tell me how well the sauna is working since I rewired it for you." He grinned and popped the meat in his mouth.

Siobhan smiled and proceeded to detail how much better

the sauna worked now, and how many people were using it. They were telling their friends about it and the new infrared lighting Adam had installed. "It's pretty much perfect," she said.

"Like you," he said as he winked at her.

When the couple finished their dinner, Siobhan did the dishes while Adam buried the dead bird in the back of their yard.

The storm worsened as they got ready for bed. Black clouds began rolling in, and the sky darkened on the horizon as heavy rain pelted the windows.

"It's getting after it," Adam said as they made their way to bed.

"It is," she said.

"Good luck tomorrow." Adam pulled the covers back from his side of the bed. He took off his watch and climbed in.

"Thank you. Interviewing is so new, and you won't be there to help," she said as she flopped into bed.

"You'll pick the right person. You know people. I prefer tools to humans.".

"Maybe. I'll text you if he's the right person." She adjusted to get comfortable in the bed Adam had when they met.

"Okay. Goodnight," Adam said, closing his eyes.

"Night."

*

BAM!

Siobhan woke with a start and sat straight up in bed.

"Adam," she whispered. She picked up her phone off her bedside table to check the time. 3:33 a.m. *What the hell was that?* She had heard something.

She flung the covers off and glanced out the window in their room. Raindrops struck through the streetlamp's golden glow. *What had made that loud bang? It was a loud bang, right? How could Adam have slept through that?* He would wake up to a mouse sneezing in the neighbor's yard.

She tip-toed around upstairs, mindful not to turn on any lights as the rain beat lightly against the roof. Nothing seemed out of place.

She got back into bed, and her hand unconsciously covered the tiger's eye crystal resting on her chest. It had a subtle warmth to it.

BAM!

Siobhan jumped and gasped.

Okay. Calm down, Siobhan, she told herself as she stared at Adam's curly black hair in stark contrast to his white pillow. *It's nothing. He'd wake up if it were something.* She tried to calm herself down by trying to convince herself that a tree branch had hit the house in the wind.

She had no trouble falling asleep amid the slowly creeping fear surrounding her.

The next morning, Siobhan got up with her alarm at five o'clock, leaving Adam asleep in bed.

She dashed down the stairs and made coffee. Still muggy from last night's storm, the morning air smelled fresh. As she leaned against her counter in the kitchen, holding the warm mug in her hands, she replayed the previous night's event. The two loud bangs pounded in her head, leaving a boom in her ears. Adam's heavy footsteps on the stairs pierced her thoughts.

"Good morning," Adam said as he came into the kitchen. He yawned and poured himself a cup of coffee. "Did you sleep well?"

"I…" Siobhan started. Then she took a sip of her coffee, trying to clear her head. "Yes. Weird night."

"Yeah, with the crazy rainstorm."

"Right," she said, looking into her mug.

"So, I have to get everything installed at the big house on the hill, but let me know how your interview goes," Adam said.

"I will. It's at eight a.m."

BAM!

He had to have heard that one. Siobhan looked at Adam through her eyelashes. Adam sipped his coffee and slowly lowered his mug as his eyes burned into hers.

"Again?" he said.

"Again! So, you heard that last night, too?" she asked, standing straighter.

"No. I mean, another bird slammed into the window, like it did when we were eating dinner," he said, his voice dripping with condescension.

"Are you sure that's what it was?" Siobhan asked uncertainly.

"I'm positive," Adam sighed. "Come on; let's go look."

"I'm taking this with me," she said as she lifted her mug.

"I'd expect nothing less," Adam grinned.

He slid open the door to the patio and stepped outside as Siobhan followed.

"Yep. See. Dead bird. Oh wow. Yeah, there are three out here," he said.

"That's what I heard last night," Siobhan said. A chill ran down the back of her spine. "That's four birds into the same window in less than twelve hours. Does that happen?"

"It must because it did. You can go inside if you want. I'll bury these with the other one toward the back of the yard," Adam said as he waved her off, motioning toward the door.

"Okay. Hey, thanks for taking care of this," she said, shaking her head. The hyper-awareness of her necklace resting against the skin of her chest beat through her veins.

"For sure…" he muttered as he made his way around the house toward the garage.

Back inside, Siobhan shivered as goosebumps popped up on her skin. Closing the door behind her, a cool breeze flew over her, bringing a mild, musky smell with it.

Slightly unbalanced, she topped off her cup of coffee and sat on the couch in the living room. She sipped the hot black liquid, which acted as a salve to her frayed nerves. "I love coffee," she said out loud, resting her head on the back of the couch.

"Me too," an older female voice said. Siobhan slowly lowered her mug and put it on the coffee table.

"Hello?" she asked out loud. She stood and made her way to the kitchen. "Is someone here?" she asked.

Eerie silence that took up space filled her house. She stood on her tiptoes and squinted as she looked out the window over the sink. Adam knelt at the back of the yard, a dark shadow against the dimness of the early morning light as he dug into the damp earth with a shovel.

Siobhan shuffled back into the living room and checked their TV. *That was strange.* Maybe the weird night with all the dead birds had her on edge. She grabbed another cup of coffee and tried to shake off the cold chill that kept creeping up her spine.

In the creeping silence, the faintest whisper of a click resonated through the house. The sound remained so quiet that it did not register as a concern.

Click click click

CHAPTER 2

As Siobhan drove to The Flex, she marveled at how the storm had arrived and cleared out as quickly as it had shown up. At seven in the morning, the heat of the July sun had already become noticeable. Not a drop of dew remained on the grass, although the air held a still dampness and the soft scent of clean rain.

Siobhan scanned her key card and pushed open the heavy glass door. Already a busy morning, she smiled and let out a breath. Thursdays tended to be busier, and fantastic for her business.

She set her purse under the counter near the safe and pressed the power button on the computer. She checked her schedule on her phone.

Eight a.m.: Interview with Jesus.

She let out a breath.

The first person to respond to her ad looking for help had been a man named Jesus Velasquez. She needed someone to help with the simple but time-consuming day-to-day chores. They were becoming too numerous for her and Helen to handle on their own.

While the computer booted up, Siobhan checked the locker rooms and stayed busy. As soon as she stepped around the counter, a woman pulled on the door. Since the gym didn't open for nonmembers until eight a.m., Siobhan reached over and opened the door to let her in.

"We don't open until eight unless you're a member," she said.

"Okay. Thanks," the woman replied as she turned to leave.

"Wait," Siobhan said. "I'm already here. Do you want to come in and sign up?"

"That would be great," she said.

"I'm the owner, Siobhan." She reached out her hand.

"Melina," the woman said, not making eye contact. Her gaze drifted to Siobhan's hand a little too long before she gave it one single pump.

"What kind of membership are you looking for?" Siobhan asked as she made her way to the computer. "Unlimited use means you'll have access to the sauna and tanning bed and all classes. Or you can pick and choose which of those you want. Here's a menu you can choose from. Prices are listed here." She flipped the laminated paper around for Melina to look at and pointed to the right side of the page. "The packages are here, with a box around what's included."

Melina tilted her head toward the laminated page, but her eyes darted around the gym. She put her hands on the counter but withdrew them and balled them into fists before grabbing the shoulder strap of her large tote bag.

Melina's wavy black hair fell almost to her waist, cascading over her shoulders. Her sharply beautiful, angular features had a shroud of melancholy laced into them. The cat-eye liquid eyeliner had been impeccably applied. She wore all black, looking sleek in the tank top and bike shorts.

"I want the classes and the gym," Melina said coolly.

"I recently upgraded the sauna with an infrared light, and it—"

"No. No, thank you," Melina interrupted as she waved her hand. She glanced at Siobhan's necklace and curled one side of her mouth into a small, lopsided smile.

The differences in the two personalities created a barrier of tension as their energies rubbed strangely against each other.

"Yeah. Um… Alright," Siobhan said. She wiped her face with her shoulder and grabbed a new key card to program it. She slid the menu off the counter and back to its place behind her computer. "Thanks for choosing The Flex," Siobhan said as she handed Melina the card.

"Yep," Melina replied as she flung her long hair over her shoulder and spun on her heel.

"Do you want me to show you around?" Siobhan asked.

Melina paused. "Nope," she said, keeping her back to Siobhan. She adjusted her large and heavy black tote on her shoulder. "Nice necklace," she said in a monotone voice as she meandered toward the women's locker room.

Siobhan flattened her palm over the tiger's eye crystal necklace.

Bleep.

Siobhan picked up her phone.

Bleep.

Helen had texted. She indicated she would be there to help cover the front desk before the first interview. Siobhan breathed a sigh of relief.

After thanking Helen via text, she leaned on the counter with her forearms and jumped back.

It felt like sticky, wet cobwebs had been built on the surface of the glass counter. Siobhan put her hand flat on it and withdrew it. She rubbed her right palm. All the hair on her arm stood at attention, and she tingled like tiny mites were wiggling around on her skin.

She reached under the counter and grabbed the cleaner and a towel. She aggressively sprayed and wiped down the glass countertop. A gym-goer came in. She recognized him as one of the regulars.

"Good morning," he said.

"Morning," she replied with a forced smile as she continued to clean the counter. She replaced the towel and cleaner under the counter, then leaned on it again.

She glanced at her arms, sure that they were covered in..

what? Invisible cobwebs? She turned her hands over, inspecting them as the strange tingling sensation started to subside. The little mites that didn't exist crawled as they wrapped her whole forearm in discomfort.

Siobhan let out a deep breath. She reached up to stretch, and her hand skimmed the tiger's eye necklace Melina had commented on. It had warmed ever so slightly, and she chastised herself for noticing.

Of course, it's warm, dummy. It's against your skin.

She shook her head and grabbed the laundry basket with dirty towels in it. She kept it near the front desk for people to drop off overnight, but today, she used it as an excuse to stay busy.

She caught a glimpse of Melina out of the corner of her eye. Her long black hair had been pulled in a tight ponytail, and she stood by the mats laid down for stretching; her slim, pale legs were several shades lighter than Siobhan's sun-kissed skin.

Melina locked eyes with Siobhan for a moment before narrowing her eyes. She lowered herself to the floor and started stretching with her back to Siobhan.

Siobhan shook her head a few times. She felt goosebumps radiating up both arms, mingling with the slight discomfort she still had from leaning on the counter.

When she'd finished sorting the towels, she made her way back to the front. Helen stood at the front desk using the computer.

"Hey!" Siobhan said excitedly, happy to see her friend.

"Hi!" Helen said as she reached one arm out to wrap Siobhan in a half-hug. "Have you had enough coffee yet?" "Is there ever enough?" Siobhan asked, pressing her head into Helen's red curls as she stepped into the hug.

"I will make us some," Helen said, grabbing the pot.

"You know how to become employee of the month."

"Since I'm the only employee, that won't be difficult," Helen joked as she grabbed the empty coffee pot from the back counter and bounded away.

Siobhan glanced at the time on her phone. 7:39 a.m. She wrung her hands as she waited, her dry mouth desperately needing coffee. She bounced one foot and put her head in one hand to check on members' key card scan errors.

Helen returned in silence and finished making the coffee. She poured herself a mug and slid one across the back counter toward Siobhan.

"Thanks," Siobhan muttered, not lifting her head.

A tap on the front door snapped Siobhan's attention to it. A Hispanic man stood outside, cupping his hands around his face, and peered into the tinted glass door, his eyes darting around.

She pushed open the door with one hand. "Hi. Are you Jesus?" she asked, holding the heavy door open for him.

"Yes, I am," he said with a thick accent. "I'm sorry I'm so

early."

"No, please don't apologize," Siobhan said. "I'm Siobhan, and I prefer early over late. This is Helen. She's covering the front desk today until her class."Helen set down the coffee pot, rattling it loudly and then catching it. She extended her hand, eyes wide and sparkling.

"It's very nice to meet you," Jesus said as he shook her hand, never looking away from Helen's eyes. "Maybe I will take one of your classes sometime," he added with a big, crooked smile.

Helen swallowed. "I hope you do," she said hastily as she lowered her eyes and pushed some of her thick red curls behind her ear. "Would you like some coffee, Jesus?"

"That sounds great. Thank you," Jesus said, offering yet another crooked smile and a dimple on one side.

Helen's cheeks had morphed into a slight pink hue under the scatter of freckles that dotted her pale face.

"Are you ready?" Siobhan asked as Helen handed Jesus a paper cup of coffee.

He nodded. "Let's go," he said, then took a sip of the hot black liquid. "Perfect coffee, Helen," he added as he snuck one last glace at her.

"Well, that was fast!" Helen exclaimed as Siobhan rounded the corner.

"He's a hard worker and reliable and really wants the job. I offered, he accepted, and he starts tomorrow," Siobhan said, smiling as she motioned toward Jesus.

"Thank you, Siobhan. It was nice to meet you, Helen. I will be here tomorrow at seven to start. Will you be here?" he asked, staring at her.

Helen smiled and blinked several times in rapid succession. "I don't normally come in on Fridays until ten, but I can make an exception this time. If it's okay with the boss," Helen replied, sipping her coffee and holding her mug with both hands. She returned Jesus' gaze, her eyes not straying from his.

"It's fine with me," Siobhan said. "I have some errands to run, and nothing opens until eight. So, if you can get Jesus started tomorrow, I would be grateful!" Siobhan said, letting out a sigh in a long breath.

"Well, it's a date then," Helen said as she raised one eyebrow. Her entire face blushed, and she grinned ear to ear.

"See you tomorrow," Jesus said with a smile and nod.

"I'm glad that went well," Helen said as soon as the door closed behind Jesus. Her gaze lingered on him as he rushed into the parking lot.

"Me too. And hey, thanks for offering to get him going tomorrow. I appreciate you going above and beyond," Siobhan said.

"No problem," Helen said coyly, a smile curling up her lips.

Siobhan smiled and shook her head, elbowing her friend. "He seems very excited about being here. Your first class today is at ten, right?" Siobhan asked.

Helen nodded. "I guess I should go set up my music and equipment. It's a cardio-weight training circuit today. Want to try it?"

"Maybe next time. I woke up in the middle of the night to birds killing themselves on my dining room window," she said with a yawn.

"Really?" Helen said, crossing her arms over her chest. "Birds? As in more than one?"

"Yeah," Siobhan said. She took a sip of coffee. "We have lived in that house for six months, and that has never happened before."

"Weird," Helen remarked as she wrinkled her forehead.

Siobhan nodded pursing her lips. "Adam didn't even hear the ones that hit the window overnight."

"Probably just because of the storm. Don't birds act weird during storms?" Helen asked, shrugging.

"Yeah. That's probably all it was," Siobhan said, a cold chill running down the back of her legs.

"Oh!" Helen said perking up. "This counter is sticky today.

I cleaned it off, and it seems fine now, but it had something wet on it."

Siobhan tilted her head to the side. "I cleaned it off right before you came in."

Helen laughed as she shrugged. "I have no idea. Maybe you could ask Adam. Or Derek. Or, maybe it was gunky."

"Yeah," Siobhan said, biting her lower lip.

"See you after my class, boss?" Helen said as she grabbed her phone, making her way around the counter toward the classroom at the back of the gym.

"I'll be here! And stop calling me 'boss'!" she said to Helen's back as she leaned over the counter.

Helen waved her hand with her phone in it and kept walking.

Siobhan leaned onto the completely normal counter she remembered. She absent-mindedly set her hand on the necklace again.

"That was fun!" Helen exclaimed as she rounded the corner with a spring in her step.

"Are you done?" Siobhan asked, looking up from the computer.

"Yep. I had two classes today, back-to-back," Helen said as

she bounded around the front counter. "Hey, you should get someone to teach yoga. I'd do it, but I don't know anything about that. Some of the people in my class asked about it today."

"Do you know anyone who can teach it? I'd take yoga," Siobhan said, her voice perking up.

"I don't, but I can ask around," Helen said, raising her eyebrows. "It would be a great way to cool down after my more intense classes."

"True," Siobhan said. "Plus, we can have a class early, like six a.m., and dig into the early birders."

Helen rolled her eyes. "Like you?"

"Ha ha . And yes. Like me," Siobhan added, shaking her head with a smile.

"Sounds awesome. I'm on my way out. Need anything before I split?" Helen asked, grabbing her bag and bouncing her way toward the front door.

"No. Thanks. I'm good," Siobhan said, putting her palm on her forehead. "I forgot to text Adam and tell him I hired Jesus today," Siobhan said more to herself than to her friend.

"Get on that! I'll see you…and Jesus tomorrow," she said, a big smile unfolding on her face. "Do you know what time you're coming in?"

"I don't," Siobhan groaned. "I'll get Jesus a login before I leave today. I'll text you his temporary password if you don't mind."

"Not at all! Happy to help," Helen said, winking. "See you tomorrow! Say 'hi' to Adam for me," she added as she flung open the front door of the gym and stepped into the engulfing summer heat.

"Will do!"

Siobhan grabbed her phone and pulled up Adam's information. Before she could begin typing a text message, he called.

"Hey!" she said as she answered his call.

"Hey. Um…" Adam trailed off.

Siobhan sat up straighter. "What?" she spat out.

"I have to tell you something," Adam said calmly.

"Okay," Siobhan said, jamming her phone between her head and shoulder. Then, she started entering Jesus' employee information into the gym's database.

"I got hurt today," Adam said. The words smacked Siobhan like a two-by-four across the back of the head, and she stopped typing, pulling her hands away from the keyboard to grab her phone. "A few minutes ago. Derek is driving me to the emergency room."

"Oh my God, Adam! What happened?" Siobhan shrieked.

"It's not a big deal," he breathed out. "I probably need a few stitches. I was helping Derek cut some pipes and I slipped and cut my arm."

"Is it—" she started.

"I'll be fine!" Adam burst out. He paused for a moment, and Siobhan gritted her teeth. "The bleeding is slowing already, so you don't need to worry," he corrected in a forced attempt at a calm voice.

"Okay. Do you want me to meet you at the emergency room so Derek can get back to work?" she asked as she started shutting down programs on her computer.

"Sure. It should be quick. I'll need you to take me back to Keller Estates for my truck. It's my left arm, so I can still drive. I don't drive an ancient artifact like you do," he said jokingly. Derek laughed deep and loud in the background.

"Ha ha, funny guy," Siobhan said, shaking her head. "I'll be there soon."

She ended the call and gathered her things, letting out a small groan as she opened the front door. The summer heat punched her in the face as she dashed toward her Jeep.

She called Helen and pulled open the Jeep's door to toss her purse in.

"Hey! Miss me already?" Helen asked, her happiness cutting through the apprehension pressing down on Siobhan.

"Well, yes, and always. Can you help me? Adam got hurt. I'm heading to the ER right now. It's a cut, he said…"

"Is he okay?" Helen asked.

"Yeah. He needs stitches," she said as she wiped the sweat forming on her brow with the back of her hand. "I'm going to meet him at the ER." She wrenched the phone between her ear and shoulder and started unzipping the back window.

"Glad it's not serious," Helen said.

"Me too. I'm headed to the ER, so could you set up Jesus' login?" Siobhan asked as she wiggled the zipper down on the passenger side window.

"I'll do it tomorrow. I'm already coming in early. Besides, it'll be good practice for me. You know how I love a good early morning," Helen said sarcastically.

"I need to give you a raise," Siobhan said, smiling as she pulled the top of the Jeep down.

"Nah. We're friends," Helen said energetically. "Take care of Adam."

"I will. If there's any way I can repay you, let me know," Siobhan said.

"Deal."

"I hope it goes well tomorrow," Siobhan said.

"It'll be fine. Later, gator!" Helen said.

Siobhan tossed her phone into her purse, stood on the front seat, and threw the top back before jumping down and settling into the driver's seat and pulling out of the parking lot.

A few cars dotted the road leading to the hospital as the sun beat down on the asphalt, sending up a distinct scent of burning tar.

As she made her way toward the bland building, she passed Derek's brand-new white truck, parked toward the front with the blue Conrad Construction logo on it. She scurried past the pristine vehicle and yanked open the door to the emergency room entrance.

A blast of air-conditioned, bleached breeze smacked her in the face. The pungent odor of the cleaning supplies seemed to mask something else in the air—something sour and sickly. She wrinkled her nose for a moment as the astringent stung her nostrils.

She made her way to the front desk, passing no one, where a heavy-set woman sat balancing a pencil on her right index finger. The name on her staff ID was Irene.

"Hey. My husband came in. Adam Keller. Is there any way I can see him?" Siobhan asked.

"He didn't have any of his paperwork done, so could you do that?" Irene asked as she set her pencil down and smacked her gum.

"Yeah. Is he okay?" Siobhan asked, shifting her purse from one arm to the other.

"They took him back already," she said as she shuffled papers onto a clipboard.

"Can I go back there?" Siobhan asked meekly.

She slid the clipboard to Siobhan through the small space

under the clear glass window.

Siobhan took the clipboard and opened her mouth to confirm she'd start the paperwork, but Irene cut her off. "Fill that out," she said, pointing to the clipboard. She stood and pushed herself out of the chair.

Siobhan lowered her head and trudged over to a green chair against the wall. The sound of the pen scratching against the clipboard annoyed her as she busied herself with the menial task of writing her address several times in different places.

"Siobhan?"

She snapped her head up.

"Derek! Hey," she said as she set the clipboard and pen down on the chair next to her to stand. "How's Adam?" she asked as she gave him a short side hug.

"He's fine," he said, returning her hug with one arm. "He's getting some stitches. I had to tell him to be more careful next time.".

"Can I go back there?" she asked, pointing to where Derek had come from.

"Probably. I came out to use the bathroom. Thought I'd see if you were here yet. Did you ask the lady over there?" Derek asked as he jerked a thumb toward Irene's desk.

"I did," Siobhan said, clenching her fist. She withheld an eye roll.

"Well, come back with me. I know where he's at," Derek said as he motioned down the long hallway. His long fingers waved, and he pushed up his shirt sleeves to reveal his tattoos all over both arms.

"Let me grab this," she said, smiling at the tall black man as she slung her purse over her shoulder and picked up the clipboard and pen.

"How are you?" Siobhan asked as she tried to keep up with his long gait.

He blew out a long breath of air. "Good. Working," he said, jamming his hands into his pockets. They rounded the corner. "He's in here," Derek said as he pushed back a curtain on the right.

The doctor kept his head down, busy putting stitches in Adam's left arm as Adam watched. He talked to the doctor but stopped and looked up when Siobhan and Derek came through the door.

"Look what I found wandering the halls," Derek said, motioning with both hands toward Siobhan. "This pretty lady."

"Easy, she's taken," Adam said, winking at her.

"How are you?" Siobhan asked Adam.

"I'm fine," he said, rolling his eyes before looking back down at the doctor's handiwork.

"He's getting ten stitches, but this wasn't a clean cut. It had a slight tear to it. I'm having to take extra time to close it up," the doctor said without missing a beat.

"Thanks, doctor…." She trailed off, waiting for his name.

"I'm Doctor Richards," he said as he looked Siobhan's way over his glasses.

"Nice to meet you. I'm Siobhan," she said.

"He's been telling me about you. You own The Flex?" Dr. Richards asked.

"We do," Siobhan said.

Adam smiled. "It's hers, though. I offer moral support," he said.

"He does more than that!" she said, taken aback. "Can I grab your insurance card?"

"Wallet's over there," he said, using his head to show direction. "On the floor by the curtain."

Siobhan knelt and timidly grabbed Adam's wallet, gingerly looking over his things. She pulled out the white insurance card.

"I'm going to run this paperwork and card to the front desk. I'll be back."

"I'll head out too if that's okay," Derek said. "Can you take him back to his truck?" Derek asked Siobhan, motioning with his head toward Adam.

"I can," she said.

"Don't come back to work today, okay? I can handle it. Rest and heal, man. And take tomorrow off, too. We're a little ahead of schedule on that house. For now, anyway," Derek said as he sniffed.

"Jeez, I didn't break anything, Derek. It's a cut. I can handle a few stitches," Adam scoffed.

"Still, take care, man. I need you on that house," Derek said as he fist-bumped Adam's good hand.

"Bye, and thanks," Adam said.

Siobhan followed Derek out and tried to keep up with his long gait. Once they made their way down the hall and around the corner, Derek stopped her by grabbing her arm. "It's a weird cut, Siobhan," he said in a low voice, looking around.

"What do you mean?" she asked, shifting the clipboard to the other arm.

"The doctor touched on it..." Derek trailed off, and his eyes darted around the empty hallway. "He cut it with a saw; I saw it with my eyes. But it was ripped open, not cut," Derek said, his low voice lowering further as he tilted his head closer to Siobhan's.

She cocked her head to the side. "So..." she started, but Derek interrupted her.

"I'm not sure what he did. After... but I saw it happen. Um..." Derek scrubbed his hand over his head. "It shouldn't look like that. I hope it wasn't something like...I don't know...after he got the cut, he tore it open himself?" Derek said as he snapped his head up, pausing as a nurse walked by, her tennis shoes making a soft thud as she trudged by.

"Oh," Siobhan said, shaking her head as the nurse rounded the corner toward the waiting area. "That's, it doesn't seem right. He wouldn't do that." She clutched the clipboard closer to her chest.

"I know," Derek interrupted, nodding. "It shouldn't look like that. I just wanted to tell you. Maybe you could watch him? He's a good guy. I need his help."

"I will," she added, biting her lip. "Thanks for everything, Derek," she said, giving him a hug.

"Anytime," he said. He pushed open the doors and left, waving at Siobhan with one hand.

Siobhan made her way to the front desk.

"Hey, I finished the paperwork. Here's our insurance card," Siobhan said, passing the clipboard and card under the window. "And here's your pen back."

The receptionist flipped through the papers, then took the insurance card, made a copy of it, and slid it back under the window.

"Do you need anything else?" Siobhan asked, squeezing herself tighter.

"Nope," she said.

Siobhan made her way to the bathroom before going back to Adam's room. She leaned down against the sink and took a deep breath before looking in the mirror, still pondering what Adam's boss had said.

Derek's comments stuck in her mind. He never minced words, and he cared deeply about everyone he knew, especially his employees. Siobhan couldn't brush off his concern.

She washed her hands and then looked back up, noticing her necklace. It appeared to have a slight glow to it. She could see the golden light bouncing off the skin of her chest. A luminescence tried to light her face from underneath as the fluorescent lights above dispersed the glow downward. She stared at it for a moment until she concluded the hospital lights must be insanely bright, even in this bathroom, causing it to have a glowing appearance.

She made her way back to Adam's room. He smiled at her as she came in. "Thanks for taking care of all that stuff," he said to her.

"Of course. You look good," she said, flashing him a smile.

"And I'm almost done, right doc?" he said, turning his head to Dr. Richards.

"I'm bandaging him up. It's going to heal," the doctor said, reaching for another strip of gauze. "Be careful. It's going to take some time to close up."

Siobhan hadn't gotten a chance to examine Adam's injury. Even though Derek had commented on how odd he'd found the cut, she didn't have the guts to ask the doctor to unwrap it so she could see.

She drifted into her own thoughts as she remembered Derek's words, getting lost in what his injury could look like under all that white bandaging.

"All set," Dr. Richards said, breaking the silence. He placed the last piece of white medical tape over the bandage. "Come back in ten days so I can see if we can pull these out. You can take the bandage off after 24 hours and let it air out some."

"Thanks, doc," Adam said as he stood. "It doesn't even hurt. You did a great job."

"Well, take it easy, though. Don't split it open again. And be careful with those saws at work," Dr. Richards said.

"I will," Adam said, extending his good fist for a bump. "See you soon," he said, fist-bumping the doctor with a smile.

"See you soon, Adam. Nice to meet you, Siobhan," he said as he flung the curtain out his way, snapped off his gloves one at a time, and tossed them in the biohazard bin.

"Well, shall we head home?" Adam said, putting his unbandaged arm around Siobhan's shoulders.

"Yep. Let's go get your truck first," she said. "Then maybe I'll go grab us some dinner?"

"Sounds great," Adam said.

As Siobhan drove back toward Keller Estates, she couldn't stop her mind from wandering back to what Derek had said and the other peculiar things she'd been experiencing.

She started to lose herself in her own thoughts, drowning out the sound of the wind rushing around as she drove.

Birds fly into windows all the time, but do four black birds smash into the same window within twelve hours of each other? Adam has been snippy and sleeping more deeply lately, too. He could be stressed at work, especially with the injury. She had heard the voice in her living room this morning, that she couldn't confirm its reality. It could have been a fabrication of her own distressed brain. The weird wet cobwebs on the counter at the gym that Helen had noticed, too, were real, right? The unfamiliar sensation caused Siobhan to ponder and chew her bottom lip.

She blew out a long breath.

"Hey, Adam?" she asked over the roar of air in her topless Jeep.

"What's up?" he said with his bandaged arm cradled to his chest, his right arm hanging out the open window.

"Derek said that your cut was weird because it came from a saw. Is everything okay?" she asked as she remained focused on the road.

"Oh, yeah. It was so weird!" he said excitedly. He shifted in the seat, then smiled as he turned slightly toward her. "I slipped, but it was almost like the saw was ripped out of my hand. It felt like someone pulled it across my arm. So weird. It was a plain cut, but then it wasn't when I got to the ER. It's an injury, and stuff like this happens all the time, though." He gave a little smirk and a quick shrug. "Derek's a good dude that he worries about all of his employees."

"Okay. So, it was some odd..." she asked as she glanced at him out of the corner of her eye.

He nodded and looked ahead. "I'm pretty sure. I don't know when it ripped or worsened. I don't know what was wrong with that saw. Hell, maybe I ripped it while I grabbed my sweatshirt to stop the bleeding. I didn't even feel it. Maybe I missed the nerves or something," he said as he stared out the windshield mindlessly retelling his account.

"Did you ask the doctor how...?"

"Nah. I needed a few stitches. It isn't that bad, Siobhan," he said, rolling his eyes. "Don't worry about me. I'm a grown man, I can handle a little injury." His voice had elevated slightly and he tapped the side of the Jeep with his right hand.

She shifted down to turn into Keller Estates.

"Well, I'm glad it'll heal," she said as she completed the turn. "Which house are you parked at?"

"Go around the corner up there, and it'll be on the right. The big one on the hill," he said, nodding toward the large estate that overlooked the rest of the subdivision like a castle. "I can get home on my own. Could you grab something for dinner?" He opened the door of the Jeep.

"Sure. Be safe. See you soon," she said, leaning over giving him a quick kiss.

"Thanks for everything today," he said, slamming her door and giving it a slap with his palm.

Still occupying Siobhan's mind were the odd events she'd experienced. She drove mindlessly to the grocery store, confused and unaware of her surroundings. She wanted to put Adam's injury behind her, but Derek's concern lingered. Adam had also been honest in his assessment of the injury, and maybe even annoyed that she had asked about it, so perhaps she overreacted. It had been a long and weird day. She chalked it up to needing a good meal and a decent night's sleep. The stress of being a business owner could be finally taking its toll on her.

After grabbing a premade salad, some pork chops, and a bottle of wine, Siobhan headed back home. It was after five o'clock when she pulled into her driveway, and as soon as she exited her Jeep with their dinner, she could see through their front window.

She pushed open the creaky front door and found Adam sitting on the couch, cradling his injured arm with his feet up on the coffee table.

He punched the pause button on the remote, stopping the movie in its tracks and leaving a scratching silence behind.

"Hey! Glad you're back. Wanna watch a movie tonight? I'm not working tomorrow," he said shrugging.

"Well, I'll watch one movie with you after dinner, but I have to get a good night's sleep tonight. I have a new employee," Siobhan said as she made her way to the kitchen with the groceries.

"Oh yeah!" Adam said, standing up still. "I want to know how it all went!"

"I hired the first person I ever interviewed," she said, shrugging. "Helen..." she licked her lips quickly, then continued: "offered to come in tomorrow and get him going so I can run my errands," she said gaining excitement as she spoke.

Adam smiled at her as he slid into a barstool. "Awesome," he said.

"I need the help. Helen and I..." she said trailed off as she got the wine opener out of the drawer. "Wine?"

"Yes, please," Adam said.

"Anyway, I haven't gotten him in the system yet to log in, but Helen said she would do it tomorrow and show him around," she said, wiping her jaw with her shoulder. "His name is Jesus." She finished opening the wine. She reached to get two glasses out of the upper cabinet and set them on the counter.

"That's great," Adam said as he stroked his bandaged arm, his eyes following her as she poured the wine.

Siobhan nodded as she pushed a glass of wine across the counter toward him, looked at his bandage, took a sip, and leaned against the counter.

Adam tapped his finger on his bandage. Siobhan lowered her glass. "You okay?"

He flicked his head. "Oh. Yeah. I'm annoyed I did this," Adam said, shaking his head, and then he took a sip of his wine. "I like that necklace." His eyes glazed over as he looked at it.

"I like it too. I've gotten several comments about it. A girl who signed up today commented on it," Siobhan said, then took a sip of her wine. She opened her mouth to tell Adam about the elusive Melina but snapped it back shut.

"Interesting," Adam said. "She probably thought it looked nice," he added, shrugging.

"Yeah, of course," Siobhan said, nodding rapidly as she gazed toward the window of their dining room.

"Do you think you'll hire anyone else?" Adam asked as he spun his glass in his fingers.

"I'm not sure. I'll see how it goes with Jesus first. I am considering a yoga teacher for some early morning classes."

"That's a good idea. That's why you're the boss," Adam said as he polished off the rest of his wine. "Good wine. Maybe some more?"

"Glass number two. Someone must have had a rough day,"

Siobhan said as she raised one eyebrow with a smile.

"You can say that again," Adam said as he patted his arm while she poured him another glass. "What do say we watch that movie?"

"Sure. Let me get dinner started."

"Don't forget to top off that wine glass before you come out here," Adam said as he made his way to the living room.

CHAPTER 3

Later that night, Siobhan jolted awake. She opened her eyes, leaving her fallen head in Adam's lap. She sat straight up, straining her ears. Adam slept, his head to the side, braced on the back of the sofa. He had his right arm on Siobhan's ribs, and his bandaged arm rested on the arm of the couch. His neck had cranked his head at a sharp angle.

She sat up slowly, pushing off Adam, then slid out from under his arm. She stayed as still as she could, scanning the room. She couldn't hear anything, but an unsettling pressure radiated in her bones—something watching her, just beyond her perception.

An eerie silent glow flowed from the TV and cast its gleam onto the floor and the coffee table in front of her. The air thickened, and the faint musk smell blew past her nose. She exhaled a long puff of air.

Click click click

The faint sound came from all around her, like it had eyes on her. The low volume sound had a real stiffness to it, although its difficulty to hear had her questioning if it was real or just a trick of her mind. Siobhan yawned but couldn't muster up the strength to walk around and find the source. Her necklace warmed on her chest, offering some mild but disconcerting comfort.

Slowly and gently, she pushed her arms over her head to

stretch, making small movements in hopes that she'd disturb Adam enough to wake him. He remained still; his breathing deep and slow.

She reached for her phone on the coffee table, intentionally causing more movement and bouncing on the couch. She tapped the screen and checked the time.

3:33 a.m. Wasn't that the same time she woke up last night when the birds struck their window? She couldn't remember.

She shoved the phone into the back pocket of her shorts as Adam's phone lit up on the coffee table. The picture of them both looking at the camera on their wedding day glowed on his home screen. She couldn't tear her gaze away from the photo. Something about Adam's eyes drew her in. They looked different. She cocked her head to the side and squinted at the image. She'd seen this picture hundreds of times and those eyes thousands.

As she tilted her head to the other side, the photo began to morph. Adam's brown eyes were fading, becoming a colorless mass of white. A twinge of fear spiraled its way up the back of her legs, and her heart rate quickened as her stare intensified.

The phone's screen went black. She snatched it off the coffee table and pressed the button on the side of the phone to light it up again. Deep brown eyes were looking back at her. As her heart rate started to slow, she tried to make sense of the change in the photo. She concluded that she needed some sleep. She yawned loudly.

Her hand shot up to touch her necklace. It warmed against her skin, and it felt alive under her palm.

She gently placed a hand on Adam's chest and shook.

"Adam," she whispered. His head jerked slightly and settled back to its awkward angle. "Hey, Adam," she said, shaking him again.

His eyes shot open; his head still tipped to the side and braced against the back of the couch. She pulled her hand away and balled it into a fist. She looked at his blank, empty expression and soulless eyes. "*Adam!*" she yelled.

He lifted his head slowly, keeping it at the same angle, and turned to look at her. Then he started to smile in a long, thin line that crossed his face as he twisted his head. She scooted back away from him on the couch.

"Adam, *stop it!*" Siobhan said forcefully. "That's not funny!" His eyes dimmed to solid white, exactly like they had been in the phone picture, as his skin tightened across his face. "*Adam!*" she screamed while pulling her legs under her on the opposite side of the couch, as he stared at her blankly, without looking directly at her.

She sat, frozen in fear, breathing heavily as his ominous smile widened further. He had never smiled like that before— sinister and unnatural.

His head snapped to a normal position, and his eyes softened like his soul had come back to his body. "Oh, man. We must have fallen asleep," he said, yawning.

"Why did you do that?" Siobhan shrieked, her voice cracking. She shook as she slapped his arm. He lifted his arms up, confused. "Whoa! What did I do, Siobhan?"

"The scary face and the creepy smile. *It freaked me out!*" she cried as she put her face in her hands. The warmth of the tiger's eye crystal spread to touch the skin of her forearms.

"Hey, what in the...I didn't do anything," he said as he reached his right arm around to hug her. She cradled her own face but leaned her head into his chest.

"That was crazy, Adam," she said. "And your eyes on the phone..."

"My what?" he interrupted. A cold bead of fear-laced sweat fell down her hairline as she contemplated whether she'd lost her mind.

"I'm sorry. Maybe I was dreaming," Siobhan said. "Or not fully awake; I don't know. I must be tired."

"Probably. Should we head to bed?" he asked, stretching his long body upward over the back of the couch. "We probably both need to get a few more hours of some good sleep."

"Yeah," Siobhan said lifting her head and looking around. She could feel eyes burning into her back. They stood, and Adam put his bandaged arm around her.

Click click click

The air vibrated slightly against each click, even though they were barely imperceptible.

Siobhan whipped her head toward Adam and opened her mouth to ask if he had heard that clicking sound but slammed it back shut. The quiet sound didn't have a source point and she couldn't guess where it had come from. A muscle twitched in Adam's jaw.

Adam leaned on Siobhan, his left arm around her waist. A warm sensation crawled into her skin, coming through his bandage. His arm radiated heat into her body; the warmth circled around her midsection and fanned out from the point of contact.

She glanced down but couldn't see anything in the dark. When they got to their room, he released her, letting her enter the bedroom first.

Adam took his shirt off to get ready for bed. "Siobhan!" Adam called, startling her. She flicked on the bathroom light.

"What's happening?" Adam asked.

"Adam, what…"

He fixed his gaze on her and extended his left arm, still wrapped in bandages. Blood seeped from beneath the white gauze and tape, the fabric repelling the flow. The lowercase t-shaped wound blazed red, and the blood dripped from Adam's fingers, splattering as it hit the carpet. A dark pool formed at his feet.

"Oh my God!" Siobhan panicked. She took her shirt off to wrap around his arm.

The tiger's eye crystal had gotten warm, and she tried to ignore it.

"Here," she said, her voice trembling in time with her body. Icy panic shot through her veins, lighting each limb up like a tree getting struck by lightning. She wrapped her shirt around his arm tightly. "Hold this," she said. "That's a lot of blood. I'm going to take you to the emergency room," she said.

Adam sat frozen and unmoving. Confusion twisted itself around panic as she tried to understand his calm demeanor as blood rolled off his hand.

"We need to go to the hospital," she said, looking into his lifeless eyes. "There's blood everywhere! Get in my Jeep while I get my keys" Her heart raced and blood hammered her ears. Adam's silent form remained sitting on the bed.

Siobhan grabbed a clean T-shirt from the folded stack of laundry on top of her dresser on her way out of the bedroom, putting it on as she bounded down the stairs. Adrenaline throbbed in her muscles. She rushed, missing several steps in the process.

"Adam! Come on, let's go!" she yelled up to him as she grabbed his cell phone off the coffee table. His screen had lit up, but she ignored it.

"Go where?" Adam yelled back.

"We're going to the emergency room!" Siobhan responded as she unlocked the front door.

"What?" Adam yelled to her. She dropped her keys on the floor and rushed back up the stairs.

When she got to the doorway of their bedroom, he took her shirt off his arm. "What are you freaking out for?" he asked, his face scrunched up. "It's just a little blood," he said, looking at her with wide eyes.

Siobhan stood frozen and gawked at Adam. "Where..." she lifted her hands, craning her neck to look around at the floor. The blood had been in the cut shape on the bandage. No blood dripped off his fingers. No blood lingered on the carpet. Nothing stained her shirt that Adam held in his right hand.

"*I saw it!*" she exclaimed. "I saw all the blood! Some of it dripped onto the floor! Where did it go?" she asked, turning around and looking for the stains.

"There's a little blood on the bandage, Siobhan," Adam said. "Look..."

"I have no idea what's going on," Siobhan shrieked as her tiger's eye crystal around her neck heated up. It emitted a mild glow, and she caught a glimpse of it out of the corner of her eye. She put her hand over it on her bare chest and patted it. It had a soothing warmth to it. "You saw that, right? There was so much blood, Adam! You were bleeding out all over the place!" She panicked, and her entire muscle structure shook and her blood drummed in her pulse points.

"Yeah, I mean, there's some on this bandage. I may need a new one," he said, picking at the edges of the white tape.

She took several steps toward him. "But I…." she stopped and hung her head as tears poked at the corners of her eyes.

"If I were bleeding out, it would be everywhere, Siobhan," Adam said with a snort.

"So, you didn't see all that blood? Was I…"

"Look, it's been a long day. You're tired. I'm tired, let's forget it, okay? *I'm fine!"* he snarled. "See," Adam assured her, waving his hand over the bandaged arm.

She had seen it. She knew she'd seen. But he was right, wasn't he? There wasn't any evidence that he had bled profusely moments before.

Great. She could now add hallucinating blood to her lengthening list of strange incidents that had occurred since she put the tiger's eye necklace on.

It had to be the necklace. She'd solve the problem right now. She reached behind her neck and took it off, feeling an immediate pinch in her stomach.

All the strange events, like the birds, the cobwebs on the counter that weren't there, Adam's phone and expression, and the odd bleeding, and the cut itself, all of that, somehow tied back to her necklace.

She had had enough. The hallucination of the gory bloody waterfalls meant she was either going crazy, or the necklace was haunted, and she couldn't tolerate being insane.

She flipped the light on in the bathroom and dropped the necklace on the counter by her sink. Oddly insecure and incredibly vulnerable without it, she gave it one last longing glance as she flicked off the bathroom light, leaving it in the dark. She felt a twinge of emotional pain like she'd left a beloved pet locked in a kennel alone. She rubbed her temples.

Siobhan's skin cooled even though the warm air embraced her. She kept her arms close to her body. She had an internal sensation that she had done something wrong or she had lost an argument.

"Do you want me to look at it?" she asked Adam, shaking as she motioned toward his arm.

"No. It's not that bad," he said, still peeling up the medical tape.

"What I saw was…I'm crazy, Adam," she said as she sat next to him on the bed. She wrung her hands in her lap nervously while looking at Adam's bandage.

"You're not crazy," he said, leaning his head against hers. "Hey, maybe you could help me put fresh gauze on this?" Adam asked, lifting his head and smiling down at her.

"Yeah. Stay here; I'll grab some antiseptic, too," she said as she pushed herself off the bed to stand. She chewed the inside of her cheek.

When she flicked on the light in the bathroom, her eyes shot to the tiger's eye necklace lying on the counter where she left it. It stared at her and called to her like it had before. She could hear it saying her name in silence. She fought the urge to put it back on as her body protested the decision and opened the cabinet door under Adam's sink.

That thing is haunted. It has to be. She squeezed her eyes shut hard and rubbed them with her fists.

What a stupid thing to even think for someone who doesn't believe in ghosts, Siobhan thought as she pawed around, looking for the supplies.

Siobhan's mind raced with images of blood laced with a vibrational clicking that pricked her eardrums from inside her head. A strange, cool breeze rolled up her back. She paused, and her heart rate picked up.

STOP IT! she screamed inside her own head. She already knew she would never erase the image of her husband bleeding like that. The permanent stain on her mind made her painfully aware of just how insane this situation had become.

She resumed her search for the medical supplies, telling

herself, "I'm not crazy; the necklace is haunted." She repeated it silently, her lips moving as if to control her racing thoughts.

With a firm grip on the gauze, she pulled backward as something fell onto the top of her head. It tangled in her blonde hair as if it were wiggling closer to her scalp. She put her hand on her head. The necklace rested on it.

Siobhan ripped it off her head, taking several strands of hair with it. She dropped the gauze and held the necklace in the palms of both her hands. The crystal had a warm feel to it. It generated a faint light that she could see bouncing off her palms and settling in the lines of her fingers. She wanted to put it on but resisted the urge.

Opening her drawer, she dropped it inside, vowing never to put it on again. A wave of depression flowed through her veins at the ridiculous promise she had made. She slammed the drawer closed a little too hard, squeezed the bridge of her nose, and fought back the tears that were prickling her eyes.

She grabbed the gauze and antiseptic and shut the cabinet.

"It is beginning," the same old woman's voice said—the same voice that talked to her that morning. She lost her balance and dropped the gauze and antiseptics as she fell backward.

The voice pounded and came from low to the ground, but it had been there. She blew out a breath, trying to steady her nerves.

Ghosts aren't real, Siobhan. Cut it out.

She pursed her lips and grabbed the first aid supplies, with the voice in the back of her mind, along with her probable descent into mental illness, and shuffled toward Adam.

Siobhan needed the alarm to wake up the next morning. She did manage to sleep some, but not enough. Her entire body tensed under her achy muscles and she yawned. She reached over and tapped the screen of her phone a little too hard, upset. Her muscles protested the lack of sleep. She sat up, yawned again, and looked over at Adam as he slept peacefully. She narrowed her eyes at him.

She snorted, tossed the covers off, and trudged to the bathroom. She flicked the light on, and all the previous night's events came flooding back to her. She could sense the necklace looking at her from inside the drawer.

She scrubbed her face hard and rubbed her tired eyes, then scratched shampoo into her hair. When she had finished, she peeked into the bedroom once again and snorted at Adam's sleeping form.

She resisted the urge to grab the necklace from her drawer and put it on like she had last night. After blow-drying her hair, she pulled it up into a ponytail and put on mascara and eye cream, so she'd look less tired. She knew it wouldn't help, but she did it anyway.

She took another glance at Adam, trying to cull the annoyance creeping up on her. She took a few deep breaths, then tossed on some jeans and a plain black T-shirt. She shut the bedroom door behind her before plodding down the stairs.

Siobhan made coffee, then sat on the couch drinking it, huddled into a small ball. She pondered the night's events. The last two nights had been strange, but last night, everything escalated. The strangeness had gotten to a whole new level of…what? Hallucinations?

None of what happened made any sense, and she had a hard time wrapping her head around it. And she couldn't stop thinking about that damn necklace. She wanted to put it back on.

Click click click

The clicking started faintly this time but each click got slightly louder than before. Lowering her coffee mug, she strained to make out the strange clicking sound. It hung in the room with her, and it wanted her to hear it. The noise acted like a sentient being. It made changes in the air and caused her skull to protest at its presence. It didn't come from the walls or the ceiling but from the ether all around her.

An odd chill surrounded Siobhan, and she bristled as the volume of the clicking increased.

Click-click-click

click-click-click-click-click-click

She shivered as the vibrational patterns it caused rippled across her skin. It sounded like a tongue clicking the roof of a mouth, but that wasn't quite what it sounded like either.

Siobhan glanced around at the living room, stairs, and dining room, ensuring none of the electronics had malfunctioned. She felt her breath catch in her throat as she couldn't pinpoint where the sounds were coming from.

The sound shifted around her as she tried to look at it. It vibrated off her body, but she couldn't see it, and as she got closer to it, it disappeared. When she turned, it turned away from her, as if it was autonomous.

Click-click-click

What the hell?

She swallowed a lump forming in her throat.

She made her way to the kitchen, blinking quickly and scanning the room for the source of the mysterious clicking. She found the tiger's eye necklace right next to the coffee maker and stopped in her tracks. Siobhan knew for a fact that she had tossed it in the drawer last night after it had somehow fallen off the counter onto her head.

She stomped over to it, held it up, slammed her coffee mug down, then picked up the necklace and examined it. Beautiful streaks of brown and gold held on to the radiating glow.

She sighed and put it back down. She slammed the front

door shut and marched to her Jeep.

Ghosts aren't real, she told herself over and over as she drove.

CHAPTER 4

Siobhan stepped out of her Jeep with a large bag of towels she had recently purchased for The Flex. She reached into the back seat and grabbed the other bag with toner in it to make the printer functional once again. By the time she arrived at her gym with her hands full, it was approaching nine o'clock.

Helen and Jesus were standing behind the front desk, looking at the computer. Helen pointed to something on the screen as Jesus peered over the short redhead's shoulder. Siobhan used her foot to tap the door and get their attention. They both looked up, and Jesus jogged around the counter to open the door for Siobhan.

"Good morning, boss," he said, offering her a small smile as he held the door open.

"Hello, Jesus. And you don't have to call me boss," she said as she made her way behind the counter.

"What's up, boss?" Helen said with a wink and a large grin. "Did you get your errands done?" She sat back in the chair behind her and spun the chair from side to side using her toes.

"I did," Siobhan said coolly. Helen shot a look at Jesus and gritted her teeth.

"Thanks for coming in, both of you. And stop calling me boss." Siobhan yawned. "You've already been here for two hours, right?"

"Yes," Jesus nodded. "Helen showed me around and gave me a fast lesson on where the janitor's closet is and how to use the washing machine."

"And he started a load of towels and cleaned the mirrors while I got him a login," Helen added, looking at Jesus through her eyelashes. "We'll work the front desk together today a little bit later."

"Great! You're both lifesavers!" Siobhan said as she dropped the bags and plopped into a chair next to Helen.

"Let me wash those towels," Jesus said as he reached for the bags.

"Thank you, Jesus."

He slung the bag over his shoulder and shot Helen a wink and a large grin before leaving.

"I like him," Helen said as she blew out a breath. She pointed at the computer screen. "I got him logged in, but I can't figure out how to get his clock-in time to say seven am. He was a little early, too.".

"Here," Siobhan said with another yawn. She stood and stretched herself up. "I'll show you." Helen pushed the chair aside as Siobhan stepped toward the computer. "Click here, the little clock icon in the lower right corner.".

"Are you okay?" Helen asked, putting her arm around her friend and cupping her bicep with her palm.

Siobhan paused, then nodded, her mind drifting to her necklace and then to Adam's bloody arm.

"Yeah. I mean, I don't know. I've been..." She stopped. How did she tell her best friend she had been hallucinating because she'd put on a haunted necklace?

Helen raised her eyebrows.

"I haven't been sleeping well," she breathed out. "It's not a big deal," she said, forcing a slight smile and tapping the counter next to the keyboard.

"That's good. Not that you're not sleeping, but that's all it is. More birds?" Helen asked.

"No. Probably stress," she said, waving her hand around. Her stomach lurched, and she looked down, staring at the keyboard's G key.

"It'll get better. You have me and Jesus," Helen said, giving Siobhan a squeeze.

"I know," she said as her body tensed.

She finished showing Helen how to adjust clock-in times, and after her friend bounded off to teach her class, Siobhan brought her attention to the printer. Once she finished fighting the toner cartridges and her fingertips were all black, she wiped her forehead with her forearm.

She gathered the trash, threw it away in the dumpster outside, and then held up her hands to examine her blackened fingers. She trudged to the locker room to wash the toner off her hands.

Oblivious to the several women chatting and moving around her, Siobhan's mind drifted once again to the strange events from last night. Out of all of them, her hallucination of Adam, bleeding profusely out of his wound, was, by far, the oddest. Or was it her peculiar attachment to the necklace she still hadn't stopped thinking about?

Siobhan couldn't stop the itching sensation spreading through her brain. She put her hand on her chest where the crystal had been, and a twinge of sadness washed over her. She had a hard time focusing on anything else besides that damn crystal, and she started to worry about her attachment to it and the hallucinations that had come with it. She caught a glimpse of herself in the mirror and didn't look at her own face. She stared at the empty space on her chest while she dried her hands, the loss consuming her energy.

She plopped in the chair behind the counter, leaned forward and grabbed her phone. As soon as she had it in her hand, Adam called her. She jumped to answer. "Hey! How's the arm today?"

No sound came from her phone.

"Adam?" The line remained silent. "Are you there?" she asked as she stood, rubbing her clammy hand down her jeans. A line of static pulsed through the earpiece. She hopped her way around the counter toward the front door and stepped into the scorching summer heat.

click

The single click pushed inside her own head as it pulsated and circled around in her sinus cavity like a pinball, searing a path where it had been. An icy chill bead of sweat slid down her neck.

Squinting against the radiance of the sun, she put one finger in her ear and pushed the phone tighter to her head. "Can you hear me? Adam?" White noise scratched in the background.

The line went dead. Siobhan jerked the phone away from her ear and huffed as she looked at the call ended screen. She rammed the phone into the back pocket of her jeans and flung the door open to go back into the gym.

Her phone rang again, vibrating in her pocket. It was Adam. She answered it by the door. "Adam?" she asked.

"Hey! Sorry I missed your call. How's your day?" Adam asked cheerfully.

"Um. Yeah. So far, it's fine...that was crazy. I couldn't hear you at all," she said.

"What?" he asked.

"When you called before."

"This is the first time I've called you today, Siobhan," Adam replied with a deep slow breath out and a tone of irritation.

"Oh. Are you sure?"

"Oh my God. I'm sure. I'm not *stupid*, Siobhan," he spat out. She recoiled. He cleared his throat. "Uh, yeah, that's crazy," he said.

"How's the arm?" she asked, kicking a rock in the parking lot.

"It's still disgusting under this bandage, but it's not painful or anything."

"Good," she said. "I was a little worried about you last night."

"I know," Adam breathed out.

"I am glad you're okay," she said as a flashback of his white eyes staring at her and his arm dripping black blood onto their carpet surfaced in her mind. She squeezed her eyes shut, trying to block out the hallucinations.

"Well, I wanted to check in after I missed your call," he said.

But YOU called ME! she thought as she gritted her teeth, gnashing them. She rubbed her forehead with her fingertips.

"Um. Things are good," she said calmly instead of snapping at him. "Take care of yourself today; relax and rest."

"Anything for you," Adam replied. "What do you want for dinner tonight? I was going to head to the store and get some stuff to snack on while I'm here anyway."

"You pick. I'm sure it'll be great. I'm going to try to be

home by three today," she said.

"It's Friday, we could decompress tonight," he said.

"Sure." She tried to feign enthusiasm. "Hey, the counter here is all… weird. It's like… staticky, and I thought you could look at it sometime."

"I'm sure it's nothing. But yeah, if it makes you feel better, I'll check it out," Adam said condescendingly.

He thinks I'm making it up.

She sucked in a deep breath. "All right. Thanks," she said.

Siobhan's mind drifted to her necklace once again. She missed the peculiar warmth it gave off.

"Why'd you leave your necklace here?" he asked.

"Where?"

"Jesus. By the coffee pot, Siobhan," he snapped.

"Oh, sorry. I decided to take it off for a day," she said, her eyes starting to sting.

"But why did you leave it here?" Adam barked.

"I didn't…" she started. "I took it off, then spaced it. You can put it upstairs in my bathroom drawer if it's in the way."

"Nah. It's not in my way. Besides, I don't want to touch it," he said.

She furrowed her brow and through gritted teeth asked, "Why not?"

"I don't want to, okay? Is there a problem with that?" he

spat back.

"No. No. I thought—"

"Well, I don't want to touch the damn thing, Siobhan. You can deal with it when you get home. You left it there, not me!" he yelled at her.

She bit back the tears welling up. "Adam, I'm sorry, I think…"

"That's it, Siobhan. You're thinking for me. I don't like it! Can you leave me alone sometimes?" he yelled as his voice got increasingly louder.

"Wow. I didn't expect…" She put her hand over her face as the tears started to roll down her cheeks.

"*Well, what did you expect?*" he shouted in an animalistic growl. She yanked the phone away from her head to keep her eardrum intact.

"Adam…"

"I'm tired. I'm taking a nap. Have a *great* day!" Then he hung up the phone without saying goodbye.

Siobhan scrubbed her hands down her face as more tears welled up, threatening to fall. Her bottom lip quivered as she opened the door to the gym.

She fell into the chair behind the counter and loosely lay in it like a mannequin. She tried to steady her breath as she pondered Adam's descent into anger. The image of her necklace sliced through her mind like a chainsaw. She could see it lying by the coffee pot, begging her to put it on.

She leaned forward and put her elbows on the counter and her head in her hands. She jumped back. That strange cobweb sensation crept up her arm again. *It's nothing. It's static,* she told herself, rubbing an elbow.

She slammed back into the chair, breathing heavily, and stared at the counter, trying to make sense of it all.

The front door made its tell-tale sucking sound as it opened. Melina strode in, her black hair up in a messy bun, with lengthy pieces weaving down over her shoulders. She wore solid black flare-leg leggings and a black T-shirt.

"Hey. Welcome back," she said, hoping Melina wouldn't notice her swelling and tired eyes.

"Hello. How have you been?" Melina asked.

"Stressed," Siobhan breathed out slowly. "Sorry!" she said right away putting her hands up. "I…I…" she inhaled slowly.

"You know, yoga could help you relax. I'm a certified instructor. If you ever want to try it, let me know," Melina said. It still came across as monotone and melancholic, but Siobhan couldn't help but pick up on sincerity.

"You're a yoga teacher?" Siobhan asked.

"I mean, not right now, but I am certified. I used to do yoga all the time to deal with a very traumatic and stressful childhood," she said then paused.

"Oh, I'm so sorry about that," Siobhan said, meaning every word. "My husband lost his parents at a young age, so he doesn't remember much of his childhood," she said empathetically.

Melina nodded. "I lost mine and my grandmother. She had a necklace like yours. You're not wearing it today, though," she said leaning forward. Lowering her voice, she said, "You should be."

Taken aback, Siobhan stammered, "What? I should be?" She raised her eyebrows and put her hand on her chest. She regretted doing it immediately because she noticed the necklace's absence. She withdrew her hand as quickly as she could. She jammed it into the back pocket of her jeans.

"It was meant to be with you," Melina said.

"Well, I'm not sure I'll put it back on. It's..." She almost said haunted.

But it can't be haunted because ghosts aren't real.

Her stomach flipped again.

"Okay," Melina said. She shrugged and turned toward the locker rooms.

"Wait!" Siobhan called after her and hurdled from behind the counter. Melina turned her head, keeping one hand on her shoulder over the strap of her large black tote bag.

"I've been wanting to hire a yoga teacher... if you're

interested," Siobhan said, while the image of her necklace seared in her brain.

"Yeah?" Melina said as she shifted her weight to one hip and put her hand on it. "What kind of schedule are you looking for?"

"You can do it anytime you'd like as long as you make sure it won't interfere with Helen's schedule," she said, digging behind the computer. "She doesn't do classes until ten because Helen...well, she's not into mornings." Siobhan handed the laminated schedule to Melina. "Feel free to come in and teach on holidays or take them off if you want. It's up to you."

"So, this schedule... Mondays and Wednesdays look completely open. And most early mornings?"

"That's right."

"What about some really early morning classes so that participants can come before work?" Melina asked.

"That would be great! I'm an early bird. I fell asleep on my couch last night at probably eight o'clock and didn't..." Siobhan stopped and shook her head, clearing out the imagery that threatened to surface and flinging her back into that place where she was fully confident that impossible things existed.

"Six, maybe? Too early?" Melina asked, slicing through Siobhan's thoughts.

"No. No, not at all," Siobhan replied. "Sorry, I'm just..."

she paused. "Tired today. I'll get you a login so you can clock your hours. I need to refund your membership. Employees have free access to the gym,"

"Can we do that when I'm done?" Melina asked, pointing her thumb behind her toward the gym.

"Sure. I'll work on getting this new schedule printed. Do you want to start Monday?"

"Sure," Melina said shrugging. "I'll be here even if it's only me."

"Well, I'll be in your class Monday morning," Siobhan said with a forced smile, trying to narrow her focus to the conversation.

"Fun," Melina said over her shoulder as she marched into the gym.

An hour later, Melina made her way back to the front.

"Hi, boss," Melina said in her monotone voice.

Siobhan groaned and rolled her eyes. "Why does everyone say that?"

Melina stood silently looking at the counter, appearing reluctant to touch it.

"You can call me Siobhan; I don't care for the boss nickname."

"Okay," Melina said, shrugging.

"What's up?" Helen asked as she bounded around the corner and dropped her bag. She pulled her ponytail out of its hair band to readjust it.

"Not much. This is Melina. She's our new yoga teacher," Siobhan said, motioning toward her new employee.

"Welcome, Melina! I'm Helen. It's nice to meet you," she said, smiling widely and reaching out with her hand.

Melina shook it and said, "You, too."

Helen flopped into one of the chairs and twisted it from side to side as she looked at the schedule Siobhan had up on the computer screen. "Ugh. If I can get up early, I will come to your class on Monday," she said, gritting her teeth.

Siobhan managed a grin. "Well, I'm going to head home," she said as she bent to gather her purse and phone. "Adam is..." she clamped her mouth shut.

Melina dropped her head and looked at the floor.

"Ok," Helen said nodding. "Hey, call me sometime this weekend. Maybe we can go hang out or something," she suggested.

"Sure," Siobhan responded with less emotion than she intended. "Text me if you need anything," she said with a slight wave. "See you both on Monday. Have a great weekend."

CHAPTER 5

Siobhan drove home, her mind stuck contemplating her mental stability and desire to put the necklace back on. She opened the creaky front door, and a mild but musky, now familiar stench flew into her nostrils.

She sniffed hard to try to clear it, but at the same time, the faint clicking sound found its way into her head. Her skin vibrated. She glanced around for the noise once again and not finding the source, she conjured up an image of her necklace.

"Adam?" she asked.

"Hey!" he said as he peeked out from the kitchen. "How was your day?"

Siobhan looked around, trying to pinpoint the clicking sound that increasingly pressed into her. She locked her eyes onto the farthest corner of their dining room, near the window the birds had flown into.

"Um. It was fine. Can you hear that?" she asked as she set her purse down on the counter.

"I don't hear anything," Adam said right away.

Click click click

Click click click Click click click Click click click

"That!" Siobhan shouted. "Did you hear a clicking?" she asked as she spun around.

"No," he said. She gritted her teeth hard.

Click click click Click click click Click click click

That sound drove her to the precipice of insanity and worked its way into her body by burrowing through her skin. How could he not hear that while she had *felt* it?

"I didn't get groceries. Do you mind going back out?" Adam asked, cutting into her thoughts. "I didn't feel like it. This thing…" he said as he lifted his injured left arm, "doesn't hurt, but it's not scabbing." "It has only been one day. Is it infected? We could go back to the doctor," she said, looking under the kitchen table.

Click click click

"Nah," he huffed watching her with bewilderment while trying to hide the anger etched on his face.

"I'll head out to get some things," she said as she backed toward the front door, hoping another drive would allow her to forget about the haunted necklace and the clicking sound.

A muscle twitched in Adam's jaw and a vein bulged on his neck. "Maybe it's because it's under the bandage. The doctor did say I could take it off," Adam said as if Siobhan wasn't standing there.

The outline of the crimson lowercase t on the white bandage where the blood and plasma had seeped through stuck out like a sore thumb.

The necklace isn't haunted because ghosts aren't real, she told herself

The image of blood pouring out of his wound onto their carpet flooded back into her mind.

"I'll grab some sandwiches," Siobhan said quickly, trying to shake the creeping insanity that had welled up inside her chest.

"Cool," Adam said, staring at his arm as he started peeling up his bandage. His detached aloofness hit at Siobhan's emotional well-being like a jackhammer.

Click click click Click click click Click click click

"Be back soon," Siobhan said as she slammed the door on the horrific clicking.

Once in the grocery store, Siobhan found the deli sandwiches and bent over to get a better look.

"Hi."

"Oh!" Siobhan exclaimed as she put a hand on her chest, jumping up. She felt the absence of her necklace. "Melina! You scared me," she said as she composed herself, swallowing hard.

Melina had changed into black ripped jeans, combat boots, and a black tank top with a gold star on the front of it.

"Sorry. I wanted to say hello," Melina said. She still had her hand on her shoulder over her massive tote bag, and her black eyeliner looked perfect. Her hair hung down and would have blended in with her shirt if it weren't so shiny.

"It's very nice to see you. You live around here?" Siobhan asked, crossing her arms over her chest.

"Yes. Around the corner. You?"

"Yep! I'm up on White Crest," Siobhan said. "This store is kind of right between us, huh?"

"Sure is.".

Siobhan's mind filled with images of dead birds in the rosemary bush.

"I wanted to tell you to put the necklace back on," Melina said with some urgency, tilting her head lower.

Siobhan wrinkled her forehead and cocked her head to the side. "What?"

Melina nodded but said nothing.

"What are you talking about?" Siobhan said, shaking her head and feeling a cool breeze swell up from the floor. "Are you trying to freak me out?" Siobhan shrieked, eyes wide.

"No. Sorry," Melina said, putting her hands up. "Put the necklace back on as soon as you get home."

"What is it with you and this necklace?" Siobhan asked, her voice cracking.

"It was my grandmother's. Wear it, Siobhan," Melina said, taking a step back. "Good to see you. I can't wait to start on

Monday."

"Wait, it *was* your grandmother's? I thought it was *like* hers?" Siobhan said, emphasizing the words as she took a few steps toward Melina.

"Put it on, okay? I don't want anything to..." Melina stopped abruptly.

Siobhan sighed. "To what?" she asked. She liked the tiger's eye crystal necklace but she still grappled with the idea that it could be haunted.

It's not haunted because ghosts aren't real.

"To... happen," Melina said.

Siobhan shook her head and threw her hands up. "That's not an answer. I love that thing, but it's..." Siobhan snapped her mouth shut.

"Haunted?" Melina asked, raising an eyebrow.

Siobhan's eyes widened, and she opened her mouth. "What?" she exclaimed a little too loudly before clapping her palm over her mouth. She and Melina looked around.

"Trust me. I know it's weird. Text if anything..." She closed her eyes and took a deep breath. "Wear it." Melina's smile faded as she became serious.

"Okay," Siobhan said, tossing her hands up. "But because I like it," she said, pointing a finger at herself.

"Fine. See you soon," Melina said. She turned around and

left jogging. She had left without buying anything.

As Siobhan drove home, the warm air whipping her blonde ponytail around her face, she contemplated the ramifications of putting the necklace back on. Too many weird things happened when she wore it, but weird things happened without it, like Adam's childish temper tantrum. But she loved the necklace, even though she couldn't pinpoint why.

The damn birds were killing themselves, and the incessant clicking pushed her closer to the edge of madness. The horrible sound had burned itself into her brain, causing a distress it felt like there was no escape from.

Then there were the hallucinations and all the blood. Why was her brain doing this to her? And why had Melina been insistent that she wear the haunted necklace? How did it end up at Siobhan's wedding if it belonged to Melina's grandmother?

Siobhan's unanswered questions continued to boil in her mind. She had to find answers, at least to some of them, but all she knew right now was that she needed that damn necklace. She fought the urge to jam the gas pedal to the floor as she sped through her neighborhood.

Her stomach tied itself into knots as soon as she pulled her Jeep onto the driveway.

She sighed heavily and slammed the door on the old TJ. She reached in the back seat for the sandwiches she'd bought for dinner.

The energy in the air around her rushed closer to her body, suffocating her on all sides. It squeezed her and tightened around her chest.

A thick haze had collected around her house, washing it in a light gray hue. The curtains were open, and Adam lingered inside. She cocked her head to the side and squinted through the fog.

Siobhan dropped her purse and the grocery bag and ran toward the front door. The quicksand air restricted her movement and breath. It was as if she had entered a nightmare. She tried to move but couldn't go anywhere. She tried harder to push her way through an energy force field that held her back. She sprinted but didn't go far as the world pressed inward. She couldn't slice through the thick, dark air, and she couldn't breathe.

The air contracted again and became heavy, like an invisible boulder being slowly rolled into her. She tried to take a deep breath, but the thick air caught in her throat and stuck in her lungs.

She took the steps two at a time, pushing through the mucky atmosphere that had bubbled up all around her.

She pushed toward the door with everything she had.

"Adam..." she squeaked out with limited breath.

She strained her muscles to reach for the doorknob. She

twisted and then pushed, but it wouldn't budge, being held closed from the inside.

Click click click Click click click   Click click click

Click click click Click click click   Click click click

She pushed harder, using her shoulder to ram the door. The clicking jumped from neuron to neuron in her brain as it reverberated through the dense air pressing down on her.

Panicking, she started violently pulling and pushing the door. She grunted as she pounded into it. She cried out as she started banging on it with both hands.

The door flung open so hard that she fell to her hands and knees on the tile as she crossed the threshold of their home. A twinge of pain shot into her right knee as it slammed into the floor.

"Adam," she croaked out before lifting her head slowly and looking up at him.

Adam faced her. She froze and stared at him as her mouth opened as the air tightened its firm grip around her ribs, squeezing her lungs.

Adam floated above her and she gasped for more oxygen.

Her heart tried to fall into her stomach.

The thickness of the atmosphere wrapped her closer in a dark blanket.

Adam's arms were outstretched, palms facing forward, and his legs crossed at the ankles. Still in his pajama pants and white T-shirt that he'd slept in last night, he hung swaying in the air.

Siobhan couldn't make a sound even though she tried to scream. The thick and distorted air wouldn't let her breathe, and it choked the life out of her.

Adam's cut on his left arm dripped blood. It flowed in a charcoal cascade of slick mercurial oil onto the carpet. Everything around the house was devoid of color except the blood staining the injury.

His head was turned up, but he stayed motionless. His eyes were the same solid white she'd seen yesterday, and blood trickled from them as it dripped onto his shirt, soaking it. The blood spots spread as the droplets made contact.

Click click click Click click click Click click click
Click click click Click click click Click click click

Each click coursed through her veins and settled around her lungs as they compressed with the tension of the space around her. The sound felt like claws were stuck in her ears, poking her brain.

Siobhan tried to scream, but the air itself had its hand around her throat.

She got dizzy and light-headed, but she couldn't look away from her husband.

His bleeding eyes were as soulless as the t-shaped cut on his arm. She stared at him as the blackness started to come closer. She could see the haze of unconsciousness move in, and her blood thudded in her ears.

She tried once more to make a sound, but she couldn't even whisper. The air thickened as it stuck in her mouth. She was lost in a place without time—a place where there was emptiness and horror and nothing else.

The invisible vice that churned the air into a pressurized tank tightened even more. The atmosphere got heavier by the second, and her vision narrowed to Adam's arm wound. She started to panic and her blood hummed in her ears. A vein bulged in her neck as she fought for air. *Is this what dying feels like?*

Siobhan registered the black tunnel she headed down, with a horribly bleeding cut at the end of it. The lowercase t shape glowed red hot as it wriggled its way deeper into his flesh. Her pulse raced faster, and her ears protested at the constant clicking sound she couldn't drown out. The strangely silent noise was deafening at the same time.

Her consciousness throbbed against the tight grip the energy of the air had on her. The horrific clicking that had started to scratch at her eardrums was the last thing she remembered before she passed out.

"Siobhan? Siobhan? What's the matter with you?"

Adam's voice came at her, fuzzy, and she couldn't see him.

She tried to move her head. Her eyes cracked open and a blurry Adam in a pristine white T-shirt looked at her.

"What the hell happened, Siobhan? Are you okay?" Adam asked, concern laced into his voice. He had drawn his face tight, and a vein in his neck bulged.

"Jesus. I almost called 911," he said as he tossed his cell phone toward the stairs. "Can you talk to me?" he asked as he wrapped his arms around her body.

"Adam," she squeaked out.

"Thank God," he said, tilting his head up. "Are you okay?"

Siobhan's body curled into the fetal position. She raked her mind for the memory of what had happened. Her eyes snapped to the spot where Adam had been levitating, bleeding, his eyes open and white.

He had been hanging there, suspended in the air that had been squeezing the life from her. Terror flooded through her senses as blood flowed off him. She remembered being in the tunnel, and then the darkness claimed her.

"Adam, are you...?" She stopped. His brown eyes looked directly into hers. They weren't white. They weren't bleeding. He wasn't hanging in the air above her. She gazed at his arm and the cut grazing it. He'd removed the bandage, but it wasn't bleeding. A simple cut with some stitches blazed in her vision.

"How did...?" She pushed herself up slightly to look at the

carpet where blood had been pooling from his gaping arm wound.

Everything had returned to normal.

But it did happen! Did it?

Was she hallucinating? Another hallucination. She shivered and it had nothing to do with the temperature.

The clicking started up with a low volume.

No.

Click click click

Click click click click click click click click click click click click

"You okay?" Adam asked, his voice combining with the clicking.

"I.. what? I don't..." She opened her mouth, but no more words came out.

"I came in from the kitchen to see you on all fours, then you rolled over and passed out. You were out for maybe two minutes! We should go to the emergency room," Adam said, a look of worry crossing his face.

"What? No. No doctor," she said as she pushed herself to a sitting position. She pulled her knees up to her chest and hugged them tightly. A bruise was developing on her right knee, where it had slammed into the floor.

"What happened to me?" she stammered. "You were..."

"Yeah. I want to know, too. You left the front door open,"

Adam said as he nodded toward it. The door was open, and her purse and the grocery bag littered the driveway.

Click click click click click click click click click click click click

"I got dinner. I saw… you were…"

The clicking began to get more obvious, but Adam wasn't showing any indication that he had heard it. Instead, he raised his eyebrows high like he was waiting for her to finish.

Click click click click click click click click click click click click

"Siobhan?" he asked, raising his eyebrows at her.

"You can't hear that?"

"You should rest," he said, shaking his head. "I'm not sure what you're hearing, but you *were* unconscious, and you may have hit your head," he added.

She was losing her mind. It was so real.

Was it a figment of her imagination in an unconscious state?

Nothing at all would give an indication that Adam had been levitating and bleeding in their living room.

"You… were…" She kept looking up at the empty space that she was sure Adam had been suspended in moments before.

"I was… *what?*" Adam said forcefully. "You sure you don't need a doctor?" he asked as he shifted back to give Siobhan some space.

"No, no doctor. I must have… I've never done that before," she said. The confusion had officially set in, and she couldn't get the frightening image of Adam out of her head.

That had to be a hallucination. He's obviously fine.

"Let's get you up," Adam said, as if he was talking to a child. He reached out to help her, and she leaned against him. He held onto her and led her to the couch. "I'll go grab your things."

Adam went out to the driveway and returned a few moments later.

"You're probably hungry," he said as he entered the kitchen with her purse and the grocery bag.

She stood and followed him.

"But how are you…?" She cocked her head to the side. "I mean, I'm confused. I thought I saw…." She trailed off and caught a glimpse of her tiger's eye necklace glowing on the counter. It illuminated the side of their stainless-steel coffee maker in a radiant orange aura.

Click click click click click click click click click click click click

She snapped her head up, her eyes darting around the kitchen. The goddamn clicking threatened to send her straight off a cliff into an abyss of mental torture.

"Maybe you should sit back down," Adam said.

"Maybe," she said as she snatched the necklace off the counter and slid onto a barstool. Adam opened the refrigerator and grabbed her a can of sparkling water.

"Here," he said as he cracked it open. A satisfying hiss of carbonation escaped the can.

"Hey, why don't we relax and eat?" he suggested.

"Sure. Sorry, Adam."

Click click click click click click click click click click click click

Adam smiled. "Tell me if you need a doctor, okay??" he said as he squeezed her shoulders, and she winced at how unfamiliar his grip had become. "Meet me on the couch?" Adam asked as he leaned down to hug her from behind.

"Sure," she said, furrowing her brow. This couldn't be Adam. It felt like a different person had touched her.

Her eyes shot to the necklace in her palm. Its glow had decreased, but it still contained its comforting warmth. She unclasped it and put it around her neck. The familiar yet uncanny tepid strength it brought with it spread from the point where it contacted her chest to the rest of her body.

"It's back," the older woman's voice said.

As if in reply to the old woman's voice, the clicking began again.

Click click click click click click click click click click click

click

"Yep, I'm going crazy," Siobhan said, breathing out and shaking her head.

Siobhan grabbed her can of water and made her way to the couch. The necklace's slowly cooling warmth encapsulated her like an embrace from a long-lost friend. She knew the crystal was where it should be, and that offered some comfort as she descended into psychological anguish.

She resolved to do two things tomorrow. First, she would start looking into her symptoms and try to figure out what kind of mental illness she was sinking deeper into, and second, she would call Melina and get more information about the haunted necklace that bordered on being a living thing.

After all, this crystal has more of a soul than Adam right now.

CHAPTER 6

Siobhan struggled with a fitful sleep and she tossed and turned most of the night. After she got up from her unconscious fall in the doorway, she spent the night teetering between dozing off and complete restlessness.

She rolled over in bed. The sheets were pushed back, and Adam's spot had been vacated. She pushed up on her elbow to listen, and she could hear him moving around in the kitchen. She slammed her head back into the pillow and crossed her hands over her belly, not bothering to remove the piece of hair that had fallen over her eye.

Siobhan pursed her lips together hard. She needed to talk to Melina and do some research. Maybe Melina could at least explain that the necklace was haunted so Siobhan could strike severe mental illness with visual and auditory hallucinations off her list of possibilities.

But if she had to start believing in ghosts, that was probably a different type of mental disorder.

So, no matter what it is, I am going crazy.

Tossing back the covers, she made her way to the bathroom to take a long, scorching hot shower. She towel-dried her hair and looked at her face in the mirror. Dark circles had formed under her eyes. The mental distress had wriggled its way into her mind, and it gripped a hold of her.

Click click click…..click click click click click click click

The sound in the walls or on the walls came from anywhere and nowhere at the same time. While it flowed everywhere, even inside her own brain, it had a fakeness to it, like it belonged somewhere else.

She had heard an old lady's voice when there was no old lady there. Her husband had levitated and bled out right in front of her. Her untrustworthy mind played tricks on her.

Everything appeared foggy, and she couldn't explain it. It was like a gray film had covered every surface.

Shaking her head, sure she should be medicated for some kind of psychosis, Siobhan looked at the necklace. It wasn't glowing right now, but it had that oddly comforting warmth of it being in the right place.

Siobhan made her way down the stairs and could hear Adam moving around in the kitchen. She rounded the corner, grabbed her phone from her purse, and plugged it into the charger by their kitchen table. She tapped the screen of the dead phone and it failed to come to life.

"Hey! You slept in," Adam said, keeping his back to her. He scraped at the pan with a spatula. "I'm making scrambled eggs and bacon. Want some?"

"Nah. Coffee," Siobhan said, looking out the window the

birds had been flying into. Dawn's first light danced across the sky in streaks of yellow and gold.

"I made some already," Adam said with his back to Siobhan.

"Thanks. Sorry about last night," Siobhan said as she got a large mug down.

"It's okay. You seem better this morning. Maybe you got lightheaded?" Adam suggested, still not looking up from his eggs.

"Yeah," she said as she poured a cup of coffee. She leaned back against the counter and took her first sip.

The image of Adam suspended in the air flooded back to her. She winced. She could not figure out where these gory hallucinations were coming from.

Click click click click click click click click click click click click

Hot tears stung the corners of her eyes. She took a long drink of her coffee, hoping it would cull the emotions bubbling up.

"How's your arm?" she asked through a cracking voice. If Adam noticed she was slipping into mental illness, he didn't act like it.

"It's not healing. I thought it would be scabbed up by now," he said.

"Strange," she muttered, taking another sip of her coffee.

"Yeah. I'm not worried yet, but I generally heal faster than this. I don't remember much from when I was a kid, but I'm pretty sure injuries heal faster than this," Adam said while he scraped the pan.

"Maybe," she said. "You don't get hurt often, though, so who knows?"

Adam chuckled. "True."

"If you think we should go back to the doctor, let me know. I'll go with you."

"I could say the same to you," he said turning to point the spatula at her and smirk.

"But I won't need to. I'll bandage this thing up and be good to go by Monday morning," he said.

Her necklace had started to give off its warm embrace.

"Let's try to have a normal day today. A day where neither of us needs a doctor," she said.

He threw his head back and laughed. She grimaced. "You got it," he said before scrapping his eggs onto a plate of bacon.

BAM!

"Son of a…" Adam said as he jumped. Siobhan also jumped, almost spilling her coffee.

BAM! BAM!

"What the hell?" Adam said, turning the stove off. He peeked out the window. "More birds, Siobhan."

"What?" she burst out.

"Yeah. Three dead birds. They slammed into that same goddamn window. Dammit!" Adam spat out.

"I'll clean up the kitchen; you eat," Siobhan said. "Is the bush okay?" she asked.

"Yeah, it appears that that bush is faring much better than the birds," Adam said with a grunt. "Mother..." he muttered angrily.

Click click click.....click click click click click click click

"Thanks. I was going to deep clean the kitchen today, so I'll get started," she said, pushing the clicking noise aside.

She focused on cleaning to try to clear out the images of dead birds, bleeding white eyeballs, and a strange, unhealing injury.

When Adam finished eating, he rinsed his plate off and put it in the dishwasher. "I'll go take care of those birds," he said to Siobhan while she was wiping down the front of their refrigerator. "Can I start this for you?" he asked, motioning to the dishwasher.

"Um. Yeah. Thanks," Siobhan said.

"Be back soon."

Siobhan finished cleaning the refrigerator and stood to admire her work. She forced a smile. The gray haze had made their house strangely dim, even though the lights were on, and it was a bright day.

She stepped to the sink, rinsed off her rag, and looked out

the window. Adam crouched at the back of the yard, but he wasn't burying the birds.

Click click click click click click click click click click click click

"What is he doing?" she muttered out loud to herself, more to drown out the clicking sound than anything else. She squinted against the early morning sun.

Bent over with his back to the window, she could see that he was doing something, his hands gyrating at his sides as he did it.

His hair had fallen in waves and rested against his shoulders as he hunched over the spot where he had been burying the birds.

Siobhan slid the patio door open. "Adam?" she called. "Adam!" she yelled, cupping her hands around her mouth. A still silence in place of the chirping of birds and the buzzing of insects that circled around her, acting like it could see her. Goosebumps rose on her skin.

She took a few steps out onto the patio and toward him. "Hey!" she yelled, crossing her arms over her chest as a cold breeze fit for winter bit at the skin on her face. Her nostrils chilled with each breath as she puffed out mists in front of her. "What are you doing?" she called out.

She shivered, her necklace got warm, and her hand

instinctively found the crystal and covered its increasing glow.

"Adam?" she said, this time more quietly and more concerned. A jolt of fear shot through her core as adrenaline coursed through her veins.

Adam stopped moving and stayed eerily still.

"A-A-A-Adam," she stuttered, her hand still on her necklace. She started to shake, and she couldn't tell if it was from the icy breeze or her husband's behavior.

She wrapped her whole hand around the tiger's eye crystal, hugging herself against the cold with her other arm. The arctic blast welled up around her. It came from the ground and swirled and danced, creating goosebumps that ran over every inch of her arms and legs. A bead of icy sweat rolled down her back.

Adam grabbed at the ground with both hands on each side, picking up two dead birds, one in each hand. He paused. Then he stood slowly and robotically and started swaying slightly from side to side.

Siobhan stood, watching, her blood searing in her veins. The cold air kicked up, blasting her in the face once again, and its icy fingers dragged her hair behind her.

Adam remained still, gripping the dead birds so tightly they swelled. He slowly turned his upper body toward her, twisted in half at the belly button. His feet and knees remained locked in place, pointing away from Siobhan. She caught a glimpse of his face, which blazed with nothingness and stark white. His pale complexion was tinged with darkness.

He looked right at her with his glowing white eyes.

"You're not going to stop me," he growled in a voice that wasn't his. The growl rolled into the open air and connected itself to the clicking. It all blurred together and became so vivid that she could see the sounds spinning around her. The clicking growl coalesced in the center of her forehead, settling into a migraine.

Siobhan grimaced and put her hands up over her nose and mouth as she sank to the ground in a squat to keep herself conscious. The thickness of the air returned, and it grabbed a hold of her ribcage, squeezing.

The cool air wrapped around her, pressing her toward the ground from behind. She fell to all fours as if someone had pushed her back.

She pushed up and rocked herself back on her heels, still hunched over, with extreme nausea. A twinge of pain shot through her stomach as she doubled over again, unable to stay upright. An invisible frozen icicle cut her from the inside like it was trying to sliver its way out of her intestines while cold hands pressed her further into the earth.

Adam stood contorted, his mouth gaping open. Bits of flesh and soft black feathers were stuck to his face. He opened his mouth wider, creating an expansive cavern that took over half of his head.

His jaw lowered to his mid-chest, and his body stayed frozen in time, making space for the solid black abyss.

Chunks of a dead bird started falling out of his mouth like he was vomiting them up. He wasn't retching or heaving. He wasn't moving at all. A featherless wing dropped to the ground, followed by a lifeless head without a beak.

Siobhan vomited.

More bird parts and more blood started pouring out of Adam's mouth.

"I'm back," he growled in the same voice as before, his mouth barely moving.

Siobhan gagged as the strong musky odor she'd smelt before throttled her senses. Its intensity had increased.

Pieces of bird continued to roll out of Adam's gaping mouth and landed in the pool of blood on the ground. The continuous stream of blood carried the same color and consistency that she'd seen leaking from his injured arm yesterday as he hung mid-air. The thick, oil-like black blood rolled off him and sank into the earth.

She vomited again while the scratching noise of the clicking thumped her ears. Unable to speak and overwhelmed with a grotesque sickness deep inside her abdomen, she gagged.

Siobhan rolled to her side, unable to control the massive ice-cold pain in her guts. Needles of frozen metal pushed their way outward, stabbing at her skin from the inside. She grabbed her stomach and gagged as the blood continued in thick streaks to roll out of Adam's mouth. It cascaded in a waterfall down to the ground, spilling off him like waves of mercury and leaving its black trail behind.

Her previously strong and tall husband looked broken in the middle. His face had contorted and became unrecognizable as human.

Siobhan used all her energy to push herself up and slowly backed toward the house on her butt, scooting as fast as she could. It took everything she had to move through the pain.

There was too much blood... black and... aware.

The essence of something dark slowly filled the space around her, and she tried to move away from it. She slowly pressed herself backward, still watching Adam's twisted and grotesque form.

Siobhan pushed harder, desperately, forcing herself through an invisible barrier that had thickened the air around her. She continued to move despite heavy resistance. The air had become a cold lump of molasses.

She forced herself to lift her body into the house. She glanced over at her rosemary bush. It was vibrating. No. She was. Her body quivered with a combination of fear and cold. She reached up with a shaking hand and shut the sliding glass door, leaving a clammy palm print on it.

Adam remained unmoving while the blood continued to spew out of his mouth in thick black liquid. It created a stream at his feet that slithered toward their house. As soon as she shut the door, the tight grip on her lungs eased, but it wasn't enough. She continued to back herself toward the living room, scooting further away from Adam.

Siobhan's brain throbbed.

Click click click

The gray haze hung in the air, and her house visibly darkened. She opened her mouth to scream, but the air gripped her throat, cutting the sound off at the source. The light slowly fell away with every grating click.

Her back bumped into the front door. She couldn't back up anymore.

Siobhan looked up at the spot where Adam had levitated. Her necklace got warm, and she could see the light coming off it from below, swallowing her face. The warmth spread up her chin and swirled around her head, culling some of the icy confusion that had set in.

Paralyzed, unmoving, and breathing minimally, she allowed the warmth to ease her. It continued to spread to her whole body. She trembled but tried to slow her breathing.

She sat frozen, trying to catch her breath for a few minutes until Adam opened the sliding door and entered.

He paused, with his back to Siobhan. Blood hammered her ears, and her pulse pounded in her neck.

He turned with fluffy black feathers still on his face and shirt, his wavy black hair slightly tousled. He slid the door closed behind him and then looked right at her, wrinkling his forehead. His clothes were clean, devoid of the blood that had been rolling off him outside. There were no dead birds in his hands.

"Siobhan?" he asked, striding toward her.

She opened her mouth, but no sounds came out.

"What are you doing there?" he asked.

She tried to move but couldn't. Paralysis gripped her body.

"Adam…" She choked out his name in a scratchy voice.

"Are you okay?" Adam asked, kneeling in front of her. She put her hands up and pressed her back harder into the door.

"What are you doing, Siobhan?" he asked as he recoiled.

"I… I… I…" she stammered.

Adam looked at her through eyes that had narrowed to slits.

"Take your time," he said, rolling his eyes.

Her eyes stung.

"You okay?" he asked

She nodded. She pointed to the fluffy feathers stuck to his face around his mouth and flung her head back to rest on the door.

He put his hand up. "Oh, yeah. I was coming to tell you…"

he trailed off.

"You... you..." She dropped her hand in her lap. "You ate... you... the dead bird..." she stammered, shaking uncontrollably.

"What?" Adam said as he dropped his hands to the upright knee.

"I... there's.... vomited... feathers and blood." She shook her head, then lowered her face to her hands, squeezing her eyes shut as the tears started.

"I didn't eat a dead bird, Siobhan!" Adam shouted. He blew out a breath and closed his eyes. "One flew into my face while I was burying those things." He turned toward the backyard and waved one hand. "It hurt. I didn't bleed, though. Look." He tipped his head to the side so that she could see his face.

"You...you did bleed. So much..." she said.

"No," he said with force. "Look." He pushed his face closer to hers. She lifted her hand and placed it on his face.

Some redness had manifested on the side of his mouth, and three fluffy down feathers were stuck in the stubble on his face, which hadn't been shaven since Thursday.

"Why... why... why... why...?" She put her hands back up to her face and shook her head. "I'm... I'm... I'm..." She blew out a long breath. "I'm crazy... or I'm..." She inhaled sharply and choked back a sob.

"No, you're not. Let me help you. I understand how it looks with these feathers on my face," he said, his face softening.

That didn't explain the blood. The thick, black blood had freely flown out of his mouth, down his chin like it had come out of a faucet, before pooling at his feet. He had stood in it. It had snaked around their yard. She was sure of it.

She had vomited.

"I think I'm sick," she said.

CHAPTER 7

Siobhan needed pharmaceutical interventions. She had hallucinated another disgusting image of her husband.

"I'm sorry, Adam," she said. "I love you."

He chuckled. "I love you too, babe. Don't mention it. Get better, okay? It's Saturday. You have all day today and tomorrow before you have to do anything, right?" he asked as he helped her stand. He held her elbow a little too tightly and helped her walk to the couch.

She sat and toppled over with her head on the pillow. "I'll get you a blanket," he said.

He drooped a blanket over her from behind the couch.

"What's wrong with me, Adam?"

"You're probably sick," Adam said, shrugging. "I'm going to wash my face. I'll be back," he said before bounding up the stairs.

Siobhan had nothing to say, and she tried not to move. She was sick but well at the same time. She had every disease all at once, and yet she was perfectly healthy.

What the FUCK is happening to me?

She lay still, realizing that a few days ago, her life had been normal, maybe even boring in its simplicity. Now, she questioned her waning sanity. Where did this strange necklace come from, and how was her husband still alive after all the weird bleeding, levitating, and bird-eating while twisted backward?

The one reasonable explanation her racing, incoherent, and borderline psychotic mind could conjure was that she had a mental condition.

She listened to Adam turn the water on upstairs, then remembered she was going to call Melina and do some research on mental illness.

She tossed the blanket off herself, and her unstable legs took her to the kitchen table to get her phone. She pulled the charging cord from it and then took it back to the couch with her.

Snuggling into the warmth of the blanket, she powered on the phone. It had 62% battery life, and she had three text messages. She sighed and answered those first.

After responding to the first text, one from her mom, she read and responded to Helen. Her friend wanted Siobhan and Adam to go out with her and Jesus. *Come with us tonight! Jesus asked me out! We are going to an early dinner, then drinks at the new fancy cocktail bar on Raven's Beach. Jesus would love to meet Adam!*

Siobhan typed a response to Helen: *I'm happy for you! Sorry, but I'm actually sick right now, so I'll be resting. Raincheck?*

She sent the text and then meant to read the third text, but

Helen responded right away. Her text read: *I'm so sorry you're sick. OK. Raincheck accepted. Let me know if you need anything.*

Siobhan typed back: *Thanks, I will. Have fun!*

The last text was from Adam. She sat up and cocked her head to the side. The text had come in at 7:33 that morning. That was right around the time she hallucinated him eating a dead bird.

He had sent an emoji. A devil. A smiling devil. Her lungs decompressed as she expelled all the air they had been holding, and her hands started shaking.

She found Melina's number while her mind shifted to her necklace.

Weird things are happening, and they have to do with the necklace. Can you call me when you get a chance? Thanks.

She gripped her phone tight and heard Adam come down the stairs.

"Hey," he said as he leaned on the back of the couch. He had cleaned his face of the bird fluff, but a slight bruise remained, along with his unshaven stubble.

"Hey," she replied, frowning. "Did you send this text?" She showed him the emoji.

"Uh, no. Must have bumped the phone. I don't like emojis. You're still beautiful, even when you're sick," he said, resting his chin on his hands on the back of the couch. Her eyes dragged involuntarily to his injured arm.

"Sorry to mess up the day we were supposed to be having," she said.

"It's all good. What if I head to the gym and make sure everything is OK for you? I can check the towels and the sauna and make sure the tanning room is clean."

"You're the best, Adam," she said. "But you don't have to."

"I have to head to that big house in Keller Estates anyway. I need to get a tool I loaned to the new guy so I can change the oil in my truck," he said as he stood.

"Oh. Well, be safe," Siobhan said as she rolled over to face the TV.

"I'll be back for dinner. Love you," Adam said as he grabbed his keys from the tray near their front door.

"Love you too," Siobhan muttered without looking at him. The front door creaked open and closed behind Adam. His diesel truck roared to life, and she waited until she couldn't hear the engine anymore before sitting up and checking her phone.

She stared at it, hoping Melina would call. The background light switched off, and the picture of her and Adam went black. She put it on the coffee table and then lay down. She shut her eyes to rest and dozed off.

Siobhan meandered through the dark house she had lived in as a child. She put her palm on the wall and pushed her hand through it as the barrier swirled to life.

This was a lucid dream.

The infinite black hallway was dimly lit with a glow that came from somewhere above her. The luminescence allowed her to see even though everything was darkened by the ether. She found a formless box on the floor and stood on it. Usually, cardboard boxes collapsed, but because this was a dream, there were no rules, and she knew it. She jumped and made her way out of the house through the porous ceiling.

She landed outside in an open meadow in a forest. It was so foggy she couldn't make out individual trees or branches, but she knew they were there. It was darker in this clearing than it had been inside the house. Gray covered everything, even the grass.

All around her a black-and-white movie played on the landscape, devoid of all white. No color could be seen, and even though she recognized the lucid dream, she couldn't experience anything chromatic. The gray hues blended, forming a nothingness devoid of everything.

She took a few steps. A twig snapped behind the bushes to her left. She stopped and looked as one bush pushed itself forward and into focus.

This bush's branches curled like the clawed hands of a reptile reaching in all directions, charcoal gray against the ashen hue of the forest behind it.

"Hello?" she called. "I know this is a dream, so whatever happens isn't real," she yelled to the noise. The bush rustled, and another twig snapped.

Click click click

The clicking was so much more eerie in the gray landscape of her dream.

Click click click

She spun around, trying to find the scratching sound that rubbed against the raw nerve endings in her chest cavity.

The bush had retreated into the hazy fog of depression and made itself invisible.

"You do know I can follow you. I'm in control," Siobhan said as she took a step toward the rustling.

Click click click

Every click vibrated in her chest uncomfortably, like they were competing with her heartbeat. She put her hand on her chest, the absence of the tiger's eye necklace noticeable.

"Come closer…." A low growling voice said as it combined with the scratching clicks. She stopped, dead in her tracks. Every inch of her body stiffened in recognition. The voice Adam had used pricked her brain. "I've been waiting…" the voice growled.

The clicking and wailing screams of ghosts surrounded her. The cold air swirled around her legs, and she wrapped her arms around herself.

Another growling roar started as the rush of cool air pressed against Siobhan's chest, just as it had in her backyard. A cold breath blew on the back of her neck, sending her hair flowing forward.

Siobhan spun around and started walking toward the eerie breath, pushing through the mercurial air. She trudged forward, cutting a path through the wind toward the voice. The resistance increased. "I'm not afraid of you!" she yelled as she started to run. She wasn't going anywhere, stuck in a colorless muck in this colorless dream.

"This is my dream, and I know I'm in control!" she yelled, now trying to convince herself.

The voice laughed a deep and roaring chuckle that sent chills right through her nerve endings, fusing with the cold that left her with waning courage. "You don't scare me!" Siobhan said with a shaky voice.

The laughter stopped, and she stopped running in place. What was she chasing anyway? A voice? "I'm in control!" she yelled again. But she knew she wasn't.

The voice growled in her ear as the icy breath landed, blowing her hair into her face. She jumped back, and the voice chuckled as it clicked.

An eerie presence lingered over her and wrapped itself around her, threatening to drag her away if she even dared move.

Each tiny hair on her body inflamed, red hot against the cold wind, which remained colorless and with it a strong, pungent, musky odor like that of a dead rat.

Her skin prickled and tingled, but she tried desperately to remain unafraid. After all, this was her lucid dream.

"MINE..." the voice said as it deepened its mocking, taunting laugh.

Siobhan bristled at the presence of evil. The air spun into fingers that tightened around her neck. She clawed at her throat, trying to clear it and make room for the oxygen she desperately needed. She inhaled sharply, and what little air she managed to breathe in stung her windpipe.

"You don't know me!" she said breathlessly.

The laughter started up again and got louder. It hurt her ears. With her chest heaving and the wind gripping her neck, she put her hands over her ears. It did little to dull the aching pain. She took her hands away. Blood pooled in her palms as the laughter continued to get more sinister and increased in volume.

It suffocated her with its cold need for control. The blood trickled from her ears and landed on her shoulders before it started to drip down her chest. The laughter coursed through her body and congested in a massive migraine right behind her eyes. She couldn't block out the atrocious sound.

"STOP!" she yelled as she gasped for more of the pungent,

thick air. The laughter got louder, close to and deafening. But it was the evil that remained stuck to her and the evil that something wanted her to feel.

Her entire body recoiled as the gray earth sent up invisible bugs to wriggle their way up her legs, leaving a trail of ice-cold barbs in their wake.

The intolerable laughter forced Siobhan to fall to her knees as her body gave out. She put her hands over her ears. The blood rushed through her fingers as it welled up and fell to the ground uncontrollably. Engulfed in waves of darkness that slapped against her like a wet sheet being whipped in the wind, she tightened her pressure on her own ears.

"Wake up, wake up, wake up, wake up..." she kept repeating as she tried to wake herself up from the lucid dream that had become the most horrific night terror. In the choking cold air that cut off all of her senses as it closed in on her lurked an evil she could feel.

She opened her eyes, balled her fists, looked up, and screamed as loud as she could toward the lifeless gunmetal sky.

Siobhan woke up screaming. She sat straight up on the couch; her heart raced, and the terror's imagery rushed through her, creating an adrenaline-fueled state of dread. She put her hand over her ear and jerked it away. No blood, only she is fully awake and in a lucid state.

Relief washed over her as she calmed herself, but the monochromatic hellscape her mind had conjured remained, the terror still gripping her. She grabbed the blanket, pulled it up to her neck, and tried to stave off the chill creeping along her skin.

Her necklace warmed against her chest. "Oh, dear God, what is happening to me?" she said out loud, rubbing her fists into her eyes through the blanket.

Then she heard it—the laughter from her dream—the low, growling voice that had come out of Adam. It spoke, but there were too many voices talking all at once, and it took up physical space in her house. It was there, but it wasn't there. The voices joined with the clicking in a union that subjugated her, deafening as it filled her head.

A heaviness pressed her into the cushion of the couch. She put her hands over her ears, like she'd done in her dream, and blood rushed between her fingers.

Large hands were slowly putting weight on her chest, and she sank into the cushion.

"Oh God," she stuttered. Then, one voice became louder than the rest, growing above the clicking and laughter.

"He can't help you..." it roared as it trailed off into a booming fit of laughter.

Siobhan screamed as she did in her dream, using whatever oxygen she had in her lungs. Blood dripped out of her right ear and landed on the blanket. Sticky and hot, some of it lingered on the side of her head as a force pressed down harder on her with a violent shove with invisible hands.

She feared that if her heart rate did not go down so she could start breathing again, she would pass out and never wake up. She quivered in fear, shaking the whole couch as she sank further, and the springs dug into her thighs.

Her muscles were sore from the cortisol and adrenaline that constantly flowed through her veins, as the sound of hell pressed against her skull and forced her to hear with her eyes.

The laughter, voices, and sounds stopped. The emptiness they left created a deafening roar. The invisible hands released their grip, and she snapped back up on the couch. Nothing but emptiness surrounded her. She reached up to touch her ear. It had stopped bleeding, but the blood on her palms remained sticky and wet. Droplets lingered on the blanket.

Siobhan put her head in her hands. No answers or solutions came, only a sense of impending dread.

She had officially lost her mind. She needed a psychologist as soon as possible. It was Saturday, though, and no one was going to see her today or tomorrow, so she sat on the couch and cried, sobbing into her bloody hands.

CHAPTER 8

Siobhan woke to the front door opening and closing. Her eyes hurt, and she rubbed the crust out of them.

"Hey, honey," Adam said. "You feeling any better?" He set down what she assumed was his toolbox.

Siobhan groaned and rolled over on the couch, burying her face in the pillow. Adam knelt in front of her.

"No offense, but you look sick," Adam said.

"Adam..." she croaked out. Adam brushed a chunk of her hair away from her tanned face to reveal swollen red eyes.

"Are you thirsty?" he asked.

"Yeah," she said, but what she wanted to say was *No. My voice is hoarse because I've been crying and screaming.*

"I'll grab you some water before I head to the garage," Adam said.

Siobhan sat upright and turned her hands over in front of her face. They were clean. Drops of blood stained the blanket. Was it real? How could she know? She couldn't, and that's what terrified her the most.

She flipped the blanket over so Adam wouldn't see the blood and put her hands in her lap. She stared at her shaking palms while she listened to him get her a glass out of the cabinet and fill it with some ice and water.

Click click click click click click click click

The now familiar scratching sound burrowed its way into her head. It grated against her frayed nerves, but it stopped when Adam came into her line of sight.

He set the glass of iced water on the coffee table next to her phone. "Do you need anything else before I go into the garage?"

"Thanks, Adam," she replied.

Click click click click click click click click

"Did you hear that?" she asked at the risk of sounding like she was officially mentally unstable. He stretched his neck and blinked as his eyes rolled upward, pretending to look for the sound.

"No. Are you okay?" he asked.

"I don't know," she said. Internally, she screamed and cried for help that she knew he couldn't give her. This was the second time she'd asked, and the second time he couldn't hear it.

"Your gym looked great, by the way," Adam said, brushing off her remark. "I don't think I've ever seen the mirrors not streaky," Adam said.

"Yeah. Jesus did that," she said flatly. She wanted to smile but couldn't manage one.

"Great job on the hire, boss," Adam said.

Siobhan rolled her eyes. She got a momentary glimpse of normal, and a shred of hope wove its way into her heart. Why couldn't the rest of her life be like this moment? "Ugh. You and everyone else," she said, wincing as she rubbed her right ear.

"We're giving credit where it's due," Adam said with a laugh. "Now," he added as he clapped his hands, "it's time to change the oil in my truck. Can I get you anything before I head out?"

Click click click click click click

Siobhan's wide eyes scanned the room frantically as she shook her head slowly. "I'm exhausted. I'm going to rest," she said as the awful scraping percussive sound of hatred tried to find its way into her brain stem while it rebounded off every surface in the house.

Adam picked up his toolbox. "Feel better," he said.

Siobhan listened to the garage door open and the slam shut. She glanced at her phone. No flashing blue light appeared to indicate she had a text message waiting to be read.

Click click click click click click click click

Siobhan put her head in her hands, trying to dull the throbbing migraine forming from the clicking. Her crystal warmed up on her chest, and she opened her eyes enough to notice a luminous glow coming off it. A cold breeze blew from her right, the open side of the couch. It skimmed across the skin on the back of her hand.

She wasn't alone.

The air cooled, and a blast of adrenaline shot through her body, stiffening her muscles.

She kept her head down as someone sat on the couch next to her. Lifting her head, she slowly turned to look at the cushion, and her heart picked up speed in her chest.

The couch cushion depressed, as if someone, *no, something,* perched there. It wasn't a human shape. It had sharp edges.

Siobhan's breath came in sharp bursts as the shape moved. It had twisted toward her. Whatever was using its being to look right at her. Eyes she couldn't see burrowed into her psyche, invading her personal space from afar.

She pushed back into the arm of the couch, trying to get some distance, but it leaned forward, closing the space between them. The presence made itself known to her and spun around her.

The gray haze swirled around her house, making space for something invisible. A cold and evil breath blew into her face. It smelled of decay, burned hair, and rotting meat.

She sat perfectly still, hoping it would go away, but it kept leaning closer. Another icy breath blew across her face, carrying the horrific smell of decaying meat and rodents with it. It blasted around her, and she tried to scream, but the pungent odor held her throat tight.

An ice-cold claw dragged down her temple and ended with

a poke to the middle of her chin. She jerked her head away, sucked in a breath, and held back the tears forming.

She scanned the room, looking for it, and it grabbed her upper arm. She tried to scream, and another jagged, bony hand clasped around her throat, cutting the sound off. The fingers dug into her flesh as they gripped, making a point where each of the claws impressed into her skin. She could see the depressions in her arm as it held tight and she felt the icy hand around her throat.

These hands were not human and did not exist.

Siobhan choked as the dense air sucked itself toward her.

The laughter started up again.

She pushed back as something kept its cold grip on her and laughed in her face with breath so foul she wanted to vomit.

She struggled and pulled back against something invisible.

The grip released, and she shot backward, flinging over the arm of the couch. She sat up on the floor and strained her eyes, trying to find what had held her. Her breath came in rapid spurts, and her heart raced, sending adrenaline-fueled blood through her veins.

Her arm inflamed and turned red where fingers had gripped it, and pointed indentations from the claws remained in her flesh.

Panicking, she jumped up and picked up her phone. She tapped the side button. Nothing. It had died again.

Siobhan threw the blanket back on the couch and shuffled

to the kitchen for her charger. She unplugged it and brought it to the living room with her, plugging it in next to the sofa with shaking hands.

Even though they'd let go, the claws of ice holding onto her arm and squeezing her throat were still present.

Her nerves were shot, and she yawned loudly against the fatigue.

Click click click click click click click click

And that goddamn clicking. Everything about it hurt. It tapped on the aching points deep inside her ear like it punctured her brain. *There has to be an explanation.*

She could hear Adam working in the garage, moving tools around and shuffling along the concrete floor.

She wanted to tell him what had happened, but she knew he wouldn't believe her and would assume she was going insane. *But I am.*

A flashback of her hallucination of Adam levitating in their living room lit up inside her head. The blood coming from his eyes and his arm had been unsettling and so real in its blackness. The same colorless tone that the bush had been in her dream, a blackness devoid of anything with no other explanation, filled her head.

The mental pressure threatened to shatter her spirit into a million slivers, never to be put back together. She had been flung into a reality that had been broken and forever contorted.

She remembered her phone's battery had been at 62% before she fell asleep and had her nightmare, but she couldn't be sure of anything anymore, so maybe she was wrong about that too.

Everything had been flipped on its head and fragmented into a sick and disgusting existence. She was going crazy, and no one was going to be able to help her.

Siobhan snatched her phone off the coffee table, shoved the power cord into it, and hit the power button. She bounced her foot as she waited for it to charge enough to boot up and go to her home screen.

Hurry up! she screamed inside her own head. *Hurry.*

She Googled *hallucinations*. Other than a few articles telling her to go to a doctor to find out why she was hallucinating, she found useless information.

She read one article claiming schizophrenia could be a possibility. She found out that schizophrenia was a severe mental disorder that affects how a person perceives reality and relates to others.

That sounded right. She probably had schizophrenia. She would need medication and therapy. Perfect. That's exactly what she needed.

Her ear still throbbed as a reminder of her dream.

She caught a glimpse of the droplets of blood on the

blanket and snatched it toward her, pulling it over her icy legs.

She checked her arm and could still see small red indentations where the tips of sharp claws had pressed into her skin. Three punctures stippled the inside of her bicep.

"Yep. I'm going crazy," she said out loud before picking up her phone and mindlessly scrolling but desperately searching for any information that could be helpful.

Tomorrow was Sunday, but Siobhan was determined to see a mental health professional. She revamped her search and looked for a therapist, psychologist, psychiatrist, counselor—anyone— who could help her on the weekend.

She had little luck, but she did notice one therapist had "emergency appointments," but those were for already existing clients. She bookmarked the website and put the address in her map app so she could at least drive by tomorrow and scope the place out. Maybe someone would be there, and she would accidentally be able to get the help she needed.

Siobhan called the number listed on the website, but no one answered, as she suspected. An emergency phone number was given, and she wanted to call it. But she couldn't force herself to call it. Instead, she punched the number into her phone and saved it.

Something pulled her toward the address across town, even though she'd never been there. She needed to get to the physical location, so she followed her instincts as she'd done with the necklace.

Siobhan set the phone down and wished she could talk to Adam about all of this. She depended on his opinions, even more so than her own.

She let her mind drift to the questions she needed answers to. Why wasn't Melina calling her? Should she text again? Call? Leave a voicemail? Maybe she was busy, but this was important. Siobhan knew the necklace had something to do with her hallucinations, but she couldn't figure it out on her own.

Click click click click click click click click

Siobhan put her hands on her face, trying to dull the vibrations the awful clicking sound caused. Each click poked inside her brain, and the immense pressure gripped her head.

Each click sent her closer to the precipice of insanity.

Maybe I DO believe in ghosts. One attacked me. No, that wasn't possible. Her mind had played a trick on her.

Siobhan believed in the physical reality that she could see, touch, and experience. But her reality had become an expanding hellscape of dull torment that lacked any sense of realism.

Or maybe not. *I am going crazy, after all. I am hallucinating. The clicking is also a hallucination.*

The blood droplets speckled the blanket and made her aware of the painful burning sensation still present in her ear while ice-cold pins prickled on her arm.

Adam opened the garage door, and it shut with a loud thud. He poked his head around the corner. "Feeling better yet?" he asked.

She moaned as she rubbed her arms to warm up. Siobhan shivered, even though the hot summer day radiated inside their house without air conditioning.

Her hand covered her necklace feeling its warmth against her frigid skin.

"Siobhan?" Adam asked.

"What?"

"You hungry?" he asked, crossing his arms over his chest.

"I…. no. I need to let my stomach settle some more," she responded as confusion set in. Her mind scattered her thoughts all over the place, and she had trouble focusing.

"Okay. I'll make myself an early dinner, then finish up in the garage. Need some water?" he asked.

"Sure, yeah. But I can get it. I need to move a little. I don't lay down all day normally," she said.

Adam chuckled. "Hopefully, no one does that unless they are sick."

"Yeah," she said. "I may have to try to see a doctor tomorrow if I don't feel better," she said. She wanted to tell Adam she should see a psychiatrist. Or psychologist. Or therapist. But saying doctor made her sound more normal.

"Okay, yeah. Do what's best for you. You still have my insurance card, right? From my injury? You can use it. I added you right after we got married," Adam reminded her.

"I do. Thanks," she said.

Siobhan's phone beeped, and she jumped up and grabbed it. Her blanket fell to the floor and pooled around her feet. *Please be Melina.*

She dragged her finger across the phone screen. She had a text message from Melina. It read: *I'm sorry I missed you today. I can meet you somewhere tomorrow.* Even her texts came across as emotionless.

She typed: *Thanks. Let me know when you are available. I really want to talk to you.*

The relief Siobhan craved never came. She couldn't explain anything, and she wouldn't know how to, if any of it was even real. She had spent all day waiting for that goddamn text message, only to find out she'd get no answers until tomorrow.

CHAPTER 9

The next morning, after a night of deep dreamless sleep, Siobhan woke up with no pain in her ear, no prick marks on her arm, no nausea, not even the slightest body ache. She was... normal.

She jumped out of bed, ready to go about her day. *FINALLY!*

Adam had already gotten up, leaving his side of the bed crumpled and his pillow askew.

Siobhan showered and brushed her teeth while she pieced together yesterday's ominous events. In the back of her mind, she had a nagging suspicion she was still going crazy.

Her hallucination of Adam eating the bird had been so real. Her lucid nightmare made her realize lucid and normal dreaming could blend into reality, and the sounds that permeated the natural world through those dreams could make her ears bleed while she had been in an unconscious state.

She grimaced as she remembered the feel of the invisible, bony, and jagged-clawed hand that had gripped her arm and the evil presence that had breathed the smell of death into her face.

Nothing made sense. But she had to find answers, figuring she must be stressed and in a problematic mental space right now. A therapist could fix it, and she had to make sure of it.

After she put on some shorts and a T-shirt, Siobhan

descended the stairs. Drops of blood were splattered on the steps starting halfway down.

She paused. *Was the blood from her ear bleeding from yesterday?* Her hand shot to her ear. She pulled her palm away, turning her hand over and inspecting it. No blood.

Adam.

She bound down the stairs and ran into the kitchen. He groaned from the couch she'd run by moments ago. The groan changed into a low growl and sunk inside her skull, probing her memories to the surface.

Siobhan peered around the corner and glanced at him. His labored breathing gargled, and blood pooled out of his right ear. It slowly dripped onto the same blanket she'd used.

She approached him with apprehension and knelt in front of him. His eyeballs were darting around behind closed lids, and his body jerked slightly. He made low groaning sounds in his throat that were not anywhere close to words as he gurgled. A small amount of saliva had bubbled up into foam in the corner of his mouth.

She put her left hand on his shoulder and shook him lightly to try to wake him. "Adam," she said. "Hey. Adam. Are you okay? You need to wake up." She was afraid he'd choke on his own saliva. He remained asleep, and the bloody stream coming from his ear increased; she got more frantic.

"Adam!" she said, shaking him vigorously. "You need to wake up now!"

She shook him while he bled and gasped for air through the foam spilling from the tiny slit his mouth had formed.

The laughter started up again. The sinister, petty, and horrifically evil laughter that had made her ears bleed the day before melded into the clicking, scraping her raw eardrums once again.

She stopped shaking her husband but kept her hand on his shoulder, unwilling to move.

"Oh, dear god..." she let out quietly. Adam lay still; the blood soaking into the blanket as the laughter got louder.

The lone sound grew in intensity as the growling and animalistic laughter that made her want to vomit, scream, and cry all at once surrounded her and split the dense air into segments.

Siobhan saw the gray haze that had descended on her house visibly darken a few shades. Her home started to look as colorless as her dream. She put her hands over her ears and slammed her eyes shut, trying to get it to stop.

"No, no, no," she said as she squeezed her eyes tighter while curling up between the couch and the coffee table. She pulled her knees to her chest, trying to make herself as small and unnoticeable as possible. Her knee grazed her necklace, and its warmth started to radiate through her entire leg.

She tried to drown out the terrible laughter, but she couldn't. It blended with the clicking that permeated and caused the air all around her to bounce in waves.

"Please stop," she whispered. Her necklace got warmer on her chest. She refused to open her eyes; instead, she froze, too afraid to look up. She tried to focus on the comforting warmth of the crystal against her chest and not the ever-increasingly sinister volume of the laughter that was not there but somehow all around her. It swirled around and grabbed at her.

Then she remembered Adam. She opened her eyes. The loud laughter stopped. Adam didn't move. He still had a small line of blood running out of his ear. His eyes were open, and the solid white orbs were looking right at her.

"Hello, Siobhan," he said in the same voice he used yesterday while he ate the dead bird. "Are we better?" he asked, following the comment with a low, sinister chuckle.

"What in the hell is wrong with you, Adam?" she managed to squeak out in a shaky voice.

She couldn't control her trembling. Her courage shrank, as if she were a mouse backed into a corner, desperate but unable to escape the inevitable.

Adam chuckled ominously and slowly opened his mouth wide, a toothy grin slashed across his face. His eyes slammed shut, and she focused on his wide-open mouth. He jerked and then flopped onto his back, his tongue rolling out of his mouth.

His head rolled to the right, and his wavy black hair fell over his face in a mass of tangles, covering his newly asymmetrical face. It looked twisted and not like him. His skin contorted on the surface of his skull, creating out-of-place lumps and a twist of flesh across one cheek.

Siobhan couldn't move. The panic and terror were searing the ends of every single capillary in her body, and they threatened to explode. She sat motionless, watching Adam.

An immeasurable amount of fear paralyzed her body and brain. She couldn't scream or cry out, and even if she managed, it wouldn't be audible in the heavy air pressurizing her lungs.

Adam's eyes slowly fluttered open. His head snapped toward her, and he looked at her with his dark brown eyes.

"Hey," he said in a hoarse voice, his face smoother than she remembered. She cocked her head to the side, noticing he now had slight nuances to his appearance that made him look a little less like himself. "I think I have your sickness," he moaned.

Siobhan stared as her body trembled.

"I hope I didn't wake you up coming down here last night," he croaked out.

What? He talked to her like nothing had happened. Like he hadn't been bleeding or talking in the most eerily creepy voice she'd ever heard. The intolerable sensation had become familiar.

This wasn't Adam. His face was his but it had twisted into a distorted version of the man she'd married. He stared at her, looking sick, so she tried to tell herself that that's why his face wasn't quite the same. She couldn't even put her finger on the exact problems with his appearance.

It was the same with his personality. It was all there, but it wasn't right.

A small amount of blood still trickled out of his ear, but nothing like before, and it had started drying and sticking to his skin.

She tried to look at his left arm, but he had it covered by the blanket.

Siobhan slowly lifted her hand, wanting to test her reality. She put her palm on Adam's cheek and his skin burned her hand with an unnatural heat. This wasn't a normal feverish heat, but one you'd expect if you grabbed a hot pie pan.

Why is this happening?

"What's wrong, Siobhan?" he asked as she jerked her hand away from his face.

She slowly and weakly pointed to his ear, and he lifted his hand to it.

"Damn. That hurts," he said, wincing. "I had this wild dream that laughter hurt my ears. I guess my body thought it was real."

Siobhan opened her mouth. She wanted to speak. She tried to get out at least something. She wanted to tell him she'd experienced the same thing, that it was real. It wasn't a dream. But that would mean they were both crazy.

He exuded logic. His body told his mind the dream had happened. That's what it was. That made sense! She had no explanation other than she had had a mental breakdown. She was the one falling into a black abyss.

"Are you..." She swallowed hard, forcing her voice to remain steady. "Okay?" she finished, her tone betraying only the slightest tremor.

"Yeah," Adam said, far less concerned about his dream than she was.

"Here," she said, lifting the blanket to his ear for him.

"Thanks. After I threw up everything I'd eaten for the last month last night, I came down here in case I got sick again so I wouldn't wake you up. I guess I was tired; that dream was vivid. Damn. I feel like it really happened."

"I'm sorry, Adam," Siobhan said, wanting to tell him she'd experienced the same thing.

It would be nice if we were crazy together, though. Two lunatics together in the gray dream of horrors.

"I always knew dreams could seem real. I'm sure it's from having a fever. I probably have some inflammation in my ear, and the dream was my subconscious mind's way of dealing with that pain," he said with certainty.

Why couldn't her mind push the crazy aside and find the Occam's Razor answer? She bit her lip and looked up at the ceiling.

"Yeah," she said, nodding. "That makes sense."

She reached behind her and pulled herself up to sit on their coffee table.

"I'm going to grab some Advil," Adam said.

"I'll get it," Siobhan said, standing.

She wanted to get away from him, but she couldn't figure out why.

"I'll grab some water for you, too," she said as she hurried into the kitchen. She filled a glass with water, took two pills out of the bottle in the cabinet, and brought them to Adam.

"Thanks, Siobhan." Adam popped the pills into his mouth. "Did your ears hurt too yesterday?" he asked out of genuine curiosity. He chugged the water, downing the Advil in one long swallow.

"Um. A little."

She opened her mouth to tell him that she had the same dream, but he spoke before she could.

"Funny how inflammation from being sick comes about," he said. "I don't feel very well at all. I understand why you considered seeing a doctor yesterday.," He set the glass of water on the coffee table and laid back down. "How did you get better?"

"I slept a lot," Siobhan said anxiously. "It helped." She slept, and she's better now. Maybe that's what he needed. Maybe it was the stomach flu. Maybe it was a fever-induced dream. Maybe he's right about everything.

He did have a decent explanation for the ear pain.

Her body trembled with sickness and inflammation. Her mind made up a story to match her emotional state. That sounded like a much saner version of events than her explanation, which included a haunted necklace, seeing her husband levitate, bleeding, and bird eating, complete with lucid nightmares that weren't lucid and the claws of hell gripping her arm as an invisible thing breathed in her face.

She blinked hard, trying to push the images out of her head.

"Okay. I'll do the same," Adam said, lying down on the couch.

"I'm gonna check the gym," she said quickly.

"OK," Adam said, closing his eyes.

He's taking this much better than I am. Maybe I'm haunted. Perhaps it's not the necklace. It's me. She was the one hallucinating. She was the one who panicked and terrified. She was the one who was not able to come up with anything logical. She was the one who was haunted. *Can people even be haunted?*

Sure, she'd seen *The Exorcist* several years ago, but...

Oh god. Is she...

"Take care of yourself. Text me if you need anything," she said.

"You got it. Thanks," he said with his eyes closed.

Siobhan made her way to the kitchen and made a pot of coffee. As it brewed, she leaned against the counter and crossed her arms tightly over her chest. Should she think it? *Possessed. Is that even a thing?* She didn't believe in ghosts, let alone demons.

Click click click

Click click click

She shivered against the cold that coalesced around her, and she grimaced as each click burned her neurons. It wasn't cold outside, but an icy breeze traveled up her spine and curled around the hair at the nape of her neck.

She hugged herself more tightly, shaking at the idea of being possessed.

"No," she said out loud, putting her hands up. *This is the mental state I'm in. I am going to be okay.* She grabbed a travel mug from the cabinet and filled it to the top with coffee. "And now I'm talking to myself," she muttered.

She sipped her coffee and enjoyed the warmth of the bitter liquid. She glanced at the clock on the stove. It was six forty-five in the morning, too early to attempt to go to the therapist's office, especially on a Sunday.

She grabbed her purse from the hook and trotted to the front door. Her house became less inviting by the moment.

She glanced at Adam on the couch.

"Adam," she said barely above a whisper. He stayed perfectly still.

She dug in her purse for her keys and headed outside to her Jeep, closing the door on the clicking sound that had started once again.

The sun blazed on another hot day, and even though it was early, the brightness bit at her eyes. Siobhan usually drove without sunglasses, but she kept some in her Jeep. Today, she needed them. Her eyes were sensitive and being in the morning light hurt them.

Maybe it was because she hadn't seen much sun yesterday because she had been sick (yeah, "sick") or possessed… *NO*. She was *sick*. She had to stop. She was driving herself crazy.

She put on the sunglasses and started the Jeep. She lowered the emergency brake, pushed the clutch to the floor, and put the Jeep in reverse.

The seat belt pressed her necklace into her skin. *Deep breaths*, she reminded herself. *You're experiencing stress. This happens. Everyone gets stressed out. You're in massive debt after buying the gym and a house. Stress. Not possessed. That's it*, she told herself. *That is ALL it is.*

The hair on her arms stood at attention, and a chill ran through her blood, icing her veins. She glanced back at the front window of her house through the darkened lenses of her sunglasses.

Was that Adam looking at her? It had to be. No one else was in there. A shiver ran down her spine, and a cold sweat formed on her brow.

Adam stood there, looking like a shadowy, dark figure, glaring at her out the front window.

Adam stood at six foot two, but was he *that* tall? Had he ever watched her like that before? His eyes, which she couldn't see, burned through the glass of the window and sent shock waves through her eyes as she stared.

She could feel pure hatred emanating from the figure. Adam seemed to blur into the gray atmosphere inside her house. She shivered as goosebumps formed on her arms.

Great. Another hallucination.

She ignored Adam and fought the urge to go back inside and yell at him for being cruel. *Be rational, Siobhan.*

Looking behind her, she backed the Jeep out of the driveway and onto the road.

"I am batshit crazy," she said out loud as she rammed the Jeep into first gear and took off toward the gym without looking back.

CHAPTER 10

When Siobhan pulled her Jeep into the parking lot of The Flex, she was no more ready to be there than she was to hallucinate her husband bleeding and levitating.

Even though it approached eighty degrees, she still had chills after Adam stared her down from their front window. This record-breaking heat wave billowed around her even though she remembered how the cold had sunk into her bones over the past few days.

She would find enough to do at the gym to keep herself busy until she could drive by the therapist's office.

She killed the Jeep's engine and reached for her phone in her purse. She checked her texts - one from Helen and one from Melina.

She opened the text from Melina. It had been sent the night before while she'd slept.

I am going to work out in the morning, then I'll call you.

There weren't many around, and the empty parking lot on a Sunday was not alarming. She did notice a red Ford Explorer a few spaces down from her Jeep and a tan Subaru station wagon parked behind her.

Siobhan sent a text back anyway, in case she missed Melina.

Thanks! I just got to the gym to check on some things. I have most of the day available.

As she expected, Helen's message was a long paragraph about how well her date with Jesus had gone. Helen had also asked if Siobhan felt any better. She typed: *I'm glad you had fun! I'll try to call later, and you can tell me all about it. Adam's sick now, though.*

She threw her phone back in her purse and made her way into the gym. She scanned her card and rounded the front counter, setting her purse on the floor and powering on her computer.

She typed in her password and waited for the screen to come to life, with her gym logo lighting up the background. She wanted to check and make sure she had Melina's login set up correctly since she started tomorrow morning.

Was she still going to take the yoga class? Was yoga right for someone losing their goddamn mind?

She pulled up Melina's name, Callaghan, M., and tried to punch in a time. It worked.

She kept busy by straightening up. She strode to the tanning room, scanned her card, opened the door, and flipped the light on.

Siobhan took her time checking for anything that needed her attention. The bed had been adequately cleaned and a fresh towel lay next to the plastic pillow with the little Plexiglas sign stating the bed had been sanitized.

Tanners were supposed to clean the bed when they were done, put out a fresh towel, and discard the old one in the basket by the door. There were several dirty towels. Siobhan grabbed the whole basket. She ensured the sanitizing spray was full, flipped the light off, and shut the door.

She spun around and ran right into Melina. "Oh!" She gasped, dropping the basket as towels spilled everywhere.

"I am so sorry," Melina said, stretching out her arms.

"It's okay," Siobhan said. She swallowed hard. "I've been…I didn't feel well yesterday so that I might be a little off today," she added as she knelt to pick up the towels.

Melina knelt to help. Perfectly applied eyeliner adorned each almond eye, and her long black hair made the sleekest ponytail Siobhan had ever seen. She wore all black again—this time, black tennis shoes, black leggings, and a black tank top with a single red stripe right down the middle of it from her neck to her waist.

"I got your text," Melina said, tossing towels into the basket. "I knew I could probably find you here. I am the only one here. I like that. It gives me space to think.".

Siobhan snorted. "I'm glad you like thinking. My mind is going nuts trying to figure out… everything," she said, dropping the last towel into the basket and standing.

"Maybe I can help—at least some," Melina said.

"Yeah. I'll wash these towels and restock, then meet me up front?" Siobhan suggested.

"Sure," Melina replied, turning to leave.

Siobhan scanned her key card, pushed open the door to the supply room, and tossed the towels in the washing machine. She credited the tidy room to Jesus.

Siobhan checked the dryer. Some locker room towels were already dry. Adam probably washed those yesterday when he stopped by. She folded them, then took them back to the front and replenished the stack near the front desk so that people could take them as they came in.

The mindless tasks kept her normal and sane, even though she still knew that things were anything but right now. She grabbed the tanning towel basket and returned it to the room.

She headed up to the front and shut down the computer.

Melina followed. "I know you probably think I'm crazy, but…"

Siobhan put her hands up and said: "Listen. I am in no position to judge anyone for any reason regarding their perceived level of sanity."

Melina sat in the chair next to Siobhan.

"So, what's the deal with this?" Siobhan asked, putting her hand over the tiger's eye crystal necklace, trying to hide her desperation.

Melina sighed. "It's a long story, and I can't tell you all of it...that's the *crazy* part," she said, using air quotes around the word crazy. "But I do know some things that may at least help," she said.

"Well, that's more than I have to go on," Siobhan said, shrugging. "I'm assuming I'm either needing to go to an insane asylum, where they dope you up all day, or my stress levels have become unmanageable. Either way, I need a psychiatrist," she added.

"Maybe you do. I don't know about that," Melina said, her monotone voice showing little indication of her emotions. "But for what it's worth, I don't think you're going crazy. You may need to manage stress better."

"All I know is that this," she said, lifting the necklace, "used to be your grandmother's."

Melina nodded. "It was. She loved it. She never took it off, except right before her death when she handed it to me. She knew she was..."

Siobhan gritted her teeth, fighting the wave of fear that washed over her. "Um, so, like..."

Melina shook her head. "No. No. It's nothing like that. She wore it until the day she died, but it didn't..." She paused.

"Oh good," Siobhan said, sighing with relief. "How did it

end up at my wedding?"

"I left it there," Melina said, looking down at her hands.

Siobhan stared at her new friend in silence. "But... why?" She shook her head.

"You needed it. And I'm glad I did because you seem to be...stressed," she said, changing her words.

Siobhan kept her hand over the necklace as Melina talked.

"My grandmother told me she was putting her energy into the crystal and that she'd warn me if I needed to let it go. She came to me in a dream and told me to leave it for you," Melina said.

"But why me? Why did I need it?" Siobhan asked, even more confused than she had been before.

"I think..." she said, trailing off and looking toward the ceiling. "I followed Grandma's instructions in the dream. I had to leave it for you," Melina said.

"Okay, so, it's normal for this thing to get warm and glow?" she asked.

Melina nodded. "Yep, I wore it until the dream," she said. Melina chewed her bottom lip and shifted in the chair.

"You snuck a weird grandmother-haunted necklace into my wedding as a gift." They both smiled a little. "I've been having hallucinations lately, and..." Siobhan confessed, dropping her eyes.

Melina sat straight up and became more alert.

"What kind of hallucinations?"

Siobhan chose not to tell Melina about the horrifying visions like Adam levitating and the dream because those still made her sound like a nutcase.

"Oh, like a feeling that my counter," she said, motioning toward it, "has some kind of wet cobwebs on it, but there's nothing there. I clean it, and it goes away, but it seems to come back." "Oh," Melina acted relieved. "But that could be anything. Like static, you know? I avoid touching it. Maybe it's the material it's made from."

Siobhan smiled and nodded. "Yeah. I figured as much. But I saw things bleed on their own. Then the blood disappeared."

"Okay. Well, that could have been your worry or concern taking over. Who was bleeding?"

Siobhan paused, unsure of how much more to say. Melina stared at her.

"It was a hallucination," Siobhan said.

Melina nodded. "I'm sorry you are experiencing these things," she said. "I hope Grandma's necklace will bring you comfort."

"I want to make sure my hallucinations are nothing, and if they are something, I need to figure out what's wrong with me and how to fix it. I found a therapist who sees people in emergency situations, and I was going to head over there after I got done here. Coming here was a way for me to pass the time," Siobhan explained.

"I hope you can get some answers," Melina said. "I have time today. If you need someone to go with you, I'd be happy to wait while you talk to the therapist," she added, looking down and seeming even more melancholy than before.

"Do you want to tell me...?" Siobhan started empathetically, sensing Melina had withheld information.

"I do. But it's going to make me sound like *I* belong in an insane asylum," Melina said, looking up.

Siobhan laughed. "At least we'll be there together. I've been crazy since the first bird slammed into my window."

"You've had birds hit your windows?" Melina asked, raising her perfectly tweezed eyebrows.

"Yeah. Several. My husband has been... Adam..." she trailed off. She couldn't explain her hallucination of him eating the bird while bleeding out of his mouth with his body twisted in half. "He's taking care of them. Burying them."

"Interesting," Melina said softly, her eyes darting around.

"Is that all a part of this necklace?" Siobhan asked.

Melina shook her head. "No, I mean, crystals can hold onto energy, and Grandmother's energy is in there, but she wouldn't fly birds into windows. My grandmother loved birds."

Siobhan put her thumb on the crystal, experiencing its familiar strange draw.

146

"Okay," Siobhan said, looking down at the necklace once again. "I would like some company when I go check out the therapist."

Melina smiled.

"I mean, I don't really want to be alone. That's when I feel the craziest."

"I will come with you. What if they aren't there, though? Should we call?" Melina asked.

"I tried yesterday. No one answered. I want to go there. I had this strange feeling that I needed to be there. Is that crazy?"

"No," Melina said, looking around.

Siobhan paused. Should she tell Melina more? Should she tell her what her overly terrifying hallucinations were? Should she tell her about Adam's suspension mid-air in their living room, bleeding from his eyes and his injury? Should she tell her about Adam eating a dead bird as a waterfall of black blood spewed from his mouth and his body twisted itself in half? Should she tell her about the weird clicking and growling and the laughter that made its way into a dream that caused her ear to bleed? Should she tell her some invisible monster had touched her? Should she tell her about Adam staring her down like a creep out their front window this morning?

As they marched toward Siobhan's Jeep, she said, "I'm being drawn to the address."

Melina's eyes shot toward Siobhan. The intensity of her unsettling gaze grew.

"Do you want me to drive, or are you okay?" Melina asked out of genuine concern.

"I'm all right as long as you're okay getting a little windblown. The top's down," Siobhan said, motioning toward her Jeep.

"Some fresh air does sound nice," Melina said.

CHAPTER 11

Melina sat silently while Siobhan drove.

The fresh air and the wind were loud, and they helped numb the unwanted thoughts that kept creeping up into the front of her mind—as well as the memories.

Melina hadn't thought about any of this for years, but she had no choice now. As she had promised, it was her job to protect Siobhan.

"Is it too much wind?" Siobhan shouted to Melina as she rounded a corner, downshifting.

"No. Not at all," Melina said. She could see her black hair swirling around her face. "I was thinking of how nice the fresh air and wind are."

"Right?" Siobhan said as she slowed down. "I think it's right around here."

"You know, some people use GPS sometimes," Melina said.

"Yeah, yeah. You sound like Adam," Siobhan said, smiling. "I don't have GPS. This thing was made in 1999, and I can't hear it anyway with the top off."

"Is that it?" Melina asked, pointing to the little building on the left. It likely used to be a house.

"Maybe!" Siobhan said excitedly. "But I don't see a sign or

address."

"There's not much parking either. Maybe you'll have to park in that church's parking lot? But it's full," Melina said, shifting uncomfortably in the passenger seat.

"Yeah. Sunday morning…" Siobhan said.

"What do you say we go get coffee or something and come back later?" Melina said nervously, trying to prolong the drive. She wanted to be anywhere else but that church. "We could head to my house," she suggested. "I have to feed my cat anyway."

"That works for me! Which way?" Siobhan asked, circling the block to get back to the main road.

"I'm off Raven's Beach Rd."

Once they got to Melina's house, Siobhan jumped out of her Jeep, relieved that she wasn't alone or at her house.

Melina's small house had a large front window, and the curtain had been closed, blocking the living room from prying eyes. It lacked warmth or an inviting personality, but it contained a safe and cozy essence.

Melina led the way up the front steps and opened the door.

As soon as the black and white tuxedo cat saw them, he lifted his head and jumped off the couch he'd been sleeping on to rub up against Melina's legs.

"Hey, Scamps," she said as she set down her tote and picked him up. His purr was loud, and Siobhan could hear it as Melina scratched his neck.

"What a cute cat!" Siobhan exclaimed. She scratched the cat's head as he rubbed against her hand, still in Melina's arms.

"He's a good boy, aren't you, Scamper?" Melina cooed, kissing the cat on his head. "He likes you," she added, offering him to Siobhan.

Siobhan took Scamper from Melina. The cat rubbed his head on the underside of her chin. "Awe," Siobhan said. "I love you too, buddy!"She cradled the cat as she followed Melina into the kitchen.

"I'll make some coffee," Melina said. "Do you want sugar or cream?"

"No," Siobhan said, setting Scamper down on the floor as he let out a protest meow. "Black is the way to drink coffee. How long do you think it'll be until church is out?"

"I don't know, maybe check their schedule online?" Melina suggested.

Siobhan started Googling. "Do you happen to know what that church is called?" Siobhan asked.

"Yeah, it's St. Margaret's Catholic Church," she said. Siobhan listened to the coffee maker brew the dark, hot liquid; ecstatic at the absence of clicking and horrendous laughter. She considered telling Melina everything right then and there.

Siobhan held tightly to what she perceived as the remainder of her sanity as she tried to find information about the church.

"Here it is," Siobhan said, still staring at her phone. "They have a mass at ten a.m. Mass? Not service? I bet it'll be cleared out by noon."

"That sounds about right," Melina said, looking off into the distance.

Scamper slithered over to his food bowl and meowed, trying to get Melina's attention. "You know you ate this morning, right?" she said as she opened the cabinet and took down a can of wet cat food.

Scamper pranced around with his eyes on Melina as she opened his food and put it in his black bowl. The cat buried his head in his food and made purring sounds as he ate.

"Sorry about taking your whole Sunday, Melina," Siobhan said, setting her phone down.

"It's no problem," Melina said, reaching for coffee mugs. She poured a cup of coffee for Siobhan and herself. Siobhan sipped it.

The two women made small talk, played with Scamper, and avoided discussing the more serious matter at hand as it crept closer to noon.

"Do you want to head to the… office?" Melina asked,

swallowing a lump in her throat. "We could get some lunch first."

"Sure. Can I use your bathroom before we head out?" Siobhan asked.

"Sure," Melina said. "It's the last door on the left."

Siobhan shut the bathroom door behind her. While washing her hands with the lavender-scented soap, she breathed the scent deeply to help calm her nerves, which had taken a beating in the past few days.

She reached for the plain black towel to dry her hands, and her eyes locked on a caddy full of bath items sitting across the perfectly clean bathtub in the mirror's reflection.

Everything had an obvious place and was pristine. Melina's level of cleanliness was second to none.

Siobhan spun around and took a step toward the bathtub where the caddy rested. It contained a lavender-scented soy candle, some more lavender-scented bath salts, some rose-scented soaps, and a bottle of bubble bath. A plain black, thick, hard-cover book sat upright in the caddy.

Siobhan grabbed the book Melina had been reading. She flipped the book over in her hands. The blank cover, binding, and back of the large, 1000-plus-page book felt heavy. She bent to put it back down, but something about it caught her attention. She jerked it back and opened it. The first three pages were blank. The third page finally told her the title: *Demonology and Exorcism*

Success.

Was it a coincidence that Siobhan questioned whether she was possessed? As she stared at the title, the pages fell as if there had been one place where it had stayed open for longer. Siobhan opened the book to that page.

On it, a simple image with no captions played on the page. The picture of an old medieval drawing of a demon stared back at her. It had three horns, none of which were symmetrical, and its legs belonged to a goat. Its hands were clawed and short like they should have been on a tyrannosaurus rex.

Those hands gripped my neck and arms.

She slammed the book shut and put it back, sensing the clawed hands that had gripped her arm and neck tightly yesterday.

Siobhan's mind started to race at the idea of demons and possession. Those things made hauntings look gentle by comparison.

"Work together," Siobhan heard the old woman's voice say. The creeping feeling of insanity coupled with the cold shiver of the unknown ran up her spine.

Of course, she heard this on the way to see a therapist. The haunted necklace got mildly warm against her chest.

Siobhan flipped off the light and made her way back to Melina's front door.

"You heard her?" Melina asked.

"What? How did you know about that?" Siobhan asked in total surprise.

Melina pointed to the necklace. "Grandmother," she said. "I heard her, too. We need to do this together."

Siobhan stood with her mouth agape, confused but comforted by the haunted necklace. She put her hand over the tiger's eye crystal and nodded.

"I'm glad you have it," Melina said.

After a quick lunch at a local cafe, Melina and Siobhan headed back to the therapist's office. Six cars were still spread out in the church's parking lot. Siobhan pulled her Jeep into a spot on the east side of the lot, closer to the office they were scoping out.

They got out of the Jeep and passed through the grass separating the properties to the house-looking therapist's office. They both cupped their hands around their faces and looked through the glass.

Four stark white chairs sat in the dark waiting room, and one hallway led to the back of the office. The building had an inviting air, even though it was devoid of life at the moment.

Opening hours and the name of the therapist were written on the glass door.

"Dr. Amanda Hill," Siobhan said, remembering that that

was the name she'd seen online. "She's the one whose phone number is given in the voicemail."

"Do you want to call it?" Melina asked.

Siobhan looked past her friend as her eyes landed on the church. "I…" She shook her head. "Why am I here?" she asked Melina.

"You wanted to check out this therapist."

"No, I mean here," she said, pointing to the church.

Melina spun around and stared at the much larger and more powerful-looking building.

"It happens to be by the office," Melina said.

Siobhan couldn't tear her eyes away from the church. "It's not a coincidence; something is wrong," she said. "I feel sick," she added as she bent in half and grabbed her stomach.

"Oh God, nope," Melina said. "Get to the grass where there's some shade," she added as she put her arm around Siobhan and guided her to the grassy median.

As Melina lowered Siobhan to the softer grassy area, edging closer to the church, she glanced toward the sky. Black birds were circling over them, high up. Siobhan took a deep breath and said, "I don't know why that nausea hit me like that." Siobhan sat back on her knees, looking at her palms. She rolled to her left and sat with her back against a tree. "It did yesterday, too."

"I'm a little worried," Melina said, the concern etched on

her face. "Are you sure you're okay?"

"I... I... Okay, I don't even believe in this stuff," Siobhan said. "But I want to tell you something." She shifted uncomfortably as she bit down on her lip hard. "I thought I was going crazy, but now I think I'm possessed. That's crazy in and of itself, though, right?" She said this nervously as she felt the weight of saying it out loud for the first time. She rested her head on the tree behind her.

"I don't..." Melina stopped herself. "Listen, I understand. We need to see the therapist to confirm it's not a mental or emotional breakdown because it could be."

Siobhan sighed. "Yeah. But this," she said, waving her hand toward the church, "has me all worried. I'm scared that everything I assume about... I might have a demon, and..." Siobhan dropped her head into her hands. "What's happening to me?" she asked on the verge of tears.

"Hey, what would make you feel better?" Melina asked as she scooted closer to Siobhan, who looked up at the question.

"I'm not sure. But..." she trailed off with her lip quivering. She slowly looked at the church. She paused and tilted her head to the side, staring at the stained-glass window of the virgin mother holding the baby Jesus.

"I'll help any way I can," Melina added, following Siobhan's gaze.

Siobhan looked back at Melina. "Tell me about your book—the one in your bathroom," she said. "Please."

"I knew someone who was possessed a long time ago. I study it so that if it happens to anyone else, I can help. I'm not an exorcist or anything, but I might want to be someday," she said, shrugging. "I don't know. Like a sort of secular exorcist."

"You knew someone who…was…" Siobhan had trouble even saying it. She'd already voiced it once, but not without difficulty. If Melina knew someone who had been possessed before, then it could be possible, and that frightened Siobhan more.

Siobhan wrung her hands and chewed the inside of her cheek.

"Look, we don't know that you are. You need to see the therapist. A lot of times, people think they are possessed, but it's schizophrenia or something else in the brain. We need to get you a diagnosis first if you have one. It could be anxiety, too. A simple pill will fix that," Melina sputtered.

"I saw schizophrenia online as a possible explanation. But why…" she trailed off and looked at Melina intently. "Why do I…?"

Melina locked eyes with Siobhan, already aware of her question as it hung in the dense atmosphere. "How did you know it was going to be me?" she asked. "That I'd be… you know… possessed."

"I didn't. And you're not," Melina said.

"How do you know?" Siobhan asked, her voice full of strain.

"I know. I went back and forth trying to decide if I should keep the necklace, but when I saw your wedding announcement…"

"That didn't help at all." Siobhan said sadly. "No offense." She glanced at the church again.

"It could be a simple medical diagnosis rather than possession," Melina said.

Siobhan took a deep breath and let it out. "I hope that's the case."

"Me too."

"Let's go in," Siobhan said, not taking her eyes off the church building.

"Seriously?" Melina asked, her eyes widening, her mouth hung open. "I mean, sure."

"We won't see the therapist today unless I can get an emergency appointment, and we're here anyway. Churches are open on Sundays."

"Okay," Melina said. "If it'll make you feel better. Do you want to go in alone?"

Siobhan shook her head. "No. No way. I need someone to support me for this. If I go in there and I'm possessed, won't I catch on fire or something?"

"I don't know. The possessed person I know... knew... never came into this church," she said.

"All right then," Siobhan said. "I guess we're going to find out... something. Crazy or demon."

"Are you sure you're okay?" Melina asked.

Siobhan blew out a breath. "I think so." She used the tree to help her stand. "I am overwhelmed with the need to go in there."

"That's fair," Melina said. Siobhan could hear her trying to keep any concerns out of her voice. "Maybe it'll help." "Ha!" Siobhan said with a full-blown grin. "Yep. Or maybe I'll need much more than a therapist. Drugs and a mental disorder would be my preference over demonic possession."

Melina smiled fully. "I agree," she stated emphatically. "I don't think you're possessed."

They both stared at the church.

"Ready?" Melina asked, unable to tear her eyes away.

Siobhan nodded slowly. They trudged side by side up to the steps leading up to the large wooden front doors of St. Margaret's Catholic Church.

"It's..." Melina started, not wanting to finish.

"It's not what I expected. I mean, I'm not sure what I expected," Siobhan said, biting her lower lip.

"Are you sure you want to do this?" Melina asked, uncertainty lacing her voice.

"I'm sure. Can you please stay with me?" Siobhan asked, peeling her eyes away from the door to look down at her shorter friend.

She had always relied on Adam during difficult or confusing times. The absence of that constant support weighed heavily on her, and she wasn't sure how to push aside her need for his approval to manage her own psychological distress.

"I will," Melina said.

Siobhan's gaze drifted up.

"That's not ominous at all," Siobhan said as hundreds of black birds circled over the church. About twenty of them made a perfect circle right over the two women.

Siobhan rubbed her upper arm with her right hand and looked back at the church.

"You got this. I'm right here. Whatever you decide to do, I'm not leaving. Besides, you drove," Melina said. Siobhan cracked a slight but uncomfortable smile.

Still holding her own upper arm, Siobhan slowly ascended the stairs towards the two enormous wooden doors. Melina stayed right next to her.

The large doors each had a window up high, a little higher than Siobhan's eye level. The extensive paneling made them look strong, sturdy, and older at the same time. The design choices were modern but done in a historic way.

Siobhan grabbed the weathered handle of the door on the left and yanked it open. The smell of inoffensive incense smacked her, intense in its smokiness as it clung to the space inside and coated her sinuses. The darkness inside the church starkly contrasted the brightness of the summer day.

Siobhan stepped inside, and Melina followed close behind, taking the door from her.

Melina shut the massive, heavy door as quietly as she could.

They had stepped into a foyer. Siobhan could see a hallway stretching to both the left and the right in the darkness. To the left, there were bathrooms. She could see the signs for the women's bathroom on a door down the corridor. To the right were offices. A shiver ran down her spine.

Siobhan allowed her eyes to adjust to the darkness. Three doors led into the sanctuary, where the congregation sat during mass. The doors were on a mostly glass wall separating the nave from the foyer, and it was much brighter in there, thanks to the stained-glass windows streaming the sunlight in and scattering it in colored shapes all over the walls, pillars, pews, and floor.

Inside and to the left, a table had been shoved into the corner, and it was full of candles. About half of the candles were lit, and all were in various stages of melting, dispersed in an unrecognizable pattern.

"Oh my god, what is... THAT!?" Siobhan asked in a horrified whisper.

CHAPTER 12

"That's a crucifix," Melina whispered back. "All Catholic churches have them."

"There's someone on it!" Siobhan said in complete shock as she stood horrified.

"Yeah. Catholics use the image of Jesus on the cross, not a plain cross," Melina explained, remembering her discomfort at the same image.

"But why? That's…." Siobhan shook her head. "I… I don't even know… unsettling? Macabre?" She tore her eyes from the crucifix to focus on the candles.

"I know. It can be weird. Especially if you aren't used to it. Images of dying or dead people aren't comforting to me either," she said, trying to assure her friend.

"They even painted blood on him," Siobhan said, her voice shaking. Siobhan visibly clenched her teeth to stop herself from complaining about her discomfort over the sight of the tortured man nailed to the cross.

"Do you want to leave?" Melina asked. Worry and discomfort were etched into Siobhan's face, and her blue eyes were wide, with pupils dilated to the point that they were all black.

Siobhan continued to focus on the candles. "No. But if I start to feel nauseated, take me out," she said.

"I'm here to help. Whatever you need, Siobhan," Melina said as encouragingly as she could. She glanced up at the crucifix.

Why did it need to be so lifelike? It made it even more foreboding.

Melina bit the inside of her cheek as she remembered having the same visceral reaction when she was here before. It had been years, but she still had that same awkward response to the imagery in the same way as Siobhan had.

Melina tore her gaze away from the front of the church to look at the pews. Two columns of pews led toward the altar. There were four people in the entire nave, all on their knees praying, except for one elderly man in the first row on the right. He sat with his backside halfway off the pew seat and his elbows on the backrest of the one in front of him. His head tilted down, likely in a comfortable position to pray in for his age.

A woman with a purple scarf over her head, tied under her chin, knelt in the first row. She looked up, maybe at the crucifix, and clasped in prayer.

Toward the back, on the same side as the older man but closer to the candles, a middle-aged couple knelt side by side with rosaries in their hands, obviously reciting prayers. Occasionally, they changed beads on the rosary to keep count.

Siobhan's body held onto the tension and kept involuntarily shivering.

"I don't know if I want to go further, but I'm compelled," Siobhan whispered to Melina. "Is that stupid?"

Something Melina couldn't quite explain nudged her psyche as Siobhan spoke and called her inside as well. She shook her head, not offering an audible answer.

The crystal resting against Siobhan's chest got warm, and she put her hand on it. Melina's gaze snapped to the tiger's eye crystal.

Neither said anything; they waited. The crystal slightly glowed, but no one noticed.

"I think we should go in," Siobhan said.

Melina nodded. Her grandmother tried to communicate something to them through the necklace.

Siobhan appeared stuck and unable to move forward. Melina grabbed her elbow. "Come on," she said quietly.

Siobhan nodded and let Melina lead the way to the glass doors in the middle of the wall separating the foyer from the nave. Melina opened the door and then motioned for Siobhan to go in first.

Siobhan passed the threshold and made her way to the last pew in the middle row. The lights coming through the stained glass danced around in a soothing cadence as Siobhan put her hands on the back of the last pew and gripped it a little tighter than necessary.

Melina tapped her arm and said, "Let's sit here. " She pointed to the pew right in front of Siobhan. Melina stepped around to the right and made her way to the middle of the pew, Siobhan close behind.

As they sat, the woman in the front pew with the purple scarf snapped her head down and put her hands over the scarf on top of her hair, checking its placement. She stood abruptly, slammed the kneeler up, and stormed out of the church; her shoes made a deep clacking sound with every quick step as she exited through the same set of doors Siobhan and Melina had entered. She looked straight ahead on her way out, and the other three patrons remained unbothered by her sudden and loud exit.

"I thought praying was supposed to calm you down," Siobhan whispered as she leaned closer to Melina, who cracked a half smile.

"You would think," Melina said.

The incense smell increased as she sat there, engulfing her, sticking to her clothes and clinging to the inside of her nostrils. She fought the urge to sneeze.

The couple, who were praying the rosary in the next row of pews to their right, sat back. Their movements broke the silence in the church. They were putting their rosaries in bags and getting ready to leave.

"Is it me?" Siobhan whispered as the couple strolled out of

the church. Melina leaned back, "Oh, definitely. It's your fault they finished their prayers," she whispered back sarcastically.

Melina glanced up at the older man, who remained stoic. He could have been sleeping. He wore a suit jacket, and his silver hair, what was left of it, was brushed to one side of his head. He hunched over the front board stiffly.

"At least he seems unbothered," Melina said, pointing to the elderly man.

"I hope we aren't interrupting anything," Siobhan said as quietly as she could.

"We aren't. Take your time. We haven't been here that long," she whispered, her eyes focusing on the candles.

Did they get brighter with bigger flames? *No. I'm in this place again, and that's all it is.*

The energy had shifted, becoming thick and heavy as Melina's eyes drifted to the light of the candles.

They were all brighter, and the flames were growing. As they flickered, puffs of light gray smoke were left twisting upward only to disappear in the dark corner above.

One of the candles lit itself, spontaneously catching fire on its own. She blinked several times and her eyes watered. She inhaled sharply.

Melina couldn't tear her eyes away as another candle lit itself. She fought the fear rising in her chest as the eerie familiarity smacked her. It started to crawl its way up her back, a sensation she hadn't experienced in years. The energy pulled inward to her as if she created the vacuum for it.

After the third candle lit on its own, she looked at Siobhan, as she stared at the crucifix with her head cocked to the side, eyes wide open, bewildered, and horrified.

Siobhan's mouth popped open as she stared, frozen. A shiver shook the pew.

A cold breeze shot over Melina as the energy rushed in once again. The air pressed into her chest, making it harder for her to breathe.

She glanced back at the candles. All of them were now lit, with four-inch-tall flames licking each other as they flickered violently in the corner. It started to get darker in the church as if the sun had dimmed. The previously bright lights cast by the stained-glass windows were fading into a dull gray color that spread outward from the center of the church.

Melina's stomach flopped. She tried to resist the urge to stare at the very object in this church that offered her immense discomfort. She couldn't tear her eyes away from the Jesus figure on the cross, remaining compelled to stare.

Melina's mind raced with memories flooding back to her. Her body got tense in anticipation as her palms got clammy.

The candles were all still flickering rapidly as if a strong wind had blown on them. Then, in a gust of cold air, every single candle extinguished simultaneously, plunging the corner into abject darkness. Not even a hint of an ember remained on any of the wicks as the smoke from each red candle billowed upward, hiding the pillar behind them.

Melina's eyes darted around, trying to find something else to focus on. The old man in front stood slowly but efficiently, facing the crucifix. His wrinkled hands were clenched tightly into fists at his sides, and his knuckles grazed his black pants. He looked straight up, and Melina followed his gaze, and her breath caught in her throat.

Unable to inhale, she gawked. Her jaw lowered, and a wave of terror passed through her veins.

The Jesus figure on the cross had blood trickling down his face. He bled from his forehead, from every prick of the crown of thorns. Blood dripped from both hands and feet, blood coming down his toes and dripping onto the floor. The wound on his side oozed a stream of black oil-like fluid all the way down the leg and the side of the wooden cross. The mercurial liquid pooled over everything, sliding instead of dripping like the rest of the crimson liquid.

Siobhan shook, and the entire pew picked up the vibrations spreading them out. Melina's ears picked up the sounds of her breath coming fast and her heart raced in her chest. The pounding of her pulse pushed against her temples.

The gray atmosphere embraced them and sent more shivers squirreling down their spines. Melina's tendons reacted, squeezing her muscles to the point of painful contractions.

Melina's stomach clenched in agonizing defeat.

Siobhan went pale, her tanned face devoid of color and replaced with fear. She stared as the crucifix bled uncontrollably right in front of them.

Melina heard Siobhan gasp for air, trying to get enough oxygen. The church had become stuffy and full of a metallic and musky odor that coalesced with the incense that lingered. Melina inhaled the smoke from the candles along with the gray haze, as its stench threatened to choke her out. It burned her lungs as she shivered and gasped for air that didn't exist. Icy sweat rolled down the back of her neck and stabbed at her skin like claws pressing into prey.

Icy pricks poked at her skin, and her eyes refused to stop staring at the blood.

The Jesus figure on the cross looked alive. His chest heaved up and down, and his face slowly tipped down, and he looked at the old man. Blood continued to run down his face as the head finished turning.

It blinked.

Siobhan gasped and whimpered.

Blood slithered its way down the steps, filling the aisles of the church like the forked tongue of a snake, whipping around, looking for something to grab.

Melina put her arm around Siobhan, hugging her, needing as much support from her friend as she attempted to offer. Siobhan leaned into Melina and squeezed her tightly. While still looking up at all the blood coming off the bottom of the cross, Siobhan whispered timidly, "You see it too, right?"

Melina nodded. "Yes," she said. "Oh my God..."

"Your God isn't here, priessssst," said a voice. It had come from the bleeding Jesus figure on the cross. The familiar voice filled the space in the church, biting into each one of Melina's pores, sending shockwaves of sharp terror coursing through her veins. The horrible sound hissed and strung itself out until the compressing force field that had boomed in her ears silenced it.

The women looked at each other, tearing their gaze away from the crucifix. "Siobhan..." Melina said. "I'm sorry..." The throbbing of the gray air smothered them, and they held each other tighter as they sank into the pew. The figure on the cross twisted its head down even more, shifting it to an unnatural angle.

"Is he...?" Siobhan whispered in a shaky voice.

"I...." Melina shook her head. "I... don't..."

The man at the front yelled, "Be gone, demon! The power of Christ compels you!" as he held up his own crucifix. He held the foot-long relic at the bottom in strong and steady hands.

The evil entity's laughter thundered throughout the church and got louder, gliding around as it whipped around them like a serpent, sliding along the rivers of blood. Melina reached up and put her hands over hers.

"Not again," she said as she put her head between her knees.

"Melina," Siobhan said as she wrapped an arm around her friend. They were shoved with a gust of wind so powerful it took Melina's breath away. The air gyrated violently, and breathing became suffocating.

The old man tightly gripped his crucifix, holding it firmly above his head while he faced the bleeding cross over the altar. The force inside the church violently blew his wispy silver hair around.

Melina slammed her eyes shut and ducked down further as Siobhan followed suit. The roar of the electromagnetic field being distorted filled their ears and cut off all other sounds.

After a few moments, the wind stopped. Their ears took in the relief from the booming pressure. Melina, still hunched over, removed her hands from her head. They looked up at the same time.

The crucifix had stopped bleeding, and the Jesus statue hung in its painted state as it had been before. Melina glanced at the candles. None of them were lit. The light slowly returned to the church as the stained glass once again caught the sun's rays, sending them swirling around in shifting and colorful waves. The gray haze dispersed into the far recesses of the church and disappeared entirely.

Both women looked forward at the man standing still in the same place. He lowered his crucifix, dropped his head, then spun around to look right at them. His gray eyes seared holes straight through Melina's.

His telltale white collar on his black shirt denoted his position in the church. His wrinkled face bore the pain of not only this event but several others he had endured as well. This man had come face to face with pure evil and had lived, and Melina remembered him.

"It's…" Melina said, barely able to croak it out.

Siobhan remained silent as the priest made his way toward them, smooth in his motions, the sound of his shoes on the tile marking each labored step. "Hello, Melina," the older man said.

He looked up at the crucifix once again.

"It's back."

CHAPTER 13

Siobhan stared at the priest in horror as Melina nodded toward him.

"Good to see you, Father Renaldo," she choked out.

"Is it her?" Father Renaldo asked as he pointed at Siobhan with the crucifix he still clutched in his hand. Melina shook her head.

"No. Adam," she said, looking at Siobhan.

Siobhan's mind reeled. She'd seen a crucifix bleed, and then it hit her. *That is what Adam looked like as he levitated.* His cut had been oozing blood, and his white eyes dripped the black liquid while he had hung, suspended in the exact same shape in her living room. It all came rushing back to her in a flood of flashbacks.

"Adam?" Siobhan asked, still scared and shaking.

"It's okay. Let us explain," Melina said, looking at Siobhan's glowing necklace, which lit up the underside of her chin. "I'm sorry," she said, still shaking from the experience.

"What's going on?" Siobhan said, scared. Her voice came out as weak and her muscles tensed. She wanted to cry, and even though the tears had welled up behind her eyes, she couldn't bring herself to do it.

"This is Adam's wife, Siobhan," Melina said to the priest.

"She's okay. It's him."

Father Renaldo nodded. "My dear," he said looking at Siobhan. "I'm Father Peter Paul Renaldo." The priest put his left hand on his chest, still holding the crucifix in his right hand.

"What does Adam have to do with this? You saw that, right?" she asked, pointing to the crucifix while looking at Father Renaldo. "He's…" she trailed off, trying not to burst into tears.

Then she remembered Melina's book *Demonology and Exorcism Success.*

Siobhan shook her head. "I am… That," she said, pointing to the crucifix, "was horrifying! We all saw that, right? So, if I'm crazy, you both are too."

"You can't rationalize this, Siobhan," Father Renaldo said. "There's nothing rational about demons. Would you like to come into the office for a moment? We have a lot to tell you."

He remained surprisingly calm, considering what they'd all seen.

"Can I say something first, Father?" Melina asked. "I need to tell her…." She trailed off as Father Renaldo gave her an approving nod.

Siobhan looked at Melina. "You knew about this?" she asked harshly, tears streaming down her face.

"No! The cross thing and the blood? No, I didn't know that would happen! I told you I'd seen a possession before. But that's because…"

"I know, and you gave me the necklace and…"

"Oh, you did give it to her? When?" Father Renaldo interrupted, looking at the tiger's eye crystal hanging around Siobhan's neck.

"At her wedding a month ago," Melina said before returning her eyes to Siobhan's. "Look. I had to warn you. I've seen a possession before, yes. I told you that. So had my grandmother. She was…" Melina paused. She glanced at her hands in her lap, then turned in the pew to face Siobhan. "She was killed by a demon, saving someone else."

"I'm so sorry," Siobhan said, choking back a sob. "I don't know what I've been seeing lately, and if I'm possessed…"

"It's not you, Siobhan," Melina said, grabbing both of Siobhan's forearms. She glanced at Siobhan's arms and hung her head. "It's Adam. It was him before. He's my…" she stopped and took a deep breath, then let out a long exhale of air. She waited for Siobhan to look at her before she said it.

"Brother."

Siobhan's mouth opened. "Adam doesn't have any siblings," Siobhan said, shaking her head.

"He doesn't remember anything," the priest said. "Most of his childhood is gone, too. The demon wiped a large chunk of his memory. After his possession, we felt it was best that he not know what happened. He was always empathetic, and he would not have survived if he had known his grandmother had died trying to save him."

"What? I…" Siobhan put her head in her hands, confused and scared. "This is too much," she said.

"Let's get out of here and go to my office, where we can talk," said Father Renaldo. "I'm going to use the restroom. Melina, you remember the way, right?"

"I do. Thanks, Father," Melina said.

"It doesn't make sense," Siobhan said, resting her forehead on her arms in the priest's office. "Why would Adam not tell me?" She had bent forward in the chair and laid her arms on the priest's desk.

The humble office welcomed them with its old wood and aged books. A crucifix hung between the two windows on the wall behind him, resting against the decades-old layer of paint. A large cactus occupied a corner by the door.

A small bookshelf, sitting on the right wall, overflowed with textbooks and journals that had been shoved into it. An opened amethyst geode rested on the middle shelf. Several books were stacked on the floor beside it.

"My brother doesn't remember anything. The demon took his memory. What he knows, he was told by Child Protective

Services and his foster families," she said, putting her hand on Siobhan's back.

"I have a sister-in-law, and I didn't even know," she said, raising her head to smile at Melina through the mental anguish and questions her mind concocted. "We could have been friends. You could have come to our wedding. I…"

"She couldn't tell you. She promised Rosemary," the priest said. "And she promised me. It would have been too hard on him since he didn't remember her."

"Who is Rosemary, and why the secrecy?" Siobhan said. "You're telling me I have a sister I didn't know about, and my husband is possessed by a demon because he was possessed before, but he went through an exorcism…" She shook her head. "This is a lot," she added in disbelief.

"I know," the priest said in a kind voice. "Rosemary is Adam and Melina's grandmother and my dear friend." Father Renaldo had the same soothing energy as Melina. Siobhan surmised that beating back the devil might have had something to do with that. She tried to listen to the back-story but drifted, lost in a sea of tumultuous emotional responses that she couldn't process fast enough.

"Adam won't be himself. That bleeding crucifix was a message to all of us that it was going to take Adam. He's most likely fully possessed now, or he will be shortly," Father Renaldo continued.

"This is hard, I know," Melina said, looking at her hand on Siobhan's back. She started to rub Siobhan's middle back slowly in soothing strokes. "My grandmother and I had to hear in this very room that Adam was possessed, and the bishop would need to sanction an exorcism for him. I didn't think I'd be hearing it again, but when the necklace glowed, that was my sign from Grandma. It's Grandma's way of warning, and you needed it more than me. You live with him."

Siobhan put her hand over her necklace.

Melina looked at the priest.

Father Renaldo sighed. "We knew the demon would come back for Adam," the priest said, hanging his head.

"How?" Siobhan asked.

"I didn't succeed. I exorcised it, yes, but I was never able to get its name. And it…" He paused for a moment and scrubbed his hand down the silver stubble on his chin.

"Rosemary, God bless her, offered her life in exchange for Adam's soul. She thought we were going to lose the battle because we couldn't get his name," the priest said. "So, she let it take her, and it released Adam."

"We had a hunch it would be back…when Adam was happy," Melina said as one tear slid down her cheek. "I'm sorry. It wants to finish what it started," she said, wiping her tears away.

"Grandma and Adam were the only family I had. She died, and then I had to cut contact with my brother."

"Demonic possession is not easy on anyone involved," Father Renaldo said, reaching across the desk and laying his palm flat.

"He told me his grandma died of a heart attack, so he had to jump around through foster families," Siobhan said.

"He's right about jumping around foster families. But how do you tell a fourteen-year-old boy that his grandmother offered her life in exchange for his life and soul?" Father Renaldo asked. "Rosemary made a deal with a demon, and they don't play fair," he added sadly.

"I guess," Siobhan said, lowering her head again. She started to understand why Adam had never told her much about his childhood.

"Here, do you need more water?" Melina asked, flicking away a tear. Her usually perfect black eyeliner had been smeared all over the side of her face.

Siobhan saw it for the first time. Melina had the same features, albeit more feminine, as Adam. Her black hair bounced in the same color as his, and she had the exact same curve in the waves. Her perfect dark brown almond eyes and pale complexion matched his. They even had the same nose. How had Siobhan missed that?

She took a drink from the bottle of water. "So, is there any way we can be sure before we..." Siobhan paused and redirected her question. "What do we do next anyway? This is all new to me, and I am still having trouble believing any of this if I'm being honest."

She finished the water and put the cap back on it, rolling the bottle around in her hands.

"We need to figure some things out," Father Renaldo said. "Right now, Adam is still in there, and if it's anything like before, he's fighting to stay. He's been through this once, and he can beat it again. But we need to get the demon's name."

"How do we do that?" Siobhan asked.

"It's going to take an exorcism."

Siobhan gasped.

"I tried. I tried telling Adam I needed him, but he couldn't leave. You could catch snippets of him coming through and breaking the demon's grasp, but he was young, you know? I was twelve, and I couldn't be around evil on that level for very long before I started vomiting uncontrollably." Melina said.

"Vomiting. I did that. When I hallucinated Adam..." Her eyes lifted to Melina's.

"You need to start from the beginning, Siobhan," the priest said calmly. "The more we know, the more we can help you."

Siobhan took a deep breath and started from the beginning

when she found the necklace at her wedding last month. Melina confirmed she'd stayed and made sure Siobhan took it with her.

"I didn't put it on right away," Siobhan said. "But I thought about it off and on until... It was recent," she said, racking her brain. "Wednesday night. As soon as I did, though, birds hit our window."

The priest nodded.

"That's how it started for us, too," Melina said.

"I didn't think the necklace had anything to do with that. But the birds fell into my Rosemary..." Her jaw opened as she said it. "Bush."

Melina smiled.

"They always hit the same window. Above that bush," Siobhan said.

Father Renaldo, still nodding, said, "Rosemary experienced the same thing for several months."

Melina bit her lip hard and nodded.

"Can you tell us more?" Father Renaldo asked. "We need to get an idea of how infested Adam might be."

Siobhan shook her head as she flashed back to the bony hand gripping her arm and choking her. She looked up at the ceiling to avoid eye contact. "This is crazy," she whispered. "But my counter at the gym was all... sticky. I noticed that right away, and then it was..."

Siobhan's necklace started to glow. All three of them looked at it as Siobhan stopped talking.

"It's attacking," Father Renaldo said, putting both hands on his desk. They looked at the tiger's eye crystal as it started to bounce on Siobhan's chest. She jumped back, putting both of her hands up.

"*What the hell is happening?*" Siobhan shrieked as the fear crept back into her and tingled her entire body. "It's never done this!"

"It's OK," Melina said, putting her hands up in front of Siobhan. "Adam is fighting back. I know it's crazy. She is warning us," Melina said.

"That's not ominous at all..." Siobhan said, putting her head back in her hands, where it had been so many times in the past few days.

CHAPTER 14

Adam rolled around on the couch, trying to get comfortable. He didn't feel any better and grimaced at the idea of having to miss another day of work. His injury wouldn't heal, and he might have to go to a doctor.

He wasn't exactly sick; it was something else. He was diseased, mind and body, with the illness sinking in and permeating every cell. He had no recollection of anything similar and could make very little sense of what kept happening inside his body.

The wiped hard drive of his brain kept him stuck in a restless sleep, and he thrashed uncontrollably on the couch.

He had a hard time concentrating, his thoughts bouncing all over the place, mainly when it talked. The low and growling voice inside his brain attempted to scratch its way out. It became increasingly difficult to shut it out, and it made him want to yell. He had snapped a few times. While he recognized his behavior changes and tried to correct them, they had started to get more impossible to control.

The voice in his head blurred his thoughts as the clicking sound started up again. Adam had tried to ignore it and bristled at the sensation.

Adam flopped once again on the couch to his other side. He

desperately tried to ignore the sinister icy chill crawling up his spine like a scorpion stinging each one of his nerves on the way up.

He couldn't sit still. He guessed he had to have a fever. He broke out in a cold sweat, and not enough blood flowed through his body. Fire radiated along his injured arm and prickled his skin.

The emptiness pooled right under the surface, scorching and searing him from the inside, while his stomach clenched in soreness. Ice-cold slivers filled his guts and tried to wriggle their way to freedom through his abdomen.

He needed to text Siobhan.

"I'm back!" the voice roared, echoing off the walls and striking at his face.

"Please shut up!" Adam yelled as loudly as he could, balling up the blanket he used and throwing it into the corner. An unbreathable gray film saturated every corner and covered each item in a hazy film.

He sat up and put his head in his hands while the laughter increased in his ears.

His ear kept bleeding. It had started Wednesday night after the first bird smashed into the window. He had wiped it away before Siobhan could see it.

"You don't remember," the laughing demonic voice cackled as it came from inside Adam to pool around his head. It mocked him deep inside his brain as it scratched its way down his neck.

Claws raked over each vertebra in his back, causing him to arch up as he attempted to squirm away from the tearing happening under his skin.

He reached for his phone on the coffee table and with shaking hands, grabbed it, pulling it toward him. He fumbled it for a moment, unable to hold on.

Get a grip. He tried to find Siobhan's text message thread.

His body wouldn't let him type. He stood there, the energy from close by going into his phone. It swirled around the device like invisible smoke and pressed on his hands, rendering them useless. It danced like static on his skin, electric and prickling. He bristled. His phone began flashing, then switched off.

What the hell is wrong with this thing?

"Worm?" the voice said, screeching through the haze. Adam looked around, dizzy and unable to see the source of the sound his ears had picked up. His brain pulsed hard against the inside of his skull, creating a dull and constant migraine so forceful that it made his hair hurt.

The voice laughed deeply. A few short chuckles radiated through the atmosphere.

Adam didn't understand what was so funny. He wasn't having a good time. His body was a wreck, and his brain was even worse.

He couldn't remember ever feeling like this, but he

couldn't remember any of his childhood either. But on some deeper level beyond his comprehension, he knew - whatever had been watching him for years had shown up here.

After his parents died in a car accident when he was five and his grandmother took him in, he hadn't focused much on building memories. They were unimportant and unnecessary. Or maybe he had forgotten. Or perhaps he didn't care. He didn't know, but it had never bothered him until now. A nagging feeling tore at his mind and he shook his head.

His grandmother died of a heart attack when he was fourteen, and after that, the sense of being followed increased even more. The events leading up to his grandmother's death were a blur, and since he was an only child, the gaps couldn't be filled in by anyone.

He stayed with foster families until he was eighteen, then chose to go to a trade school and become an electrician, using the money left to him by his family. Working with his hands had always made him happy. But he was still always being watched. The feeling subsided a little when he met Siobhan, but after they got married, it continued to worsen.

He wasn't being followed today. Instead, dark invisible hands strangled him. They belonged to whatever had been following him. His oxygen-deprived body reacted as if it had a major parasitic infestation, one so bad that the bugs crawled along the inside of his skin over every inch of his body. Something held onto and squeezed his lungs, and it wouldn't let go.

He had never told Siobhan about the constant watchful eye, or the awareness that something continually monitored him. She would have called him crazy, and she would have been right.

He searched through his memories in his throbbing head, trying to recall anything that could help him right now.

Adam remembered the day he met Siobhan at the gym she now owns. She had been working there, her hair pulled up into a messy ponytail, bits of blonde hair stuck to her sweaty forehead. She'd finished working out and was completing her shift at the front desk. She always smiled—all the time, not just at him, but at everyone. He knew he needed to make sure that smile never left her face.

She liked to say she hoped she got wrinkles early from smiling so much all the time. She was beautiful and quirky and had such an infectious zest for the simple things in life which really appealed to him. It was an integral part of her; he'd never seen it in anyone before.

He remembered her white jeans and black shirt she'd worn on their first date. How could he forget? So where were the rest of his memories? Did his life begin when he met her?

Of course not. He remembered going to trade school to become an electrician. He remembered a few of his foster families, although not as many as he'd had.

He had spent countless hours pondering his lack of memory. He had no family to share anything with. As an only child of parents who were only children, he had no aunts, uncles, or cousins to help fill in the gaps left by the traumatic deaths of his family members.

So, what now? The sinister voice said Adam had forgotten all of it. Of course, he did. Supposedly the result of trauma, his amnesia had been dismissed as a trauma response, and childhood PTSD.

He tossed his dead phone onto the coffee table and then snatched up the blanket he'd thrown in anger. The blood droplets had dried on it. He couldn't remember if he had bled. He looked at his arm. He hadn't covered it today, and the stitched-up cut retained some moisture but had stopped seeping blood. It remained unhealed and didn't show signs of scabbing. He caught a glimpse of the stairs. Blood dotted the steps.

Was Siobhan bleeding? Why wouldn't she tell him? The horrific and aggressively antagonistic laughter started up again. It stopped after a few moments. The deafening silence came from nowhere.

Click Click Click

Good Lord, not the clicking.

Adam's mind reeled, spinning inside his own skull like a

top. He dropped the blanket on the couch and glanced at his blank phone screen, annoyed that it refused to work.

But should he even care? He's sick, and she's not here to help him. He shook his head. Where were these negative thoughts coming from? They can't be his. He wasn't an angry person. He was usually very slow to anger, patient, and relatively calm. People described him as overly nice and accused him of toxic positivity. He had been told it was likely a trauma response from so many family deaths at such a young age.

clickclickclickclickclickclick

The spinning pressure in his skull spread. His lungs pressed against his chest from the inside. He sat, trying to catch his breath. The air carried evil with it, thick and heavy, and he needed to chew it instead of breathe it.

He looked up. A large and looming black shadow hovered above him. Paralyzed, unable to move anything, he stared as an invisible rock lowered onto him. The dark shadow sank toward him. The two glowing red orbs in the center of the shadow pierced through his brain, poking like thorns deep into his psyche, latching onto his consciousness.

The shadow surrounded him and seeped into his skin. It wriggled its way into his body with force. He jerked uncontrollably as he flopped off the couch onto the floor. Adam seized up as foam came out of the side of his mouth. He couldn't stop it.

Adam knew in his gut he'd been taken over. He knew he had lost himself. His consciousness had been replaced, and he had no control over anything. He felt not entirely in his own body. Halfway in, a part of him hung outside of himself like the tongue of a sleeping dog, and hovered in front of his forehead.

What the fuck is going on? Was he dead?

No, he couldn't be. His consciousness continued to reason, but it wasn't attached to his physical vessel anymore. He lay on the floor, unable to get up, foaming at the mouth.

His vision blurred, and his eyes looked around. He saw his house from a perspective he'd never experienced before. Images came together in front of his eyes.

He looked through a cloudy red haze of crimson distortion. Everything looked uglier but more perfect somehow.

He hovered partially outside his body, looking at himself. The twisted and sickly-looking weakling he saw barely registered. Something else used his eyes and generated the images imprinting in his mind.

"Do you remember?" The voice came out of Adam's mouth. The snarling voice of an angry sociopath filled the space around his head.

He couldn't answer. He vomited blood and choked on it as it spewed out of his mouth. Black blood mixed with foam sprayed the front of the couch; then, his body lay still for a moment. He looked at himself, his eyes open and white, unmoving.

His left arm twisted, and his white eyes glimpsed the cut he'd gotten at work. With black blood and foam still trickling out of his mouth, his cut began to bleed a bright crimson color and drip slowly off his arm. His body smiled the most sinister grin it could manage, and then a snake-like tongue flung out of his bleeding mouth to lash the wound on his arm.

He tried to scream as the agony racked upward from the injury.

He pushed hard, clawing all the way back into his body. He pressed his consciousness against himself, unfolding as he slithered further inside. He managed to push hard enough to get back inside all the way.

The limited space for his consciousness became tighter inside his own body. The pressure of sharing himself threatened to split his skin at the seams.

Something else had total control over Adam and everything his body did. Something wanted his energy, his essence, and his soul. Now that it had his body, the clock was ticking against his life.

He had to force himself to stay inside himself right now, and he wouldn't be able to let down his guard if he were to have any chance of regaining his body and saving his soul.

After Adam pushed his energy back into his body, he tried

to figure out what to do. The entity inside him had stood and paced back and forth between the stained couch and the coffee table. The speed was much too fast and agitated to belong to a human. It was as if Adam had been put on fast-forward.

Then his body stopped, frozen in time.

Did I do that?

"You're a fool," the evil voice said, coming out of Adam's mouth and surrounding his own soul from the inside of his body. "You won't beat me again. They are bringing me the same one," it said, chuckling.

"Who are you?" Adam demanded.

"You don't know, do you, worm? They lied to you. You can't trust anyone. But not to worry. I am in control now. Soon, you will tire, and Grammy isn't here to save you this time," it said as the ear-splitting laughter joined up to create the clicking sound.

"I'll fight you," Adam said.

The roaring laughter shook the walls of the house and rattled glasses in the cabinets.

"Nooooooo," the voice growled as it uttered the word, dragging it out. The tension increased as it folded over Adam in waves. A short chuckle followed. "You won't. And would you like to know why?"

Adam did want to know why. But a part of him was content in the unknown. Even though he had no control over his body, he agonized in pain, like someone was repeatedly using a hot poker to stab at his skin.

"You like it, don't you?" the entity said, forcing a lopsided sinister grin to appear on Adam's face. The pressure increased until his left arm caught fire in front of eyes that weren't his.

The flames licked up toward his shoulder as red-hot pain shot through his fingertips.

He wanted to yell out in pain.

He couldn't look away from the bloody, burning red upside cross being etched and blackened into his skin by the blaze rolling upward.

He tried to scream in agony, but the sound failed to manifest. He used all his energy to push against the entity. Then it started laughing again, fading the laughter into the slow staccato of the clicking sound.

"We can finish this later," the low voice promised. "You should rest now. A bigger battle is coming. I have marked you again, worm. You will feel every pain I am about to give, worm, and you are powerless to stop it."

Severe pain coursed through Adam's body. His perfectly burned arm, right over where his injury had been, seared into a cross in his flesh. The stitches had melted away, revealing the mark of the sinister beast within; an upside down cross.

"This is who has you," the evil voice said, raising the left arm into the air. "You'll die like this! Marked FOREVER!" The voice trailed off into a cesspool of screeching animal sounds before it died down and became the clicking sound once again.

The arm began bleeding red hot black blood as the walls vibrated from the demonic laugh.

This is what it must be like in Hell.

The agony held onto his nervous system as he worked to remain in his body. He tried to reduce the pain until he could somehow get it back.

Adam solidified his resolve. He would beat whatever the hell this was. He wasn't sure how to do it, but he knew he couldn't give up.

"You took that well, worm," the voice said. "You didn't like it much when you were a boy." It started laughing as the pain subsided to a degree, and the bleeding slowed. The blackened, bloody cross deeply etched into the flesh of Adam's arm rose up red, sore and open. It hurt like hell.

"Torture begins," the voice said through its own laughter. It surrounded Adam's body and bounced off the walls to create waves of reverberation that sunk into his bones.

CHAPTER 15

The vibration of Siobhan's necklace slowly subsided.

"What happened?" she asked sternly, looking back and forth between Melina and the priest. Both shared a look of concern.

"I don't know," Father Renaldo said, deeply furrowing his brow. "It is strong. Rosemary tried to come through. Warning." He pointed at the crystal.

"That's how she communicates. But sometimes, I will hear her voice," Melina said.

"I've been hearing her voice too," Siobhan said. "Like at your house. She told me we need to work together. But I kept telling myself it was in my head." Siobhan looked at Melina. "She told me she liked coffee."

Melina smiled. "She loved coffee. She's with you. She's in spirit form, so like we said," Melina said, motioning to the priest, "she can't physically interact the way the demon can."

"It's her life's mission to see this demon flung back to hell permanently, but it can only happen if we can get its name," Father Renaldo said through gritted teeth. The frustration wore on him, and he clenched his fists tightly. "They guard their names with everything because of that."

"If we have its name, we have control over it. Father

Renaldo can command it much more easily. Without a name, we can make… suggestions," Melina said.

The priest raised his eyebrows toward Melina. "I'm impressed. You've been studying. You know so much now," Father Renaldo said.

"Knowing is only half," Melina said. "We are going to need to finish hearing out Siobhan. It keeps interrupting us."

"The sooner, the better," Father Renaldo agreed. "Please, Siobhan. Can you continue?"

She sighed. She'd gotten to the part about finding the necklace at her wedding and putting it on to see birds fly into a window.

Her mind reeled as it processed its compression into thoughts of demons and possession and exorcisms and her husband's well-being.

So many things were stuffed into her head and at the same time, she needed to get so much information out that thoughts were overwhelming and bordered on being painful. Discomfort held Siobhan hostage as she spoke, relaying her story.

She told the priest about the wet cobwebs on her counter. She told them that Adam had had a "slip" at work, and they ended up at the ER to make sure it wasn't serious.

"Now this, this is where I am going to sound like a crazy psychopath," she said. Her eyes darted around the office as she worked hard to focus.

"I know how you feel. I've said some hard things in this office, too," Melina said, trying to keep Siobhan as calm as possible.

"I saw Melina in the grocery store on Friday night. Do you remember?" Siobhan asked. "Of course you do; it wasn't that long ago, but what I mean is, do you remember what you told me?"

"Yes. I told you to put the necklace back on because you didn't have it on that day," she said.

Siobhan nodded. "Yeah. And I thought it was weird, you know?"

Melina smiled. "I do."

"Well, I went home after that," Siobhan said. "And I had a hallucination."

"It wasn't a hallucination," the priest said. "I don't mean to frighten you, but based on what we saw in there…" He pointed toward the crucifix above the altar of his church. "We know it was an event."

Siobhan shook her head. "I hope it was a hallucination. Because Adam was suspended. He was hovering in the air, his cut was bleeding…" Melina's eyes snapped up.

"Cut?" Melina said, interrupting. "You said accident. Work accident. A slip. Was it a cut?"

Father Renaldo leaned forward on his desk. "He got cut?"

he asked emphatically in time with Melina.

"I mean, yeah. It was a work accident. I thought …"

"The way you talked, I assumed a fall, or a twist, or a sprain or something. You said 'slip,'" Melina said. "You need to back up."

"I'm sorry. I didn't harp on it because it wasn't part of my story. It was a slip…" she trailed off.

"No, it's a part of the story, Siobhan. This is serious. How did it happen? The cut? The injury?" the priest asked, seeming quite worried as he squirmed in his seat.

"Um. It happened at work. I didn't see it happen. He slipped with a saw while cutting some pipes. That's the story I got from his boss anyway," Siobhan said.

Father Renaldo opened a drawer in his desk. He cocked his head to the side, took out a pencil, then slammed the drawer shut. He stomped over to the short bookcase, grabbed a notebook from behind the amethyst, opened it, and flipped through the pages. Not satisfied, he put the notebook down and grabbed another. He looked through it briefly, then found a blank page. He set it down and slammed the pencil on top of the notebook in front of Siobhan.

She jumped back as the priest banged around.

"Draw it. The cut. Draw it to scale and where it is on his body," the priest said.

Siobhan slowly, with shaking hands, picked up the pencil.

"I'm not a very good artist. But it's his inner left forearm. Like, the underside right here," she said, motioning to the spot on her own arm, dragging her finger downward toward her wrist.

"Draw it, Siobhan," Father Renaldo said impatiently. "Please..."

She did her best rendition of Adam's injury on the paper provided. "This is his wrist; this is his elbow," she said, pointing to her drawing. She spun the notebook around on the desk.

Melina had gone white. "That's it," she whispered. The priest leaned forward, his eyes glued to Siobhan's drawing.

"What?" Siobhan asked. "What's *it*?'" She made air quotes while still holding the pencil in her right hand.

"It's his mark," the priest said. "It claimed him that day."

Melina looked at Siobhan, "It's an upside-down cross," she added. "See?" She pointed to the paper across the desk. "It did this before, too," she said, looking at the priest. "It's probably worse already."

Father Renaldo nodded. "I agree. If this demon succeeds, Adam will not make it," he said forcefully.

Siobhan took a deep breath and let it out in a long sigh. The information she'd gotten from Melina and Father Renaldo filled her head, and she tried to make sense of everything she had to comprehend.

"I should check on Adam," she said, reaching into her purse

for her phone.

Father Renaldo sat still, staring at the drawing Siobhan had made of Adam's demonic mark, which she assumed had come from a work injury until a few moments ago.

Siobhan pulled out her phone and tapped the button to turn on the screen. She cocked her head to the side.

"What is it?" Melina asked in a low voice. The priest reached down and opened a drawer at the bottom of his desk, pulling out a brown leather-bound notebook with a red ribbon as a bookmark. He ripped Siobhan's drawing out, folded it, and wedged it between two pages. He flipped one page over and started writing notes. He would reference a book on his desk and then return to writing. He all but ignored the two women as he buried his focus into his notebook.

"This didn't vibrate, or ring, or anything, right?" Siobhan asked, pointing to the phone in her hand.

"I didn't hear it," Melina said.

"Look at this," she said, turning the phone so Melina could see it. The screen lit up. Siobhan tapped the screen to reveal her notifications. She had 666 missed calls, all from Adam.

Melina blinked, staring. She put her hand on the desk. "Father?" she asked.

Father Renaldo looked up from his writing. "Look at this," Melina said, pointing to Siobhan's phone. Siobhan turned the phone and let the priest see it.

"That's not good," he said, furrowing his brow. The wrinkles on his forehead creased as he let the information on the phone screen sink in. "We need to do something," he added. "Look."

On the wallpaper screen of her phone, Adam's eyes were whited out, staring back at her in his wedding. "This is what I saw before," she said. "The night of his injury… mark… whatever. I looked at Adam's phone, and his eyes were white like this. Then, during the… levitation, the bird-eating, they were white, like this."

The priest set his pen down. "We should do a house blessing, Siobhan."

Melina shook her head. "Father, we…" she started.

"I know." He waved off her concern with a hand. "But we need to gauge the level of infestation, and the way to do it is for me to come in and see what happens during a house blessing. I may be able to get it to give me information to help us beat it," he said.

"What is a house blessing?" Siobhan asked.

"It's a simple ritual I'll do to bless your home and your space. It'll irritate the demon and give me some kind of idea of how deeply it has embedded itself in Adam," Father Renaldo said. "I will bring a test. A religious artifact I'll try to hide from him. If he senses it, that's a good indication that the possession is fully manifested. A blessing won't cast out the demon, but the test will let me know if that's what we're dealing with," he said, his gray eyes softening with sorrow.

"So how do we do this?" Siobhan asked.

"Well, I assume that you know Adam isn't himself, so could you stay somewhere else tonight? We can do the blessing tomorrow," Father Renaldo said.

"You can stay with me if you want," Melina said. "I have a spare room, but we'd have to share the bathroom."

"Yeah. I mean, I don't know what else to do. Should I tell Adam I won't be there? I don't have clothes or a toothbrush or anything, and the gym..." Siobhan said, concerned about her schedule and its conflicts.

She shook her head and reevaluated her priorities.

"We can stop and get you a toothbrush. I should have everything else. You can borrow some clothes. We should still go in tomorrow morning," Melina said. "This kind of thing... people tend not to believe it. Trust me," she added, looking melancholy once again.

"Yeah. I'm not even sure I do yet," Siobhan said, biting her lower lip.

"We'll go in. I'll teach the yoga class like nothing is wrong, and you come to the class and do your best to participate," Melina said.

Siobhan nodded. She tapped the button on her phone to

bring the screen to life again. The 666 missed calls notification seared its image across the top. "So tomorrow, Father?" Siobhan asked.

"Yes. That'll give me time to prepare. I have a video of Adam's previous exorcism locked in a safe. I will study it and add anything of importance to my notes. I might see something I could use. These things are as evil and deceptive as you can imagine, and I need to be reminded of what I will be up against," he said.

"I understand," Siobhan said shrugging, even though she didn't. Things were much less confusing when the events could be boiled down to a mental problem that could be diagnosed by a psychiatrist.

"Write down your phone number here," the priest said, pointing at a corner on the left page of his notebook as he spun it around for Siobhan. "I'll call you later today with the time. Adam likely isn't in control of himself anymore, so if you could, call his place of employment and tell them he'll be out."

"Like, say he's sick or something?" Siobhan asked.

"That will work," the priest said. "I don't often encourage lying; you shouldn't get in the habit of doing it. But as Melina said, most people tend to laugh at these kinds of things and dismiss them. The fewer who know, the better it'll be."

Siobhan dropped her head and nodded.

Melina smiled. "It'll be okay," she said.

Siobhan wrote her phone number in the priest's notebook. As she slid the book back to him across his desk, she said, "Thank you."

"Not a problem," he replied. "I'll learn what I can before I call you tomorrow. Hang in there. I've dealt with this demon before. Hopefully, we can get a name," he said with a resolute state of courage.

"Now, please tell me everything else you remember before you go," he said.

Siobhan relayed the events, including the bird eating while Adam's body twisted in half and the nauseated sickness that had landed her on the couch. She told them about the terrifying lucid nightmare which had made her ears bleed and also the awful, relentless clicking.

The priest took a few notes as she spoke and interjected questions for clarity once in a while.

Two hours later, Siobhan and Melina pushed open the wooden doors of the church and stepped outside. The hot summer air scorched the skin of their faces, and they had to squint their watering eyes against the harsh sunlight.

"Well, this has been a horrible day," Siobhan said, still not fully believing what she had seen and heard since they entered the church over two hours ago.

"I'm sorry," Melina said. "I can't imagine how hard this is

for you."

Siobhan paused, unsure of how to respond. While grateful for Melina's help, she still wished she'd known Adam had a sister sooner. "I'm glad you are here," Siobhan said. "I'm not sure I could do this without you."

"I bet you could. You're much stronger than you give yourself credit for," Melina said.

She shook her head and looked at her feet.

She and Melina got into the black Jeep. "Let's head to the store first, then get your car," Siobhan said as tears stung her eyes. "I..." she sighed. "I hate the idea of even being alone right now and seeing.... crazy things again."

"Whatever is best for you. We've got several hours to kill, and we should try to use some of them to relax and eat a healthy dinner so we can be ready for the house blessing," Melina said.

"Thanks again," Siobhan said as she jammed the clutch down and put the Jeep into first gear. She used the drive to try to calm her racing mind and overly exerted heart.

CHAPTER 16

Adam's body paced violently back and forth, this time between the kitchen and the living room. Adam's body filled with impatience as it forced itself to move.

He stayed subdued even though the pain surging in his veins blasted at his nerves. He desperately tried to remain hidden lest he make his existence known.

The entity knew Adam still had a presence inside his own body.

The pain of its takeover and the searing burn on his left arm were still present. He couldn't control his eyes, but occasionally, the entity would acknowledge Adam's presence by making him smile with a wrinkled nose as if admiring its handiwork.

Adam's thoughts were still his own, and they were not being controlled, but if he let his guard down for even a moment, he knew that it could read his mind and answer those thoughts.

Claws were wrapped tightly around his spinal cord from the inside, digging into the back of his lungs. The sharp pains all over his ribcage sometimes abated, but they always came back. Every capillary wanted to explode and bleed onto every single nerve in his body.

Red hot bugs crawled under his skin in all directions, leaving burnt trails of lava-like heat behind them. His lungs strained as they were being gripped tightly by thorny hands. Those same hands were simultaneously gripping his backbone, and every breath caused him an immense amount of searing pain.

Adam's body breathed, but it came in short bursts and often gargled.

He had to contact Siobhan. He needed her to know he wasn't himself anymore. His phone battery had died, and the entity wouldn't charge it.

He dropped his guard momentarily out of concern for Siobhan, and the entity chuckled. "She's coming back. With him," it said out of Adam's mouth. The voice was neither masculine nor feminine, and it carried a sing-song tone.

Adam's mind registered the pain of the presence inside him as a hot burst of energy pushed his flesh away from his bones.

"What do you want?" Adam asked it.

"To finish what I started," it replied, followed by three short chuckles that melded into the clicking and dispersed into the ever-graying atmosphere. The outward force from Adam's skeletal structure increased, and his skin spilt from the pressure.

"And what was that?" Adam asked—a twinge of sharp pain shot through his left arm as the mark burned.

It chuckled, shaking the entire house with its vibrational laughter that rebounded on each click. "To take you with me," it replied in a childlike voice. The entity cackled with its sinister growl.

The red-hot pain in his arm flared up as the pressure in his elbows increased to match that of his rib cage. Steeling himself against the pain once more, he asked, "When are you going to leave?"

It laughed again. *"Never!"* it roared. "I will prevail this time. Stop fighting me, worm," it said as it twisted Adam's left arm over his head and bent it behind his back at the shoulder. His bones and tendons bent in ways they shouldn't and snapped under the stress. His arm was mangled around him, and the aching pain within it confirmed that. The muscles popped and strained against the pulling as his arm held itself in that twisted shape.

"Who are you?" Adam said as he continued to contort beyond recognition. More laughter filled the house, coming from the twisted body but not coming from Adam's mouth.

"I am Hell. I am death. I am WAR!" it said, dragging out the last word and pushing pain into Adam's belly. Adam braced himself for the pain. Something was tearing his flesh from his bones.

Adam shut down, unable to take any more trauma to his pain receptors. He used his energy to turn off any association with his body, allowing the entity to stew inside alone.

"We'll rest now, worm," the entity said as it slammed Adam's body into the couch, putting it to sleep.

Even though he slept, Adam felt the dull throb of pain, especially in his left arm and along his spine, as the agony continued to make itself known. He couldn't see. His eyes were closed by whatever lived inside of him. He lay twisted on the couch and in an uncomfortably painful position that the entity in control relished.

The being had quieted. The present swirling energy failed to manifest pain outside of the homeostatic level of agony Adam had become accustomed to.

Adam tried to wake himself up, but he had no control. His body stirred a little. He tried to open his own eyes. His left eye cracked open slightly. His own eyeball looked through a different perspective. He mainly saw in black and white, with a crimson fog glazing over everything.

Trying to remain calm so he wouldn't tip off the entity, Adam attempted to push the pain behind a wall of steeled determination to open the other eye. As he blinked it open, he killed his excitement at being able to control his body to avoid agitating the entity.

Whatever had taken him hostage had loosened its grip on him for now.

Everything Adam could see through the red and hazy distortion had painted the entire atmosphere of his house differently. The heavy and crushing oppression weighed his body down.

He took advantage of the entity's absence, sat up, and grabbed his phone. He tried to move smoothly so he could get a message to Siobhan before whatever attacked him came back and forced him into submission with pain.

Click click click

He ignored the grating clicking sound that smacked his ear drums.

He put the phone on the charger in the kitchen and sat by it. "Come on," he said, trying to get it to charge faster. He needed a little more—enough to send a text or a quick call to Siobhan.

His body, racked with pain, could sense the entity as it burrowed deep inside, resting under his ribcage.

He looked around at his house, which looked different than it used to. The red haze of the perspective colored everything, turning his home into a warped hellscape. The windows blurred into crimson waves, and the walls wriggled around like they were alive. The dining room table churned in his vision like it had been made from burnt wood and liquid magma as the bright orange swirled up its legs.

His arm hurt, and he glanced at the horrifyingly disgusting wound. He could see an infection festering, with bits of yellow and green pus oozing out of it. The red and inflamed wound throbbed for a whole half an inch around the lowercase t shape. It had continued to morph into a sharp and recognizable cross.

He looked back at his phone. 2%. *Jesus Christ*. This is taking forever. He hit the button, trying to power on the phone anyway. It let him know that the battery still lacked enough energy.

He shifted his gaze to the clock on the stove. Through the fiery ashes floating in his vision, he squinted to read it. 3:19 pm. Siobhan had been gone for most of the day, and he hoped she had found enough to keep her busy and away until he could figure out what was going on in his own body.

His impatience lingered, and he started to worry that the entity would come alive inside of him again and regain control. *Stay calm. Don't make any sudden thoughts*. His insides turned over.

Shit. 5% battery. He couldn't wait. He powered on the phone, and it jumped to life. He left it on the charger, hoping to get enough time to send a text message. He waited, unmoving, for his phone to charge and boot up.

His background lit up. Ignoring it, he swiped open the phone and found Siobhan's number. His stomach lurched again. Something rolled around in his intestines and clawed its way upward.

Hurry. Hurry.

He typed up his message and hit send. Less than one second later the entity pushed him aside and took Adam's body over. The pain intensified like a lion raking its claws down his back.

The entity lifted his body out of the chair, made its way back to the couch, and laid it across the cushions.

Silence cut into the thick air as it put Adam's body back to sleep.

Click click click

Click click click. Click click click

The clicking sound began to surround Adam again. This time, it bore down on him. He hardened his resolve against the sinister minion and hoped his message had found Siobhan.

Adam wanted some rest, too. Exhaustion racked his mind but he needed to figure out how to defeat whatever had taken control of him. He hoped he could do it before the pain became too much and it killed him.

The torture had already made it difficult for him to think, and it intensified and worsened. He thought about ways to remove the agony before his mind shut down.

Be safe, Siobhan. He had to come up with a plan. But the throbbing, dull ache surrounding his entire psyche stole his will.

CHAPTER 17

"I don't understand why we can't do the exorcism now if you guys think he's… possessed," Siobhan said, taking a sip of the sparkling water she'd bought at the store earlier.

Melina's dark aesthetic was reflected in her quaint living room, matching the rest of her home and her standard attire. The dark gray couch contrasted with the stark white carpet, but the gold accent wall where the TV sat brought some much-needed color to the living room. In addition to the sofa, Melina had two chairs but no coffee table. She had a massive black corner bookshelf with antique books and forms of skulls on it.

Melina even had glass jars shaped like skulls sitting on the bookshelf, adorning her book collection. The antique tomes were the most numerous items in the sparse room. The living room even smelt like a library, but not a library on a college campus. Her room smelled like an old museum where scholars sat researching intelligent topics like quantum mechanics and the origin of life while others studied languages on ancient scrolls.

"Well," Melina said as she set her can of water down. She leaned back in the chair and looked up briefly. "The priest can't do an exorcism without the consent of the bishop. They control everything. And he's not really an exorcist. Those are few and far between these days. He did it for Adam before because we waited three months, and they didn't approve it. That is part of why I needed to stay so quiet about the whole thing. He could get in a lot of trouble if anyone finds out."

"It seems like an exception can be made this time, too," Siobhan said.

"And he might make one again," Melina said, shrugging. "He wants to protect life first before following stringent rules. We have to wait until tomorrow, and then we'll know more. He will do the house blessing to see where things are at."

"I hate that you know how this is going to go, but I am also thankful for your help in explaining it all. I'm not sure I even believe it," Siobhan said.

"Make sure you stay calm tomorrow. A demon will do some very interesting things to try to get you upset. The more it can affect you, the more it will clamp down on Adam, making it harder for him to fight back and easier for the demon to control him," Melina warned.

Siobhan sighed as hot tears threatened to fall. "It's going to be a long night, isn't it?" she asked.

Melina nodded. "I think so."

Siobhan's phone vibrated in her purse. She reached for her purse on the other side of the sofa. She pulled out her phone, and the telltale blinking blue light indicated she had received a text message. She pulled it up.

Her eyes widened in shock. "It's from Adam," Siobhan said in surprise.

Melina stood and came over to sit by Siobhan. "From Adam? Or…" Melina looked worried.

Siobhan shook her head. "Let's look together."

Her thumb hovered over the notification, ready to open the text.

Melina nodded before she leaned in to look.

Siobhan tapped the notification and opened the text.

"Oh my god…" she muttered. "It was him."

The text read: *Something is wrong. I love you. Don't come back here.*

The next morning, Siobhan woke up after getting a surprising amount of dreamless sleep. She opened her eyes and sat up in the full-sized bed in Melina's spare bedroom, the cream-colored linen bed sheets tangled around her legs.

She tossed the comforter aside and flicked on the lamp by the side of the bed. Through the adjacent wall, she could hear Melina in the bathroom.

She threw on the white T-shirt she'd bought at the grocery store and the plain black cropped leggings she had picked up. She put her dirty shorts and shirt back in the plastic bag.

Her brow furrowed as she reeled over her first night away from Adam since they moved in together.

Siobhan pulled open the door as Melina came out of the bathroom. "It's all yours," she said. "I left the shampoo and body wash in there for you. I'm going to make coffee."

"Thanks, Melina," Siobhan said. She took a quick shower. The hot water seeped into her muscle temporarily, making her feel less sore even though she had rushed through it. She brushed her teeth and put her grocery store outfit back on.

Siobhan tossed her bag of dirty clothes on the floor.

"Do you want to wash those?" Melina asked.

"Nah. I'll drop them off at home," Siobhan said as Melina handed her a mug full of hot black coffee. "I'm hoping to grab some things if I'm going to be staying awhile," she added before taking a sip.

Melina nodded. "I'm excited to do this class, but it seems strange now that…you know…" she trailed off.

"Yeah. But you're right. People think this stuff is for those who are clinically insane. I thought I was. Hell, I still might be, who knows?" Siobhan said, shrugging her shoulders as she fought against the sting of tears.

She set her coffee mug down and pulled the hair tie off her wrist, tying it in a wet, wild, and messy bun. She picked up the mug and took a big drink of coffee from it.

Scamper came into the room meowing and rubbed his side on Melina's ankles, tangling himself between her legs.

"Hi, buddy," she said, setting down her mug and reaching down to pick him up. She hugged him and scratched the side of his face. He purred and rubbed his head against her chin. "I love you too, Scamps," she said as she sat him down by his food dish. The cat eagerly began eating the food she'd already gotten into his bowl.

"He's such a good boy," Siobhan said.

"He is." Melina polished off the rest of her coffee and put the mug right into the dishwasher.

"Oh, here," Siobhan said as she also finished, handing the mug to Melina.

Shutting the dishwasher door, Melina asked, "Are you ready to do this?"

Siobhan inhaled sharply. "No. But do I have a choice?" she asked, picking up her purse and slinging it over her shoulders.

"You always have a choice."

"Meet you there?" Siobhan said as she fished for her Jeep keys.

"Meet you there."

"How do you do it, Melina?" Siobhan asked after her first yoga class, approaching the gym's front desk. "I feel great, even though my stress is through the roof

"I know how it feels to have… to be in your shoes," Melina corrected, looking around.

"Well, thanks. Too bad Helen missed it," Siobhan said, glancing at the clock by the locker rooms and smiling.

They rounded the corner, and Jesus stood at the computer with the employee login program running. "Good morning, ladies," he said in his heavy accent, nodding their way.

"Hello, Jesus. You don't have to come until eight," Siobhan said.

"I want to get started on some things," he said. "It might get a little messy in here over the weekends."

"It does," Siobhan said. "You can come in as early as you'd like." She lifted her nose as the aroma of freshly brewed coffee billowed toward her.

"Coffee. For you. I will go start now," Jesus said, making his way to the men's locker room.

Siobhan sighed with relief that she'd hired him.

"Good job on that one," Melina added. "A whole hour early. Wow."

Siobhan grabbed two mugs and started pouring coffee for herself and Melina.

Helen bounced in the front door with a large skip.

"You're early," Siobhan said with a friendly smirk. "Hand me another mug, please," Siobhan said to Melina, reaching out her hand.

"Oh my God, Siobhan! We had the best time! Oh, I'm sorry. Are you better?" Helen asked as Siobhan handed her a mug. She wriggled around, incapable of stilling her body.

Melina picked up her mug and sat in the chair, quietly sipping the freshly brewed coffee.

"I am. I still feel a little like I was run over by a truck, but the yoga class helped," Siobhan said, nodding her head toward Melina. "She nailed it."

"Ah! Sorry, I missed it. I'm here, though, and *really* early. Six hurts my head. I don't want to think about setting an alarm and getting out of bed for that," Helen said with a big smile. "No offense!"

Ding.

Siobhan reached into her purse for her phone. She'd gotten a text message from Derek. She had called him last night and left him a voicemail. She had told him that Adam had been having trouble with the injury and needed more time to heal.

Derek's text read: *Just got your voicemail. Hope it's not infected. Tell Adam to feel better and stay home this whole week. I need him. TTYL*

She tossed her phone back in her bag. "Sorry, Adam's still

sick," she said as Melina eyed Siobhan over her mug. "He's not going to work today, and his injury isn't healing up that fast. It's worse than we thought."

"Oh, I'm sorry to hear that," Helen said, pulling her curly red hair in half to tighten her ponytail. "Did he have whatever you had?"

Siobhan shrugged. "I don't know. Probably. But he's injured too," she said. Siobhan set her mug down and leaned on the counter. Sure enough, the sticky, wet cobwebs were there. She recoiled and sat back this time, deciding not to reach for the cleaner.

Helen bounced and kicked her feet.

"Tell us all about Jesus!" Siobhan said, forcing her mind to focus on her friend.

Melina stared at the counter quietly and sipped her coffee.

"He's so sweet. We had food at this tiny little Mexican place. But not like American Mexican food like the Sweet Burrito. We had real food with those corn tortillas that they make there! It was so good but *spicy,"* Helen said with emphasis. "Then we went to that new cocktail bar on Raven's Beach. I had some kind of drink with Rum Chata, and it was so good!" "That sounds so fun," Siobhan said, feigning enthusiasm.

"The Black Cat Fever?" Melina asked Helen. "Is that the new bar?"

"Yes! That's it!" Helen said, snapping her fingers. "We loved it. Have you been there?"

"Oh. No. I'm not a drinker. I live off Raven's Beach. I pass it every day when I come here or go to the grocery store. It looks nice," Melina said, sipping her coffee.

"It was so fancy inside," Helen said, wriggling some more. "And Jesus was such a gentleman. He opened the car door for me, he walked me up to my door, and he almost left without a hug or a kiss or anything." Helen smiled wryly.

"But I'm guessing you decided that that wasn't the right ending to the evening," Siobhan said mischievously with a crooked smile.

"Of course it wasn't!" Helen threw her head back and laughed. "He got a big kiss, then a nice long hug. I said 'thanks,' and he made sure I was inside before leaving. I even waved to him from my front window. Sometimes, it's nice having a first-floor apartment. Then he texted me Sunday saying he had a great time and wants me to come over after my last class today to have some Mexican food at his apartment," Helen said, squealing. "Of course, I'm going. I had to come early to see him!"

"Good for you, Helen! I'm so happy for you," Siobhan said with genuine happiness, although she had to force it out.

The mundane female conversation served its purpose and took Siobhan's mind off Adam and what could happen later today.

She tensed at the thought that she would get to see Adam but she was not prepared to experience more disturbingly evil imagery. That bleeding crucifix took up physical space in her mind, along with the image of Adam, in the same shape, suspended in their living room.

The mental exhaustion broke her, and she pretended to be okay by half listening to Helen relay every conversation she'd had with Jesus on Saturday. Her mind busied itself replaying all her hallucinations, which were probably not hallucinations. They were so vivid, real, graphic, and frankly, terrifying.

I saw a bleeding crucifix in a Catholic Church.

"…and then when he shut the door, he called me 'preciosa'. When I asked what that meant, he said, 'Precious.' It's like a term of endearment. How is he so sweet?" Helen continued giggling.

Melina had been silent since she asked about the Black Cat Fever cocktail bar, and Siobhan hadn't said anything either. She tried to perk up and nod at the right places as Helen spoke.

Siobhan's phone rang, tearing through Helen's happiness. Melina had gone to work out.

"I'm going to help Jesus clean the mirrors," Helen said, winking at Siobhan as she picked up her phone.

"Hello?" She said, answering and rubbing her forehead with her palm to cull the aching headache forming behind her eyes.

"Siobhan. This is Father Renaldo. Are you having a blessed

day?" he asked.

"I am. Sure. I mean, I'm fine. I'm not fine, but I'm acting fine. Anyway, I'm sure you understand," she said..

"I do," Father Renaldo said. "I have rewatched the tape of Adam's exorcism. I didn't find anything particularly useful, but I could go through it again later." The priest cleared his throat before saying, "I'd like to schedule a home blessing for today at one. Is that too soon for you?"

"No, that's fine. I want Melina to come with me. I don't have anyone else," she said sadly and looked at the floor.

"Okay. Call me back if it doesn't work. What's your address? I'll be there at one unless you need to postpone," the priest said.

She rattled off her address and gave quick, simple directions.

"Thanks, Siobhan," the priest said. "I'll see you later today, and don't hesitate to fill me in if you experience anything," he added with encouragement.

"I will. Thank you, Father," she said as she hung up.

Siobhan tossed her phone into her purse and tried to find Melina.

CHAPTER 18

The closer it got to one o'clock, the quicker Siobhan's heart beat.

"Adam did say to stay away," she said to Melina before shoveling a bit of salad into her mouth. Her stomach knotted, but it grumbled in anticipation.

"We won't know how bad it has gotten and how fast it's progressing this time unless he does it," Melina said, wiping the ketchup and mustard off her fingers that dripped down her burger and onto her hands. She sat back in her seat and put her hands on her lap. She looked down at them, averting her eyes. "I was twelve before and didn't understand." She took a sip of her water.

"How will he know?" Siobhan asked, biting her bottom lip and sitting back in the booth.

Melina shrugged. "If I remember correctly, he'll go off Adam's reaction to the blessing and the test. If things move on their own or if Adam responds to the object he can't see, it indicates a possession. Before..." Melina stopped herself.

"Before what?" Siobhan asked.

"I don't know. Do you even want to hear about how it went last time?" Melina asked.

Siobhan let out a sigh. "I might. My appetite is shot, so you may as well fill me in," she said resolutely as she pushed her plate away.

"The priest came over, and Grandma let him in. Right away, Adam smiled. But not, like, a normal smile like I had seen on my brother a million times. He smiled and didn't even look like him. He looked... evil. Bad. Like he was about to commit a horrific crime. His whole demeanor changed into one of being condescending to the priest and berating," she said.

Siobhan nodded, trying to listen and understand what she should expect in less than an hour.

"He said horrible cuss words and called the priest all kinds of awful names," Melina said. "Adam never talked like that. I mean, he was fourteen, so he cursed here and there, but nothing like the string of f-bombs and c-words we were hearing. I remember him always keeping his cool, too."

Melina paused to look at Siobhan, who stared back at her, listening without interruption. "I do remember that he had a laugh, too. A laugh that was somehow in Adam's voice, but it wasn't him. Like he was making the sounds, but he didn't laugh like that. It was a foul sound, like a laugh that was rotting away. I'm sorry," she said, biting her lip. "This is so hard to explain and so unbelievable," Melina added, throwing up her hands.

"I appreciate you telling me," Siobhan said. "And hey, I do believe you. It's this whole... I don't know." She waved her hand in the air. "It's not you. It's hard to buy this... demon thing."

"You are where I was nineteen years ago. I saw so many

things and I heard awful voices that I'll never forget. And the clicking," Melina said sadly, gritting her teeth.

"I have heard that too," Siobhan groaned. She put her hands over her ears.

Melina finished her water, and the ice banged against the plastic cup as she set it on the table. "Should we meet Father Renaldo?" she asked.

Siobhan nodded.

As Siobhan drove to her house with Melina behind her, she broke down. She started sobbing uncontrollably. The events of the past few days were too much for her.

Siobhan sniffled and repeatedly wiped tears from her eyes as they clouded her vision. The droplets fell, landing on her T-shirt. Her hair whipped around her face as the wind stung her tear-stained cheeks.

She pulled into her driveway. The looming shadow lingered in the front window like a stain on the glass. Melina pulled up to the curb and got out as Siobhan tossed her phone and keys back into her purse.

Glowing red eyes burning inside the shadow were unmoving but bore holes into her chest with their intensity.

The necklace got warm, and instinctively, she wrapped her hand around it.

Help me.

Melina got out and made her way to the Jeep's driver's side door. "Are you okay?" she asked.

Siobhan sat, unmoving in the vehicle. Her eyes were red and swollen, and tears stained her cheeks. Melina rested her hand on Siobhan's arm through the open window of the topless vehicle.

Siobhan nodded her head. She nodded once toward the front window where the black shadow loomed, and Melina narrowed her eyes at it. "It's the shadow from my night terrors. The one I saw as a child when Adam was possessed. It was always watching," Melina explained.

"You..." the low growling voice said as it trailed into a tongue-clicking sinister laugh of pure malevolent and heinous evil.

"It knows," Melina said in a whisper.

"What do we do?" Siobhan asked in a panic that she had little control over.

"We go in," Melina said.

Siobhan gnashed her teeth and shivered. She fidgeted in the seat with anxiety as her heart beat faster.

"It won't do us any good to be scared. It knows everything already," Melina said, still looking at the shadow.

Siobhan let out a long breath. "Well," she said, reaching for the door handle. "Let's get this over with," she added as Melina stepped to the side, allowing Siobhan to open the door of the Jeep and get out.

Siobhan steadied her emotions.

The shadow stared intently as Siobhan and Melina began their trek up the walkway toward the evil presence.

The long walk up to the front door filled Siobhan with dread.

The tight and heavy air forced each breath to catch in her throat. Siobhan's necklace jumped off her chest as she tried to make sure she was getting enough air. The glow from her necklace lit the gray haze that wove around her and gave her comfort. Its warmth eased the tightness in the energy field around them.

Siobhan slowly reached her shaking hand toward the doorknob. She somehow managed to get a grip on the golden-colored knob, and it shook under her anxiety. Her fingers were holding on so tightly they were turning white.

Siobhan swung the door open, and a blast of wind crushed her and Melina. They struggled to stay on their feet as they stepped inside, out of breath, searching for enough oxygen with their lungs. Siobhan shut the door behind them, stranding them in utter oppression.

The shadow had dispersed from the window. It had somehow found a way to linger in every square inch of the house without being anywhere in particular. The shadow wound its way all around them, rubbing against them and poking at their skin.

They could hear Adam's labored breathing as he lay on his

side, with his arms twisted at crazy, unnatural angles. His head turned back without a pillow, and his mouth hung open. Green foam pooled on the couch below him as it streamed out of his mouth.

Siobhan nodded to Melina to follow her into the kitchen. She opened the laundry room door and tossed her plastic bag of dirty clothes inside. They sat at the bar between the dining room and kitchen.

"I wonder how long he's been asleep," Siobhan said quietly, wrinkling her nose as she caught a smell of decaying rodents that clung to the heavy graying air inside her home.

"It's hard to say. He slept a lot before... I mean, before when this happened. He was either asleep or..." Melina said.

"I don't want to wake him up," she said. The sound of Adam's breathing chopped at the heavy air.

"I am sure the priest will agitate the demon enough," Melina said.

"I hope he gets through this. He looks so sick," she added sadly.

"He did before. We have to make sure once we expel the demon that he doesn't come back," Melina said. "Going through this a third time is not an option. Not only for Adam but for the demon," she said, crossing her arms over her chest.

Siobhan had come in with someone. He should know her. He stayed alert and let his body rest, trying not to agitate the entity.

Why did Siobhan come back here when he asked her not to? She was going to have to rely on her own instincts because he couldn't help her much in his condition.

Adam's body reeled, still in pain. Being asleep dulled the intensity of the pain that lingered after the entity inflicted torment during its active time. He hoped that he'd stay asleep until Siobhan left.

He tried to listen even though he couldn't control his ears. He could hear Siobhan and her friend in the kitchen, and he knew they were talking even though their voices were low. Did he hear the word *demon*?

Could that be what's wrong with me? This is the stuff people made up for horror movies.

Demon. Adam's logic attempted to push that thought aside as hard as it tried to maintain composure in his own body so the malevolent entity would have less power over his short-circuiting nerve endings.

His blood heated in his veins. The presence stirred. The energy of something evil butted up against that of Adam's own psyche.

At this point, Adam had no idea what to call his continued consciousness and lack of bodily function. What do you call being able to see and hear out of your own body but know someone *something* else is using its own eyes and ears instead? What do you even call it when your perspective is not your own, and you can't respond or control your own limbs?

Possessed. Adam knew it, but he couldn't admit to it.

The blood in his veins increased in temperature. The pain was incredible.

"The time," Siobhan said through the cloudy haze.

"Maybe we should grab some of your clothes before he gets here," her friend said.

Their footsteps approached slowly. He had shifted slightly, and his left arm had turned to face upward.

He sensed them stopping to look at him.

"That's much more inflamed than I remember," Siobhan said.

The upside-down cross, raw and open, with a small amount of blood congealing in the deepest part of the wound, had swollen and pulsated on his arm.

Adam's body stayed asleep, but the cut visibly throbbed, like it had its own life force. Its blackened edges peeled up like it had been burnt and the entire arm periodically jerked.

It hurt like hell, and he didn't understand the damn thing. The stitches the doctor put in were gone, and it inflamed and burned with infection. Every single irregular heartbeat in his wound pulsated.

"It's the same as before but bigger," Siobhan's friend said.

Siobhan let out an audible breath slowly, and he could hear her footsteps going toward the stairs.

What's the same as before? Who was this lady that he was sure he knew?

His blood temperature continued to elevate. The sharp prickles of rivers of red-hot lava flowing through his body caused him to jerk several more times.

It surfaced under his skin. It wouldn't be long before his body became alert and awakened by the entity possessing him.

Demon.

Click click click click click click
Click click click click click click

Siobhan rushed to find an overnight bag and threw in her hairbrush, a few pairs of shorts, one pair of jeans, and some leggings. She grabbed five T-shirts from her drawer and a few handfuls of underwear without counting.

"That should do it," she said, zipping the bag.

DING DONG

Melina and Siobhan looked at each other over the messy, unmade bed. They took one step toward the bedroom door but stopped.

"Hello, Father," Adam said as he answered the door.

CHAPTER 19

Siobhan snapped her gaze back to Melina, who stared at her with wide eyes.

"Hello, Adam. I'm Father…"

Adam interrupted the priest and said, "Peter Paul Renaldo. Right," he said. His calm voice sounded like it had come from Adam himself. His speech cadence faltered as he spoke.

"Sure, of course, you do," said the priest. "May I come in?" he asked.

"Uh. Nah. I don't feel like I need prayers today, priest," Adam said in an irritated tone of voice.

Siobhan's necklace got warm on her chest.

"Let's go," Melina said as she rushed toward the stairs. She put her hands on Siobhan's back, pushing her to move.

"Father, welcome. Please come in," Melina said. He looked up as the women stepped down the stairs.

"Thank you, but I need Siobhan to let me in if that's OK," Father Renaldo said.

"She doesn't want you to come in, asshole," Adam said with anger and gritted teeth as he looked down at the much shorter priest. His six-foot-two frame shadowed Father Renaldo in a cold darkness that the priest did not cower away from.

"Yes, I do," Siobhan said in a saccharine tone as she looked at Adam. His face held steady in its off-and-slightly distorted appearance. "He's here because I asked him to come. He's going to bless our home." She took the door from Adam, and he glared at her. His eyes flashed pure white before going back to the deep brown.

"Stupid," he snarled as he spun away and flopped down to a sitting position on the couch with his back to the front door.

He lifted his left arm and looked at his injury. She couldn't see his face, but he laughed a slow, low chortle that ground her nerves. Adam's laugh, while familiar, had a terrifying edge to it and tickled her ears.

Click click click

The laugh ran into the clicking sound she now knew all too well, and Siobhan gritted her teeth against the grating noise.

The priest set the briefcase he carried on the floor.

"How are you today, Siobhan?" Father Renaldo asked as he reached out to shake Siobhan's hand.

"I'm..." she glanced over at Adam, who sat on the couch upright, still with his back to them, admiring his injury. The mark. She snapped her gaze back to the priest. "Great, " she finished.

Siobhan shook the priest's outstretched hand and he put his palm over the back of her right hand. An object pressed into her skin. She locked eyes with the priest. He looked down, and she followed his gaze. He flipped his hand over to display a rosary, crumpled into a tiny ball. He reclasped his hand around it and dumped the rosary into Siobhan's hand. She stared at it before lifting her eyes to look at him through her lashes.

He nodded once.

"I saw that priest," said a voice that came from Adam's mouth. The word *priest* hung in the air like a curse word stuck in the dark and ever-thickening ether. Adam faced away from them, and none of them could see his face. The slow and low-clicking sound started up again, and Siobhan bristled.

The priest stooped and grabbed his briefcase. Turning it away from Siobhan and Melina, he opened it so neither could see what it held.

Siobhan gripped the rosary tightly in her hand. If she squeezed it anymore, it would break her skin.

The priest removed an item from his briefcase and reclosed the two latches. He set it upright and slid it behind him on the floor.

He held a gold metal handle about ten inches long. A ball with holes in it had been attached to the top of the handle. Siobhan had never seen anything like it before.

"Aspergillum," the priest said, setting his hand on her shoulder to ease her trepidation.

The laughter started again. A few quick chuckles came in spurts; it wasn't Adam's voice this time. The audible and ever-present hazy fog that lingered on the moving air in the house held the vibrations of the otherworldly laughter.

"Let's start," the priest said, pointing up the stairs.

Siobhan nodded.

Once the three reached the top, the priest took the aspergillum and whipped it forward. A few splashes of water came out. "I bless this home in the name of the Father," he said, flinging the water. "And of the Son," he said with another blast of water when he spoke the word *Son*.

"And of the holy spirit," he said, tossing water for the third time. The evil laughter remained as an undercurrent to the clicking, which quickened as the priest spoke. "I will bless every room," the priest said.

He entered the spare bedroom.

While moving around upstairs, Father Renaldo made sure to fling holy water and pray in each room. "Nothing is happening," Siobhan whispered to Melina as she leaned toward her. "Except for the clicking and laughing."

"But that laugh…" Melina whispered.

"What do we do?" Siobhan asked with a shaky voice and quivering lip.

Melina wrapped Siobhan in a hug. The cackling guttural laughter got a little louder, and a twinge of pain radiated in her ear again. The twisted and unnatural sound disturbed her more than it had in her lucid dream.

When the priest emerged from Siobhan's bedroom, he stepped past both women and made his way down the stairs. Siobhan and Melina followed.

Adam stood facing them. His head cocked to the side at an unnatural angle, and he had a smile that stretched far too big for any human. His white eyeballs stared into the priest.

"Did you do what you came to do, priest?" Adam said in a malicious form of his own voice, snarling as he pronounced the *s* in priest. His lips curled, like a dog baring its teeth. The priest, unflinching, lifted his aspergillum and said, "In the name of Jesus Christ, I command you to leave this house, unclean spirit!" Father Renaldo whipped holy water onto Adam. He screamed and hissed as steam came off his chest, billowing where each droplet had landed. The clicking got louder and drowned out by the hissing of Adam's burning skin.

Siobhan winced and shook uncontrollably.

"You're gonna have to do better than that, priest," Adam said in the familiar, low guttural voice. "We're gonna do this again, yesssssss?" he said, further cocking his head in a manner that should have broken his neck. He locked eyes with Father Renaldo.

Siobhan bit the inside of her cheek and held back a scream. Adam's head had twisted as if it were locked in a brutal medieval torture device.

His left arm moved. His cut pulsated with thousands of needles that were constantly and repeatedly being jammed into it as it depressed repeatedly in small pricks.

On the verge of tears, Siobhan's entire body quaked with fear as she recoiled. Her breath came out in short spurts.

An eerie gray fog throbbed strangely around Adam. It swirled and came toward her.

"The power of Christ compels you, demon," the priest said as Siobhan grabbed Melina, leaning on her. Her legs weakened as she shook more violently. "God the Father compels you! Give me your name!"

"The power of Christ compels you, demon," Adam repeated in the priest's voice, mocking him. Adam straightened his head. "That didn't work before," he said in the demon's voice. "What makes you think it will work this time, you old fool?"

"Old fool?" the priest said in amusement, with a sardonic grin. "You had better insults last time, vile serpent."

Adam smiled painfully slowly. A sinister shadow came over his face.

He laughed and clicked his tongue to the roof of his mouth. "Tsk, tsk. So did you, priessst," he said, hissing and dragging out the *s* as a long snake-like tongue whipped out of Adam's mouth and then shot back inside.

The sinister laughter started again, complete with the

clicking that merged them in an inharmonious and sinister song.

Siobhan's necklace warmed against her quivering body, but she held Melina tightly.

She couldn't drag her eyes away from Adam.

The oppressive energy pushed her downward.

"You brought the sister," Adam said, as a much too large smile peeled open on his face. He shot his gaze at Melina.

Siobhan's ears started to burn as her blood pressed hard into her eardrums. She drowned in the new sound of Adam's voice.

"You wanted to see me again, didn't you?" the demon said as Adam's left arm lifted to point at her. His arm bent at an odd angle. Heavy energy seemed to flow outward from his body. The saturated air pushed in on Siobhan's face as a shock wave rolled over her, forcing her to take a step back and grip Melina tighter.

Adam's arm remained outstretched as his wound started to leak blood. Chunks of yellow and green pus the size of dimes began to push their way out of the cut and hit the floor, landing in a pool of blood.

She wrinkled her nose at the smell that coalesced around her. The stench of decaying rodents and bitter, long-ago-expelled urine lingered in the room. Mixed, they made a pungent odor so palpable she could feel it lingering in her nostrils.

"Easy now, demon. You'll wear yourself out," the priest said as he flung more holy water on Adam. "Now give me your name, vile beast!" he shouted over the clicks.

Adam recoiled and hissed as he snapped his face back toward the priest, leaving Siobhan breathing heavily.

"Come back with your exorcism, priest. I will take him for good this time. Oh, and Rosemary says..." the demon's voice trailed off as Adam's head flung back and his eyes closed. His head snapped forward, his eyes opening; this time, solid black orbs stared back at Father Renaldo.

"Hello, old friend," Adam said in Rosemary's voice. Melina gasped and lost her balance. Siobhan wrapped her arm further around Melina to keep her steady on two feet.

Siobhan swallowed hard as her necklace got warmer. She could see its faint glow in front of her.

"You have games, demon. But I have the power of Christ," the priest said, his voice unwavering, as he once again showered Adam with holy water. Adam recoiled and hissed, falling face-first onto the sofa. The water came off his chest in steaming small wisps and rolled upward in swirling, smoky patterns before dispersing into the hazy darkness of the room.

Adam sank as the priest held the aspergillum high, as he had done with the crucifix the day at the church.

The demon slowly released control over Adam's body, and it fell into a sort of sleep. Melina and Siobhan unclenched the mutual grip they had on each other.

Siobhan's hand ached. She turned it up and the rosary she'd been gripping tightly had left imprints from the beads on her palm. She held onto it but released her grip enough that a small loop fell between her fingers.

"Oh my God. What...was...." Siobhan stuttered, barely able to get the words out.

"He's possessed," Father Renaldo said with certainty. "We need to get him upstairs and prepare the ties."

"Wait, what?" Siobhan asked, still forcing words to form in her throat. "Ties? You can't tie him up!" she protested, her breathing still fast and heavy.

"They are not for now. They are for later," the priest said.

"He'll hurt himself or us if..." Melina said, trailing off, a wave of sadness darkening her pale face.

"I'll need to conduct a physical exam and psychological assessment with a qualified medical professional before we do the exorcism. We should allow him to move about the bedroom while we wait for the examinations and exorcism approval," the priest said. "He hasn't done too much damage yet, but he may get more destructive."

"How do we get him up there?" Melina asked. "Siobhan and I aren't that big, and you're not..." She trailed off, then snapped her mouth shut, pursing her lips.

Father Renaldo smiled. "Young anymore?" he finished for

her. "My dear, I already know. We can do it. There are three of us. And I have the power of the Holy Spirit to help me," he said, winking at Melina.

Siobhan inhaled audibly, taking her first deep breath since she'd driven to her house earlier.

"He's not getting himself up there," Melina said as she marched toward Adam. The priest followed. Melina put one of Adam's arms around her slender shoulders, and Father Renaldo did the same. "As long as he stays passed out, I can get him," Melina said to the priest.

"I missed you, brother," she whispered with a hint of emotion.

Tears welled up in Siobhan's eyes. She wanted to smile, but she couldn't.

"Siobhan?" the priest said.

She snapped out of her own head. "Sorry," she said, rubbing her free hand up and down her arm.

"We'll need some rope," Father Renaldo said.

"Um, yeah," she said shaking her head. "I'll look."

She glanced at the rosary in her palm once more before setting it down on the priest's briefcase and meandering into the garage. She flicked on the fluorescent overhead light. A darkness that had nothing to do with a windowless garage followed her in.

She searched Adam's toolbox. She opened the top two

drawers on the left simultaneously and pawed around, finally finding it in the left middle drawer.

She didn't bother to shut the drawers. Instead, she grabbed the nicely coiled polypropylene rope and a box cutter from the top of the red toolbox.

She flicked the light off and let the door to the garage slam hard behind her.

When she got back in the kitchen, she could hear Melina and Father Renaldo struggling under Adam's weight as they made their way up the stairs.

Her eyes inadvertently traveled toward the sounds. A smoky shadow crawled across the ceiling, darkening its path with a dusty fog. A smooth breeze of icy air blew over her face, to be replaced with the stagnant smell of decay.

She squeezed her eyes shut, shook her head, and then trudged up the stairs.

Adam lay helpless on their bed. A few bruises were developing on his face. Through his white t-shirt, red and inflamed spots on his chest popped. Blisters full of fluid were in every spot where a water droplet had contacted his skin. He also had a few blistered spots on his neck, as if he'd been burned.

Siobhan winced, and a tear burned in the corner of her eye.

CHAPTER 20

Adam saw Siobhan through the demon's perspective. His own eyes narrowed to tiny slits preventing his sight from taking in the whole room.

The pain ran through his veins like his blood carried razor blades. The sting of a million wasps seared up Adam's left arm and into his shoulder. He had almost missed the word the entity had said earlier as the pain settled in his body. "Sister."

He pushed himself inside his own body as his presence began to shrink, taking up less space.

He wanted to tell his wife that he was sorry. He was sorry about all of this. He was sorry he had no memory. He was sorry he was possessed by a demon. He had so many things he wanted to apologize for.

Adam put up his wall and blocked everything in his psyche from the demon. He built the invisible wall and secured it using his energy. The demon rested but built its strength while it did so.

He pushed toward his consciousness. He fluttered his eyes open. The milky red haze that lit the demon's perspective still covered his vision. A jolt of searing pain shot up like lightning. The electricity shot up the back of his legs and into his core.

In a red-lit backdrop, Siobhan stood at the side of the bed. She worked to tie a rope to the bedpost near his left arm.

"Siobhan," Adam said in a raspy and dry voice. She stopped and slowly raised her head. "Help me…it hurts…" he choked out. "I'm in here," he said. Then his head dropped to the side, and he let go, receding back into the dark recesses of his own psyche.

"Adam," Siobhan whispered. The priest and Melina continued tying the ropes on the other side of the bed. She crawled up on the bed and lay next to him. She gave him a hug, even though she knew he couldn't feel it. "We will help you," she said.

She kissed his bruised cheek, then slid off the bed and sat on the floor. She backed herself to the wall, put her head in her hands, and sobbed. Tears started to fall between her fingers, landing on her bare legs.

Melina and the priest moved around making muffled sounds as they lashed the ties that would hold Adam to the bed. Melina made her way to the side of the bed where Siobhan hovered and glanced at the undone knot.

"Hey. He came through. That's a good thing," Melina said as she knelt and put her hand on Siobhan's shoulder.

"I… can't…" Siobhan said through tears that snuffed out her words. "I can't do this… without him." The burden of codependence strangled her decision-making and clouded her ability to help him.

"You can," Melina said. "We can."

"I will do anything I can, Siobhan," the priest said as he leaned over to finish tying the knot Siobhan left undone. "I am hoping to come back tonight with a doctor who can examine him. They will need to be present during the exorcism too, to protect Adam and…"

"And you," Melina said.

Father Renaldo nodded.

Siobhan stood and grabbed her bag from the floor. "I wish I could stay here with him—with Adam, I mean," she said.

"I know," Father Renaldo said as Melina stood. He put a hand on Siobhan's shoulder. "I promise, we'll record everything tonight. A physical and mental evaluation will be required. It's also a way for me to gather more information before I try to exorcise it. Why don't you and Melina get settled? I would like you to be here tonight when we examine him if you're up for it."

Siobhan nodded and wiped her tears with the back of her hand. She sniffed hard and sucked in the depressing air.

"I will shoot for five o'clock. I will let you know if that changes," Father Renaldo said.

Siobhan lingered in the doorway after Melina and the priest had gone down the stairs. She stared at her sleeping husband. His face showed signs of bruising; he had several yellowed blisters on his neck and a horrible cut deep into his left forearm that seeped blood onto their comforter. His lips were cracked, and his skin peeled up in spots along his stubbled jaw. He had several scratches in random places on his face and arms.

"Come back, Adam," she said, then shut the door behind her.

Once outside, the priest, carrying his briefcase, walked Siobhan to her Jeep.

"I will do what I can tonight," he said. "I have the liberty to do a home blessing without approval from the bishop, but I am supposed to rule out mental illness first..." He wanted to say more but looked up at the lone cloud in the sky.

"Father Renaldo, you can tell me," Siobhan said, pleading.

"I want to go forward with exorcism, Siobhan. The last time, the archdiocese didn't..." He looked up again. "I shouldn't have done it. But they were taking too long. They wanted more testing. I proceeded with the exorcism anyway. I'd like to do it right this time" He let out a heavy sigh.

"He was in trouble, and you helped him. It's the same this time, Father. Please don't wait too long," Melina said, irritated. She scratched her arm and shook her head.

"My dear, I will do everything I can to get this done. But I am one man. I will need assistants. Melina, you remember. You were too young last time, and Rosemary... she..." He paused, hesitant to finish once again and lowered his head.

"Yeah," Siobhan said, nodding. "She died of a heart attack

during the exorcism, correct?"

"That's the official story," the priest said, showing a lack of confidence. "I can get its name. But I can't let someone... I didn't enforce the rules, and she's no longer here." His eyes were drawn to the upstairs window over the garage, and sadness overtook him. His eyes welled with tears.

"It knows," he said, still glaring at the window through misty eyes. A black shadow had cast itself over the bedroom window. The white house stood in stark comparison to the blackness of the smoky haze that billowed outside of the window.

"I will come back," he said, looking at his watch. "It's after two now. I'll call when I have more information.

"Yeah," Siobhan said, her voice cracking and lip quivering.

Father Renaldo nodded. "I'll be in touch soon."

Adam steeled his thoughts, hoping the demon would forget he maintained space there while his consciousness tried to come up with a plan that made sense. The pain had gotten worse and the relentless torment ratcheted up the ante. His aching left arm began its steady throb of agony in anticipation of further torment by the demon.

He couldn't remember having a sister. How could he block something like this out? He didn't ponder these ideas for long because he knew that if the demon started to realize he was alert and had energy, it would take as much of it as it could through the torment of agonizing pain.

He'd heard Siobhan leave through the demon's ears a while ago, even though his assessment of time had warped dramatically. Alone in his bedroom with pure evil, Adam awaited the demon's torture. As if on cue, the demon prickled the inside of Adam's skull with its metaphysically textured hands, tapping on the inside of his brain. Talons scratched their way down the back of his brain stem and stabbed into his upper back.

The demon agitated inside of him, preparing itself for torment. Adam only had one idea. He could try to wrestle the demon's name out of it.

The demon smiled, which manifested itself as a gaping open-mouth grin on Adam's face. "Worm," it said, using its host's mouth before making its clicking chuckle.

The forked tongue rolled over the roof of Adam's mouth. The demon had Adam's vertebrae pressed against an invisible grater and started sliding it up and down as it sliced his skin. He recoiled in pain.

"Go to hell, you piece of shit," Adam said. In the silence that ensued, the demon responded by filling the house with its laughter so raucously that it shook the foundation. Adam's body jerked from side to side, throwing bedding in all directions.

"You think I haven't been there, you little worm?" the demon sneered as it sat Adam's body up. As stiff as a board, the whole upper part of Adam's body rose off the bed. The demon's vision tilted to the left, and it gazed at the rope tied to the bed frame. It sneered, pulling up Adam's upper lip.

Adam could see his wound from the demon's perspective. The telltale red haze that blurred everything except what the entity focused on caused Adam's eyeballs to throb in his head. A blood-colored, writhing fog painted over everything, including his wound. Worms wiggled their way upward and crawled around in the burnt skin of his arm.

The cut bled but it didn't gush. A slow drip of thick blood trickled off his arm. The dark, almost black blood, had a slight gray haze that lifted off it like it was smoldering and hot. The yellow and green pus-colored chunks clung to his skin and smelled like decaying flesh and rotten eggs.

Adam's skin was inflamed, red, and bruised around the carved-in injury. It had its own heat source and burned like someone had used a scorching hot iron to brand him. He was sure the branding iron was still pressed into his skin as it heated, never cooling or soothing. The wound now covered the entire length of his forearm.

"You like that, squishy worm?" the demon asked. "When I'm ready, I'll split that at the wrist and end your miserable existence," it said, laughing in the roar that burned Adam's ears.

Blood came out of his ear, and even if he wanted to wipe it away, he couldn't. His body thrashed about once more, ripping the sheets off the corners of the mattress. "You will bleed out while they watch you squirm," it said, adding its clicking to the voice.

Adam tried to focus through the agony. He needed any information he could get while the demon talked to him, and he'd have to do it from a demonic perspective.

"You're too much of a coward," Adam said, steeling himself against the pain he knew the demon would send. "You're so scared of the priest that you won't even give him your name!" The sound manifested into nothing but choking and gargling. The demon understood.

It tossed Adam's head back and roared with laughter. Blood started pouring out of his ear as the clicking coalesced with the roar of a throbbing heartbeat. His stomach churned in pain like someone had stabbed him.

"Stupid worm," the demon said before resorting to its clicking sounds that bounced through the air. Adam braced himself harder against the pain, which began increasing in his abdomen. The demon chuckled for a few more moments. "Maybe if they didn't lie to you, you'd know what was coming." Adam's head jolted back as he took a punch in the left eye. "Do you like this?" the demon said. "Give in. Agree to join me in the Kingdom; it can all end, worm."

Adam tried to brace his consciousness, but the pain in his abdomen intensified. He would be forced to lay low for now. He needed time to figure out how to beat this thing. He couldn't cause it pain or control his own body, so he'd need to move around within himself as a small consciousness.

Adam retreated, deep into his own vessel, trying to find himself a space behind his eyes, the place he liked the most. It held the least pain for him, and he could use the demon's perspective to at least see and hear Siobhan.

"That's right. Don't worry, dirty little worm. It'll be over soon," the demon said as it stayed upright and started to laugh once again. "I am a great Duke of Hell. I will not be commanded by you!" it roared.

"We'll see about that," Adam said as he did his best to hide while he braced for the pain. He beamed inwardly, glad he took it too far, and regretted that he couldn't take the punishment anymore at the same time. He had to give up for now as his strength waned.

CHAPTER 21

Siobhan received a call from the priest a little before three o'clock, not even an hour after she had last seen him.

"Siobhan," he said through her cell phone. "I hope you are doing as well as you can be given the circumstances.".

She shifted her weight on Melina's couch. "I'm hanging on, Father. Melina's here; I'm going to put you on speakerphone," she said, looking at her sister-in-law.

Melina leaned forward in her chair. She'd been reading her demonology book while Siobhan researched the history of the Catholic Church's exorcism rite.

"Okay, Father," she said.

"I was able to sit down and speak with Dr. Amanda Hill personally; she's…"

Siobhan snapped to attention, and her eyes locked on Melina's. She interrupted the priest and said, "The therapist by your office?"

Siobhan had a quick flashback to the nausea she had gotten in front of Dr. Hill's office building before being compelled to enter the church where the bleeding crucifix brought her to Father Renaldo.

"Yes, that's right. She's a parishioner and sympathetic to things that cannot be evidenced with scientific inquiry. She will come with me to do a psychological examination and an overall physical one on Adam today at five o'clock," he said.

"We'll be there. Hey, Father Renaldo? Is it possible Adam is… mentally unstable?" she asked without a shred of hope in her shaky voice.

"I'm afraid, my dear, that that isn't the case. Like I said, we've been through this with him before. I failed by not getting the demon's name, and Rosemary got tired of my shenanigans, so she…"

"It's been nineteen years, and what she did to save her grandson still haunts me to this day," he said with an air of sadness and distress. Every time the priest mentioned Rosemary's death during the exorcism, he shut down. The experience still stained the priest's soul, leaving him with a darkness he'd never be able to shake.

"An exorcism will scar." He inhaled sharply. "I made mistakes, and they are going to be brought up by the demon. All I can do now is make it right."

"It wasn't your fault, Father. She made the choice," Melina said, leaning toward Siobhan's phone.

"I appreciate your words, my dear, but unfortunately, they are not icing the wound Rosemary's decision has left on my heart. Now that I am sitting in my emotions, I will leave you both to it. I will see you at five o'clock," he finished sadly.

"Thank you," Siobhan said before tapping the button to end the phone call. She searched her phone for Helen's phone number. "I'm going to see if Helen can cover for me this week at the gym. With Jesus there, it should be fine."

"Good idea," Melina said. "I'll still go in early and teach the yoga classes. You can stay here if you need to. My house is your house."

"Thanks, but I'll go in and take your class. I have to try to pretend everything is normal, and I am not some psychopath who's lost her mind, right?" Siobhan said as she tapped the green button to call Helen.

Melina smiled. "Right."

Siobhan tensed her muscles and sought any inner strength that could help her rise to the occasion. She bit her lip as answers eluded her. Adam's inability to help her dug into her chest and her hands got clammy.

Siobhan relayed to Helen that Adam was still sick and that he would need to see a doctor that night. She intentionally left out the part about the doctor being a trained psychiatrist and coming with a Catholic priest to evaluate him for an exorcism.

"Oh no! I'm so sorry! Yeah, sure, anything you need. Jesus and I will handle it. Keep me posted. I hope he will recover soon!" Helen said supportively.

"You're the best. Tell Jesus I'm sorry but grateful for his

help. And you both are getting a dollar-an-hour raise," she said.

"You just get Adam better," Helen said. "I already headed home, but I could go back. Jesus is still there, I think," she offered.

"Nah. Maybe call him for me?" Siobhan said.

"Oh, I would *love* to," Helen said, giggling. "I'm sorry, that was unempathetic of me, with what you're going through."

"No, no. You're allowed to be happy and supportive at the same time," Siobhan said, although she lacked her best friend's energetic tone. "Let me know if either of you needs anything. I am going to try to make it to the morning yoga classes, and I will be there to run payroll Friday," she said, ending the call.

"Well," Melina said resolutely while standing. "What do you say we eat a quick early dinner and then head over to your place? I have some stuff to make a chicken salad in the fridge," she said, jerking her thumb toward the kitchen.

"I don't know how much I'll be able to eat, but I should keep my strength up," Siobhan expressed as she stood to follow Melina into the kitchen.

"You have to find that fire deep inside yourself. If this goes to exorcism, we will need to be strong. Mentally and physically," Melina said. "And you need to trust yourself. Feel your emotions; don't let them feel you. It's going to be hard."

Siobhan smiled. "It's tough without Adam. We were going through life together, and now I can't rely on him," she said.

"That's why you have to rely on you," Melina told her.

Later that day, as they pulled up to her house, Siobhan tried to ignore the smoky haze still lingering over the upstairs bedroom window. The shadowy figure with blazing eyes glared at them through the front living room as they approached the front door.

Nothing had changed since the last time she stepped into the house other than the potency of the frigid energy and the disturbing smell. The heavy atmosphere inside coupled with the humid pressure caused the air to push down on her like she wore a weighted vest.

The cold and lifeless environment stained with stagnant air moved its way toward Siobhan. It smothered inward all around her and gripped tightly like her rib cage was in a vice. Sitting on the couch, Melina and Siobhan simultaneously looked up the stairs at the sound of a low, animalistic growl. The tightness threatened to strangle anything it could out of the room. The thick and heavy air carried the stench of death and decay, mixed with body odor and dirty, unwashed, burnt hair and skin. As the air thickened, so did the hint of rotting meat as it combined with the already putrid odor.

Siobhan wrinkled her nose. "What is that smell?" she asked, putting the back of her hand on her nose.

Melina lowered her head. "Evil," she said.

"Well, it's bad."

The necklace warmed against Siobhan's skin, and Melina glanced at it.

"I feel her. Rosemary," Siobhan said. "It's nice to have her with me. With us. We can use all the help we can get, even if it's spiritual," Siobhan said.

"It's all spiritual now," Melina replied.

The smell increased in intensity. It could have come from anywhere, and yet it came from nowhere. It surrounded them and twisted into the deep air threatening to push them through the floor. It clung to their clothes and would remain long after they left.

The doorbell rang. Siobhan stood to answer it and a blast of icy cold air punched her so hard it flung her hair behind her and made her squint her eyes.

"Dear God," said Melina. She shuddered and hugged herself to stay warm against the air that had instantaneously dropped in temperature.

"Why is it so cold? It's *July*!" Siobhan protested, making her way to the door. Melina stayed huddled on the couch and pointed toward Adam. Siobhan pushed herself through the thickness of the space around her and, freezing with goosebumps over every single millimeter of her skin, flung open the front door.

"Hello again," the priest said. "It knows I'm here," he added, looking at the woman in her early forties standing next to him. Dressed in black pinstripe pants and a simple blue tank top blouse, her brown hair had been pulled up into an elegant, wispy bun style. She wore square black glasses that were perched perfectly on a small nose. She was beautiful but nondescript. A simple stethoscope hung around her neck, and she held a small bag in one hand and two books and a notebook in the other.

"Hi," Siobhan said lowly, swinging the door open further so Father Renaldo and Dr. Hill could come in.

"I'm Dr. Amanda Hill. It's nice to meet you, Siobhan. Father Renaldo has told me so much about you and Adam. I attend mass every weekend at St. Margaret's, and I hope I can help give you some answers today," she said, extending her hand. "I am a psychiatrist, but I am also a trained medical doctor." She wasn't boasting; instead, she came across as soothing.

Siobhan shook the doctor's hand. "Thank you. I'm sorry. I'm not myself. I feel very…" She trailed off.

"Cold?" the doctor asked. She shifted the books and notebook in her arms as she set down her bag. A lone pen was jammed into the notebook's metal spiral, and the papers stuck inside were falling loosely.

"Yeah, and it smells," Siobhan said. She pinched her nose and wrinkled it.

The doctor nodded.

"The smell is familiar, my dear," the priest said, looking up the stairs. "The cold was a sign." He set down his briefcase. "Demons often pull energy from the physical world around them. That's why it can be so cold when we are in their presence. They use it as the strength of the host wanes…"

Siobhan rubbed her temples, then plopped on the couch and started bouncing a foot up and down repeatedly.

"Well, shall we, Father?" Dr. Hill asked as she motioned to the stairs to break the tension.

"Let me grab my notebook," he said, setting down his briefcase. He unclipped both clasps and took out his brown leather-covered notebook and a book. He left the briefcase open and stood, pointing at it.

"If something happens, the crucifix and rosary are in there," he said, jamming his pointer finger toward the open briefcase. "Each of you can get one. Hold onto that crucifix." His gaze shifted toward the stairs.

Dr. Hill set down the two books she'd brought by the priest's briefcase and flipped open her notebook. She checked the top two sheets of loose paper, then flipped a few pages on the notebook. She scrawled something with the pen, then put it back in the wire spiral spine and looked at the priest. "Ready?" she asked.

"I'll go first," Father Renaldo said, heading up the stairs. Dr. Hill gave one last quick glance Siobhan's way, then grabbed her bag and followed the priest.

Father Renaldo opened the bedroom door to reveal an immobile Adam asleep on the bed. When she entered the room, the intense smell punched Dr. Hill in the face. She sniffed as it worsened as she entered the bedroom. The stench of decaying and rotting flesh took up physical space. The odor stung her nostrils and sat at the back of her eyes. She could see it in its thickness as it whipped around in the mass of hazy gray fog that pressed into her.

Father Renaldo looked around the room. He silently pointed to the far corner, where a simple gray chair sat, and lowered himself into it. He leaned back and tapped his stubbled chin. The priest took a small video camera out of his pants pocket and braced it against his leg, pushing the record button. He motioned to Dr. Hill that she could begin her assessment.

Dr. Hill used her stethoscope to listen to Adam's lungs as he slept. Adam's heavy and wet breathing was audible. Dr. Hill could hear fluid and gargling with each breath. But, when she used her stethoscope to listen to his lungs, the sound of nothing but normal breathing filled her ears.

She took Adam's pulse. Again, it was perfectly normal when she pressed her fingers to his wrist, but she could see his irregular and fast heartbeat throbbing in a large wound cut into his left forearm. She made a few notes on one of her pieces of loose paper. She couldn't verify with her medical instruments and her own hands what she was experiencing.

She rubbed her forehead with her fingers, trying to loosen the tension headache forming.

"Adam," she said as she adjusted the stethoscope around her neck.

Dr. Hill opened her bag and removed her blood pressure cuff, determined to find one instrument that could give her accurate readings. She chewed the inside of her cheek while she tried to figure out what happened inside and outside to the badly bruised and injured man in front of her.

Her eyes locked on the yellow ropes on each corner of the bed. She opened her mouth to ask the priest about them when movement tore her attention back to Adam.

"We may need to restrain him," Father Renaldo said, answering her unspoken question.

"Not yet," Dr. Hill replied sharply. "I'm not tying him up unless it's necessary."

Adam's body slowly lifted off the bed.

An icy finger traveled up Dr. Hill's spine. The cold kicked up and burned its path in her skin.

She took a step back, then stood frozen, her mouth agape. Adam's body slowly rose off the bed. His belly button led the way upward, as if pulled by a rope, while his neck strained under the weight of his own head, which tilted away from his body. His back popped into an unnatural position. He hung there for less than twenty seconds; then, the body slammed back into the bed with a thud, and his head ricocheted off the mattress.

Dr. Hill looked at Father Renaldo, her eyes and mouth wide in fear. The priest stood, his video camera still trained on Adam.

Adam's head turned and, with his eyes still closed, allowed his mouth to open. His jaw hung open and his purple tongue rolled out of his mouth.

Dr. Hill leaned forward to look at the dried blood that at one time had been coming out of his ear. He had welts in addition to the bruises forming on his face, and his left eye looked swollen like he'd been punched. The large wound that overtook his forearm aggressively glowed as it sunk further into the muscle meat. She fought the urge to gag.

"When..." She tried to talk, but words stuck in her dry throat. She coughed, but the priest understood her question.

"Siobhan found me Sunday," the priest said. "He got the mark on Thursday." Her memory rang as her brain tried to tell her something, but she pushed it aside. She needed to finish examining him.

"This is fast. I've seen one other possession," Dr. Hill said slowly and carefully. "But she had been leading up to this point for almost a year. This is fascinating," she said, trying to mask her fear while marveling at the speed with which Adam had become entirely under demonic possession.

"I still need to get his blood pressure," Dr. Hill stated as she slid the cuff over his right arm. Adam appeared to be unconscious, other than the horrific gaping smile plastered on his face.

"He's been possessed by this entity before," Father Renaldo said as Dr. Hill tried to get a reading. "I exorcised it previously but made some mistakes. So, it came back."

"It's spinning. He has no blood pressure, at least according to this. That isn't even possible," Dr. Hill said as she took the cuff off and inspected it. She narrowed her eyes at the tool. "Maybe this thing is broken…"

A horrific low laughter ripped its way around the room. Adam's eyes were still closed, and his mouth froze.

Dr. Hill tilted her head as a strange clicking sound that came from the walls and floor beneath her radiated through her body. It surrounded her, catching her in a claustrophobic stranglehold.

Adam's eyes snapped open. They were rolled up so far that they appeared to be pure white. She took another step back but kept her gaze on him. Quietly, she asked the priest, "Is he…?"

Adam sat up stiffly and robotically as if he had been controlled by a remote. His body tensed and went rigid, while another low chuckle came from somewhere. Over her head?

"Is he what, Doctor?" the demon asked in Adam's voice as he swung his head violently to look right at her.

"I... I..." she stammered and started backing herself into the wall.

"Come on, please?" Adam pleaded as his eyes returned to normal. "Come examine me," he said provocatively as he tilted his head to the side. His tongue lashed out and licked his cracked and bleeding top lip.

"Don't fall for it," the priest said. "It's trying to confuse you." She stayed staring at Adam as he bore circles into her forehead with his eyes.

"No," Adam said. "Help me, Doctor."

"I need to help him, Father," she said as she took a step toward the bed. The priest kept the camcorder on Adam.

Adam's head slowly turned toward the priest. "You're not ready, priessst," Adam's voice started, but the growling demon finished. The doctor jumped back and grabbed her notebook. She sat in the chair in the corner where the priest had previously been and started writing furiously.

"Calm down, demon. I will come for you. I promise," Father Renaldo said. "Why don't you release my friend Adam?"

The giggling transformed into sinister growls, which fused with the bizarre clicking sound that had started up again.

"He's not going to make it," Adam said as he wagged his tongue at the priest. "You're a failure, asshoooole," the demon said as its laughter morphed into the words it spoke.

The sounds sank into the walls.

"She died because of you, you know…" it said, as Adam's head flung backward.

Adam's body then released his bowels. The demon used his body to laugh and leave excrement and urine all over the sheet on the bed.

Siobhan's dresser in the corner started to shake, followed by Dr. Hill's chair. The doctor grabbed the edges of the seat and fought the urge to scream. Her glasses bounced on her nose, impeding her vision.

"Jesus," she said. "Help me." And she squeezed her eyes shut, trying to end the terrifying vision.

"Jesus help me… pigs and swine… swine… swine… send him home, Father. Pigs… and Jesus. Help me, Christ, the pig, and swine," the demon said in a sing-song cadence as Adam's head flung from side to side while still being bent backward at the neck.

Adam's body tightened, then slammed back to the bed. His eyes shut, and he lay still, breathing heavily. Covered in feces and urine, he stank and sank further away from the person he'd known.

"Doctor," the priest said, keeping the camcorder on Adam. "Please go get Siobhan. We will clean him up."

Dr. Hill nodded. "I think I've seen enough," she said, trembling.

CHAPTER 22

Siobhan fought the disturbing images of her husband as she showered. After helping clean up the mess Adam left on the bed, she felt off, almost like she had been infected with a virus. No, that was *not* Adam. He wouldn't do that, and she knew it, but she had never had to clean up a mess like that before.

Melina's water got hotter than hers, and she took every advantage of it. Using the hottest water possible, she vigorously scrubbed her body. When she finished, her shoulders red from the sting of the scorching hot water, she made her way down the hallway and pushed open the door to the spare room.

Even though she'd gotten clean, the gross sting of what she'd done lingered. She would never be able scrape the image out of her mind's eye.

She brushed her hair and then found Melina curled up in the chair in her living room, reading the demonology book Siobhan had seen in the bathroom the first time she used it.

"Better?" Melina asked, closing the book.

Siobhan shook her head. "I'm not sure I will ever be okay," she said, flopping down on the couch and pulling her legs up underneath her. She rested her chin on her knees.

"You still good to go back tomorrow after yoga?" Melina

asked.

Siobhan nodded, then put her forehead on her knees and hugged herself against the shiver.

When Dr. Hill and Father Renaldo finished evaluating Adam, and Siobhan had helped clean him up under the doctor's direction, she received advice to return the following day. The priest insisted she not go to her house at night right now.

Father Renaldo explained that all furniture needed to be removed except for one table, which would be adorned with candles and a crucifix during an exorcism. The safety of everyone, including the possessed, would be the utmost priority.

The priest asked that Melina and Siobhan be his assistants for the exorcism if they could agree to the rules that he would lay out to them in person. Siobhan reluctantly agreed, but Melina was a little more eager. She bit her lip hard as the thought of attempting to destroy this evil being forever flooded her brain.

Siobhan lacked the nerves of steel she'd need to help with a successful exorcism. She fought back tears and her body involuntarily shook as the fear spread through her veins.

"Hey. I know you're not hungry, but how about we have some decaf coffee and try to relax before bed? We could read and study. No demon talk," Melina said.

"That sounds all right," Siobhan replied.

Siobhan trudged through the gray forest again. Colors formed around her. The forest flooded her memory, and she knew she was dreaming. A moment of sheer panic shot through the core of her being as she remembered the last lucid dream she had.

She put her hands up by her head in anticipation. The forest became greener as she turned around. Flowers were blooming in every color, and the gray tone slowly washed away. She knelt to touch the little light purple flowers on the rosemary plant in front of her—but this wasn't any plant—this was hers—this was the plant she had in her backyard. She brushed her fingers over the bush, smiling at the beauty of this marvelous living thing.

"Siobhan," said an older woman. Rosemary. She raised her head but kept her right hand lingering on the bush's tiny flowers. She strained to hear. She wanted to hear her again.

"Siobhan," she said again.

"Yes! I'm here!" she said excitedly, standing. She spun in circles back and forth, looking for Rosemary. The lovely, herbal scent of the plant filled her nostrils and permeated the bright air in the forest meadow. The smell made the green of the plants greener and the blue of the sky bluer.

She spun around again and saw her. Her necklace glowed and she could see the orange coming up from under her chin. It got warm like it had so many times in the few days that she'd been wearing it.

"It suits you," Rosemary said, smiling. She had her mostly silver hair pulled into an older 1960s-style hair bun. A few black streaks were still present. Her light blue dress reached the earthen ground and buttoned the entire length of it. On each button, a flower was imprinted slightly different from the last. The short, loose sleeves blew in the wind as the skirts lightly wrapped around Rosemary's ankles. Her clear brown eyes held the utmost kindness and sincerity. Barefoot, she stood with her feet directly on the soil, her toes embedded in the earth.

"Why? Why did you do it?" she asked Rosemary, holding back tears.

"I had to. Father Renaldo is a good man, but we were losing," she said. "Right before the exorcism, I gave it to Melina," she said, pointing to the necklace. "I told her to wear it and give it to you. I came to her and wanted her to know it was going to start again."

Rosemary looked up at the sky and outstretched her hands. A light swirl of white smoke lifted from her palms and floated over her head, coming toward Siobhan.

She let the smoky aural mist come over her. It coalesced around her throat, then settled into the tiger's eye crystal Siobhan still wore around her neck. She kept her eyes on Rosemary, never focusing on the mist.

Rosemary's almond-shaped eyes opened to ensure the

energy source in the smoke had reached Siobhan. She smiled. "You could use some light," she said, dropping her hands to her side.

"Of course I can. Thank you," Siobhan said. "But how? I mean, how did you put yourself, or your words, or your…your…" Siobhan shook her head, unable to come up with the right words as she stood in that colorful forest of her lucid dream.

"I willed it. I made a deal with the devil. It happened quietly. I would let it kill me if it left Adam. And only if my spirit could go into the crystal," she said.

"He agreed? The…. devil?" Siobhan asked, wincing.

Rosemary nodded. "He did. Because he knew if the priest kept going, he would lose, and Adam would die. Demons don't care if their hosts die. They care about losing power. He was going to hold out, and I knew it. I'm sorry I never got to meet you. You are lovely," she said.

"But how did you know?" Siobhan said.

"I lost the sense of my grandson. His energy and life force was fading. I could feel it. The doctor in the room didn't seem to see it. But I knew. I had lived long enough, Siobhan. Adam was a boy. He deserved to go on," she said in her soothing and monotone voice, looking up once again. She sounded unexcitable and owned the wisdom Siobhan had yet to master.

Siobhan followed Rosemary's gaze. Clouds were rolling in thick and gray, and the colorful forest lost its luster in favor of the dim and dankness of the gunmetal hue slowly closing in.

"Melina couldn't tell you, and not even Father Renaldo knew that I had talked to the demon. It was all in silence. He only knew after, when Melina told him. I'm surprised he believed her. She was a little girl," Rosemary paused. "Our time is almost up," she said, her brown eyes sinking into Siobhan's blue ones.

"Wait! Are you going to help us? Help us help Adam!" she shrieked in a shrill voice full of fear and uncertainty.

Rosemary shook her head. "I'm gone, my dear," she said. She pointed to the necklace. "It will glow and provide heat when I am near. All I can do is warn. I cannot save Adam again. I did it once. You have to save him, Siobhan." She swirled into a translucent cloud, dissipating before Siobhan's eyes.

"No! Wait! I have so much more I need to ask! Rosemary! Please!" she yelled, jogging toward the disappearing older woman.

"Trust yourself. Adam will..." The breeze yanked her voice away as she blew around, ghost-like.

"Rosemary! I want to talk to you!" She ran right through the spot where Adam's grandmother had been standing, causing the ghostly aura to swirl toward the darkening sky in a flurry of silver fog.

SNAP!

She swung her head and whipped around, searching in the

nothingness for what had made that sound.

The low laughter started bubbling from the soil, shaking the earth beneath her feet.

"No," Siobhan whispered, putting her hands up to both of her ears. The laughter remained at the same volume and caused a sharp jolt of pain to shoot deep into her skull. Something else made a sound. Shrieks? Screams? She took her hands off her ears. The laughter continued, and in between the growling grunts of demonic evil, the screams pierced her ears. They were coming from above her head.

Black birds swirled in a small circle above her like they had done right before she set foot in St. Margaret's. They were screeching loudly, competing with the horrific laughter that came straight from hell. The birds circled around her head, and she tried to guess how many there were. Twenty?

They shot into a straight line and headed toward the spot where she had been standing by the rosemary bush when the older woman had appeared. The gray abyss threatened to swallow her, along with the shrill sound of the birds and the sinister chuckle of a demon she couldn't see.

The birds stopped midair as if God himself had hit the pause button on nature's remote. They stopped for a moment and then shot into the Rosemary bush, falling hard, impaling themselves on the twigs of the bush, and screaming in dying agony.

Every single one lay dead, their crimson blood the only color blotting the solid gray landscape.

The next day, Melina taught her yoga class to Siobhan and ten others.

Siobhan tried to focus on Melina while her mind raced. She wanted to know what had happened in her bedroom last night. Whatever took place compelled the doctor with a medical license to declare that Adam needed an exorcism.

The priest and the doctor did not give any details about what they had seen, and Siobhan couldn't read the writing on the sheet of paper the doctor brought down with her. Nonetheless, Dr. Hill agreed with the priest and said she would recommend an exorcism, but she would be there as a medical professional to check the health and well-being of everyone there, especially Adam.

Father Renaldo had said he'd like to review the recording he took to see if he could notice anything that would help him during the rite.

He wanted to bless his book and aspergillum, along with the rosary, candles, and crucifixes he intended to bring with him for the ritual. The priest also said he needed to make prayer preparations. He said he would make an attempt to get the bishop's approval but added that time was of the essence.

This was the fastest infestation that Father Renaldo could find in all texts and written accounts of demonic possession that he had access to. The priest mentioned that this entity knew what it wanted, and its goal was to finish what it had started nineteen years ago.

"And breathe out," Melina said as she pushed to the downward dog pose, snapping Siobhan out of her own head.

Focus, Siobhan. Focus.

She'd told Melina about the dream before they came into the gym. Melina said little about it, but she did seem relieved her grandmother had come through to them. But relief didn't come to Siobhan.

After class, they sat behind the front desk.

"It looks terrific in here," Melina noted. Siobhan nodded.

"It does. Jesus and Helen are doing a great job. I feel terrible putting this on them," she said. The stress had started to well up behind the bridge of her nose and she pinched it to ease some of the pressure. "I hope they will tell me if it gets to be too much."

"I'm sure they will," Melina said in her more melancholic tone. She sipped from a bottle of water. "Want to head over to your place and move some furniture?"

Melina mindlessly screwed the lid back on the water bottle.

Siobhan nodded, biting the inside of her right cheek.

Arriving back at Siobhan's house was like being smacked in the gut with a baseball bat. The air pushed out of their lungs, and they wanted to remain outside in the fresh air. The shadow figure glared at them from the front door. Siobhan looked up to see the haze around her bedroom window had dissipated some, but it clung to the ether. Her necklace got warm.

Melina looked at the necklace. They forced themselves to make their way up the steps and push open the door into the house. The heavy weight of oppression hung over them.

"We should do this quickly," Siobhan said tossing her purse on the floor, not even bothering to hang it up.

"That smell is worse," Melina said, tilting her head upward. "And I'm not sure how that's even possible." A dark gray haze infected every inch of air in the formerly bright house.

A blast of cold flew at Siobhan and Melina. The breeze blew their hair around their faces.

BAM!

Siobhan recognized that sound. A bird flew into the dining room window again. She blew out a long breath. Based on all of the terrifyingly horrific things she'd seen in the past few days, a dead bird struck her as relatively mild in comparison.

BAM! BAM, BAM!

"What is that?" Melina asked.

"The birds," Siobhan said, turning toward the dining room. She flung open the sliding glass door with Melina not far behind. The thickening, stagnant, and pungent air of the house rushed out with them, offering a mild reprieve from the pressure. Siobhan pointed. Four dead black birds were lying in her rosemary bush.

"I forgot what that sounded like," Melina said, shuddering. The same screeching bird screams that had impregnated Siobhan's dream last night interrupted her. Several birds flew in a circle over the same bush where four lay dead.

"They are going to dive into the bush!" Siobhan said as they were struck with another blast of icy cold wind that left them with chattering teeth.

One by one, forming a straight line, the birds plummeted down, diving right into the plant. Some ended up impaled on the thin twigs, leaving stains of blood behind them. Others cracked as they slammed into the earth housing the plant and expired upon impact. The sound of screeching birds and cracking bones worked its way into their ears.

Melina gritted her teeth. Still shaking from the cold, she hugged herself and rubbed her hands up and down her arms to stay warm. "Like your dream?" she asked.

Siobhan nodded. "Yeah. There was less color and more blood in the dream," she said. "I don't want to move them," she added flippantly. "Let's move the furniture like the priest recommended. I'm sick of this. I want this over! I want my life back. I want my husband back! I want the stupid and meaningless plant that I didn't even know had the same name as your grandmother back! I am tired!"

"Okay," Melina said soothingly, guiding Siobhan back inside the house.

Moving the furniture into the spare bedroom was easy. The tricky part was doing it without alerting Adam or the demon.

Siobhan and Melina worked quietly to take the nightstands and lamps out of Siobhan and Adam's room.

Adam remained still, lying on the bed, twisted and contorted. His shape resembled that of a stack of twigs. He had welts and scrapes forming on his face. The blisters from the holy water had broken open and were oozing a clear liquid.

The priest had told them to leave one small table in a far corner. They shut the bathroom and closet doors and pushed Siobhan's nightstand into place as the corner table. After removing all the contents from her nightstand drawer, they removed the dressers and chair as well, piling everything into the two small spare bedrooms.

CHAPTER 23

Without being able to see her, Adam sensed her. He braced his mind, but the demon kept his eyes closed tightly. It strengthened the longer it stayed, as Adam's own strength waned.

He made every effort to listen for Siobhan through the blackness that had mixed with static awareness. Another voice and separate movements alerted him to their presence, and he strained to hear better. She moved stuff around, pushing items over the carpet while methodically checking on him.

The annoyance at being out of control once again struck him, chipping away at his mental state.

A poke brought Adam's awareness to his neck as a tingle ran up his left arm. He tried to sense the demon lurking deep within him as he had sensed Siobhan. If it stirred, he could try to warn Siobhan.

The icy cold bit him. The sensation strange, considering something else had control over his body. The demon used heat as his weapon of choice to burn Adam, leaving him cowering like a dog.

The demon harmed him, repeatedly striking him and burning him. It took pleasure in creating agonizing pain for Adam, both mentally and physically. He had gotten punched in the face from the inside, but the bruises had welled up on his physical body.

Scrapes and welts appeared as the demon used its rough, forked tongue to scratch his face and lash him. The welts swelled and filled with fluids before cracking and bleeding.

Humiliated and disgusted that his body defecated and urinated all over the bed, Adam fought for his sanity, unsure of what Siobhan thought of him. Maybe she would leave him because he's a disgusting pig, slobbering and bleeding, out of control, and lying around broken and shattered.

He seethed at the demon with a fiery hatred that bubbled from deep inside his core. The negative energy Adam thrust out strengthened it and bit back at him.

The cold air pressed against his face and suffocated him. He couldn't see, but he used the icy air as a soothing balm for the increasing inflammation in his body.

Adam pricked his ears to hear Siobhan leave the bedroom, her footsteps no longer close. He assumed she had come with his sister, Melina. They were talking in the spare bedroom across the hall.

The muffled voices got crystal clear and the demon wanted to hear. Adam sunk deeper into the recesses behind his eyes again, forcing his will to go near an ear to listen better.

"It's crazy to see my breath inside in July!" Siobhan said.

"I remember some pretty cold days and nights from before. Demons and negative entities like to use heat to energize themselves, remember? So, when it's cold, they are...." Melina's voice trailed off nervously.

"Gassing up the tank, so to speak?" Siobhan asked with a surprisingly calm voice. Some of the fear had dissipated into resolve. Through the demon's ears, Siobhan sounded stronger.

The entity stabbed Adam's ears with an ice pick. The demon roused.

"It's glowing," Melina said.

"And warm. Let's go," Siobhan added. Before she finished talking, Adam heard their footsteps as they rushed down the stairs and the slam of the front door.

A low growl started deep within Adam's diaphragm and came out of his throat. His mouth didn't move, and his eyes stayed closed. The cold air forced the temperature to well below zero degrees in the room. He had experienced that kind of cold once when he took a trip with friends to northern Canada. He had vowed never to go there again after experiencing such a deep cold. He tried to figure out how to process his cold nerve endings while staying unavailable to the demon. The sting of ice burned his skin in its coldness.

"Wormmm," the low growling sound ground along Adam's frayed nerves. "He is coming," it said as the words meshed into the sinister chuckle Adam knew all too well by now. "Listen, worm," it commanded as the clicking sound started up again. Adam's ears picked up a conversation taking place outside.

"God, the clicking is making me crazy," Melina said. "I'll go get us lunch."

"I'll meet you back at the gym. I feel like I need to be there for a few more hours and do *some* work," Siobhan replied.

"Be careful. Adam needs you," Melina said. "Stay hydrated and keep your energy up."

"Did you hear that, worm," the demon asked in its chuckled voice. "Answer me..." it taunted. "I know you can hear me, shit-eating wormmm." The demon dragged out its words, using its own diabolical voice.

"Burn in hell," Adam spat as best as he could, using the energy he had before retreating. It dialed up the pain. His head ached like he'd been struck across the back of the skull with a board. Pain danced behind his eyes.

Three long claws dragged down the center of his chest, leaving a crimson trail behind them. Adam kept his eyes closed as the searing pain of heat blazed through the icy atmosphere. The three long gashes welled up and spilled black blood. Adam tried to scream in agony, but he had no voice.

He momentarily caught a whiff of the indescribable stench that poor Siobhan had smelled. His senses were on fire and numb. His brain racked with confusion, yet somehow he understood everything as he existed in the peculiar paradigm.

He couldn't see the long claws that had left the scratches that ran from his sternum to his navel, but he knew, somehow, exactly what those claw marks looked like, and then he got an idea.

In his agony, he understood. But he'd need to wait until the priest weakened the demon for him to try it. The demon had strengthened too much for him to do this on his own. But if this idea worked, he could be free.

The pain from the scratches on his chest blurred with the stinging of the mark on his arm. He fortified his consciousness so he could try to fight and braced himself against the gruesome agony.

Back at The Flex, Siobhan busied herself with menial tasks that she had started to miss since evil had infiltrated her life. She washed a load of towels and had started to fold them when Jesus came around the corner.

"Hola, boss," Jesus said with his crooked smile. Siobhan shook her head and sighed.

"Are you guys ever going to stop calling me that?" she asked. She tried to smile but couldn't manage one.

Jesus kept his crooked grin pasted on, though. "Helen told me your husband is sick. He is Adam, right?" Jesus asked, crossing his arms over his chest. After a few moments of watching Siobhan folding the towels, he threw his hands up, saying, "Here, let me. You sit." He pointed to the chair.

Siobhan dropped the towel on the counter and flopped in the chair by the computer. She shook her head. "I don't know how bad it is, Jesus. He's been so sick since the injury, and I don't know what to do," she said, exasperated. She found herself able to manipulate the details enough, so she'd sound sane to Jesus.

"Love him," Jesus said as he snapped a towel and then folded it in half. "My mother, God bless her soul." He made the sign of the cross with his right hand. "She always said we don't know why God put us on the path we are on. We have to trust there's a reason."

"Well, I don't like it," Siobhan said. "My mother always said you make your own destiny."

Jesus smiled once again crookedly. "We all have our own different mothers. I see yours liked crystals, too.," He nodded toward the tiger's eye necklace.

Siobhan lifted the crystal off her chest. "This? Oh, no. This wasn't from my mother. It was from…a guest. A wedding guest. Someone left it for me," she said.

"Oh, I see," Jesus replied, looking back at the towels he had folded perfectly into tight little. "My mother loved them. She had so many. Rocks too. She said they held the energy of the dead and the living."

Siobhan dropped the crystal back against her chest.

"She said they align energies and that once a person dies if they choose, they can put their spirit into a crystal of their choice so their loved ones can keep them close at all times, warn them of danger, or help them sleep," he said.

"I think they can too. Where did you grow up, Jesus?"

"Guadalajara, México," Jesus said, a wave of nostalgia crossing his face.

"Well, I'm glad you're here. You're good for the gym and for Helen," Siobhan said.

"I'm not much. I'm a poor man of God who lost my mother a long time ago," he said. "Helen is better than I will ever be."

"I'm sorry about your mother," Siobhan said, rolling the tiger's eye through her fingers.

"It's okay, boss. It was a long time ago. She said she put herself into a crystal so she could always be with me. I still have it. She was very interested in warding off evil too, so she had some… how do you say it… superstitions?" he asked, looking up. Siobhan managed to smile this time.

Melina entered the front door with three takeout bags. She set them down on the counter. "I assumed Jesus and Helen would want food, so I got something for everyone. I don't know what anyone likes, so I'm sorry if it's not quite right," she said, opening the bag.

"Thank you. I am very hungry today," Jesus said.

"Where's Helen?" Melina asked.

"Teaching," Siobhan said. "She'll be done in the next ten or fifteen minutes."

"Should we wait for her?"

"Nah. Let's eat. She'll be happy to have something when she's done," Siobhan said.

Siobhan pondered what Jesus had told her while they enjoyed a nice lunch. Is it possible that energy or life force in crystals is common? How many people housed their spirits in crystals to be with children, warn of evil, or help them sleep?

Later that day, when Siobhan picked up towels in the women's locker room, she tried to forget Adam's condition. She mentally fought her own inner demon, the one that kept telling her she needed Adam to tell her what to do. She had to focus on these chores so she could keep up before Adam's exorcism.

Her mind filled itself with unanswered questions. Had the priest gotten permission from the bishop yet? Would an exorcism even work? What would happen? What were all the possibilities?

She bent over to pick up another towel, and a blast of cold hair blew into her from behind. She faced away from the inner wall of the lockers. She squatted down and twisted to see who had flung open the door. She peeked around the pale yellow lockers lining the wall that jutted out in the center but didn't see anyone. The mirrors on the other side could not have caused a wind.

She stood, leaving the towels on the floor. The hair on her body stood at attention, and the energy moved around her in the locker room. She listened hard, trying to hear something, anything. Her necklace warmed.

Click click click

Click click click

As the last click radiated on her skin, she heard her name in a quiet voice, which she almost didn't hear as it mingled with the clicking. She strained to listen again, trying to shut out everything to make sense of the lingering sounds around her.

"Siobhan," it said. The low growling voice she'd heard before in her dream and around Adam snarled. She shivered as her hands got clammy. She clenched her teeth, spun around, and ran out of the locker room straight to the front counter where Helen sat reading a fitness magazine. She fell forward, out of breath, onto the counter. The sticky cobwebs latched onto her and pulled her forward. She jerked back, flinging herself into the front door, and banged against it with a thud as she screamed and rubbed her arms.

"Siobhan!" Helen yelled. "What in the hell are you doing?" she asked, rushing toward her friend. Siobhan's eyes were wide, and a bead of sweat rolled down her left temple. Her lips were blue, and her necklace glowed.

"Hey! Calm down! What's the matter?" Helen asked in a concerned tone. Siobhan leaned back against the door and slid down slowly to land on her bottom with exasperation and panic. She shook.

She took a few more breaths. "It's okay. Hey, it's okay," Helen said, kneeling down next to Siobhan.

Siobhan shook her head and squeezed her eyes shut. "I heard...I don't know...maybe I'm on edge, then the counter, it's...." Her phone rang in her purse behind the counter.

"Want me to get it for you?" Helen asked, jerking her thumb toward the front desk.

Siobhan shook her head. "No. I can do it. I'm fine," she said clenching her fists. "I'm stressed.". Her words were jumbled and made little sense, and she knew it.

Siobhan lifted herself off the floor by herself, not using Helen's offered outstretched arms.

"You sure you're fine?" Helen asked.

"Fine," Siobhan said, taking the ringing phone out of her purse. "I have to take this. It's Adam... I..."

"It's fine. I will cover the counter," Helen said, watching Siobhan with a side-eye. She returned to her chair, visibly shaken by her friend's sudden loss of composure.

Siobhan answered her phone and opened the front door to talk outside.

"Siobhan, hello," Father Renaldo said into her phone. A faint amount of static stung her ear, the shoddy reception hissing.

She welcomed the sun's burn on her skin after experiencing the icy wind in her own house.

"Hello, Father," she said. "Did Dr. Hill find anything else in her research yet? Did you get... permission? Did..." Siobhan rattled off her questions in nervous haste.

"Slow down. Take a deep breath. I'm calling to tell you that Dr. Hill is continuing her research, but so far, she still agrees that Adam needs an exorcism," Father Renaldo said. "I have submitted Adam's video to the bishop. He said he has an assistant priest who will watch it and let me know later tonight or tomorrow. I don't have many answers for you yet. We don't have much time either. But if the bishop says no..." Father Renaldo trailed off.

"What? What if he says no?" Siobhan shrieked into the phone.

The priest remained calm. "If he says no, I will do the exorcism anyway. I owe it to Rosemary and Adam to expel this vile creature and send him back to hell for good."

Siobhan remained silent.

"I will call you tonight or tomorrow morning with an update. Stay safe. If you need to go back to see Adam, you can do so. But please leave if Rosemary warns you. Once you're done, leave and don't go back to your house unless I tell you to," he said. "This may be your one opportunity to see Adam before the exorcism. If he can see you, and he knows you will be there, he will be more likely to fight the demon with us."

Siobhan nodded but still said nothing.

"Thank you for taking that furniture out," he said, breaking the silence.

Siobhan nodded again before realizing that the priest couldn't hear her head move. "Be safe, Father. I'll talk to you soon," she said, itching to end the conversation. She had learned no new information that could help her digest where they were at right now.

Siobhan cried for most of the drive home. She let the salty streaks flow freely down her face. The wind whipped her hair around, and she left it wild, not bothering to tame it after she pulled into her driveway.

The familiar shadow figure with glowing red eyes stared at her from the front window. She glanced up to see the gray haze still around her bedroom window. It swirled but less thickly than she remembered.

She opened the front door and glanced over where the

shadow had been consistently looming. The cold seeped into her skin and she sensed an invisible presence. The force all around her held the evidence of its existence, but her senses were unable to confirm anything.

She plodded up the stairs and apprehensively cracked the door to her bedroom. Adam slept. She sat on the edge of the bed and looked at him.

His lips were split in several places from being so dehydrated, and he had more bruises on his face. The blisters left by the holy water had festered into open sores. He had long, thin welts that had split open all over his body. The long gashes on his chest had seeped blood, staining his shirt. The familiar black-colored blood had welled up along several of the wounds.

She choked back a sob, looking at him. But at that moment, she started to see him differently. He'd always had faith in her. She needed to have faith in herself.

She reached over and grabbed his bruised hand. She winced at the heat but held it tightly.

He knew she was there; he could feel her. She touched his hand. Adam could also feel the demon, its presence still gripping a tight hold of his spinal cord and twisting its claws into his chest cavity. He stirred.

Pushing himself to the surface, and despite the pain, he forced himself to open his eyes. He could see her. She stared at the wound, the demon's mark. There would be a torturous price to pay for talking to her, but he did it anyway. His skin burned, and his vision blurred with the warped crimson stain of the demon's perspective as it pooled around her.

"Siobhan," he whispered through chapped lips. One of the cracks split, and blood dripped down his chin. She jumped back, releasing his hand. She looked at him, hands up, ready to flee. She had tears streaking her face, and her bottom lip quivered. "It's me," he croaked out.

It sounded like he hadn't spoken in years. Siobhan stood frozen, unmoved, and looked into Adam's eyes as he pushed himself to a pained sitting position on the bed. The misery in which he existed stretched across his face. He managed a crooked smile.

"Adam," she said, letting the tears flow freely down her face. "I miss you. I need you to come back," she choked out.

Siobhan glanced at his disgusting t-shirt and inhaled a sharp sob. The shirt, covered in blood, sweat, vomit, saliva, and pus, had been shredded and it held onto his body in the places where it imbedded itself in a wound.

"I'm in here. But it is painful. I need you. You need to be strong. Don't..." he grimaced. His left arm had turned up, exposing the blackened flesh inside. The grotesque mark gave off heat and diffused its soreness, looking redder than it had been.

Siobhan took a step forward as tears pelted her shirt. "Don't what, Adam?"

"Don't give up. I love you. I will fight as long as I can," he said, rolling to his side. He groaned. "Uhh." He grimaced and let out an agonized grunt of pain.

"I'm sorry, Adam. I'm here. I love you," she said, trying to be strong through the uncertainty welling up inside.

"Thank you," he said. "We can do this. Together," he added, looking into her eyes with his.

She leaned forward and gave him a gingerly hug, trying not to inflict additional pain. He wanted to hug her back but couldn't lift his right arm high enough, so he placed it on her lower back.

"I'm not...I didn't shit the bed," he said. Siobhan smiled through her blurry vision.

"I know," she said, pushing away softly to look at him. "Fight hard, Adam."

"I...yeah," he grimaced again. "You better go. It's coming," he said, gritting his teeth.

Her crystal necklace started to emit a mild glow.

"I'll be strong," she said, backing toward the door.

"Go," he croaked out. He needed her to get out of the house soon.

She gave Adam one last glance over her shoulder as he jerked against the mattress and his arm wrenched over his head. A tendon popped loudly in his arm as it twisted itself sadistically behind his body.

CHAPTER 25

Adam's body flopped hard to the bed as he groaned and then cried out in pain. His left hip crunched at an unnatural angle and then snapped itself out of place. The door closed behind Siobhan with a light thud and he listened to her footsteps take the stairs two at a time.

The solitary laugh, along with loud clicking, reverberated deep within his chest.

"Do you think she'll help you, wormmm?" the demon taunted. This time the voice came from nowhere. It surrounded Adam and, at the same time, came from him and at him in waves. The laughter struck the walls and created a sinister echo.

Adam's body burned in agonizing pain. He resolved in his determination to fight and outlast this malevolent force no matter how hard it got.

The claw marks on his chest inflamed and began to press outward in searing, hot bands of sharp pain. More blood welled under the surface of his skin as they strained on the edge of bursting.

"Fuck you, asshole," Adam said through gritted teeth, expecting more pain as punishment. But if he thought he had any idea of how bad the pain could get, he soon found out he'd had no idea at all.

Siobhan let Melina drive her to the church the following day. Melina didn't have to teach her yoga class, and Helen and Jesus could run her gym better than she could right now.

Melina tapped her hands on the steering wheel to cover the uncomfortable silence. Siobhan processed Adam's deterioration and inhaled sharply at the image of him in agony yesterday.

Siobhan had merely picked at the dinner Melina had made last night and had no desire to talk about what happened at her house when she had gone to see Adam. Melina had offered to go, but Siobhan respectfully insisted she needed to go alone.

St. Margaret's looked far more foreboding today than it had the last time Siobhan had seen the church. The stained glass looked darker, and the large wooden doors were not inviting. Siobhan looked at it through different eyes this time.

"If Adam gets through this…" Siobhan began, breaking the silence. "When—when Adam gets through this," she corrected herself. A deep breath did little to steady her nerves, but it helped seal her resolve. Melina kept her eyes forward as she pulled her Ford Explorer into a parking spot in the back row. She put the car in park and hovered her hand over the key.

"I'm going to make sure I help other people," Siobhan said, slicing the silence. "Like you. I want to help you do the…secular exorcism."

Melina shut the car off, killing the air conditioner with the engine. Siobhan stepped out of the car and slammed the door shut. "Melina?" she asked.

"Yeah?" They started their walk toward the large church's doors.

"What do you think?" Siobhan asked, looking at the stained-glass window above the doors.

"Yes," Melina said. "Let's help others. Demonology," she said, looking at Siobhan. Her head lifted slightly, and she looked more mentally stable.

Siobhan had gained a lot of strength from her decision to fight evil. Even without a plan, she had a will. Still agnostic, not believing in religion or churches, Siobhan would find a way. Melina's words "secular exorcist" rang in her mind as they started their silent walk to Father Renaldo's office.

Melina opened the front door of the church, and they entered, ready, but nervous about their exorcism lesson.

Father Renaldo sat at his desk and looked up when Melina tapped twice with her knuckle on the frame of his open door. He had a pair of glasses perched on his nose and wrote in his notebook. The black book with the gold cross on it sat unopened on his desk. He peeped over his glasses and motioned with his hands, saying, "Please, sit down."

Siobhan and Melina sat as they had before, in the same

chairs. The memory of the bleeding crucifix came rushing back to Siobhan. Her heart raced as she once again saw the black blood pooling on the floor by the altar and snaking around the church. She shivered, remembering how the tiny punctures on the Christ figure had dripped blood from where the crown of thorns had stabbed him.

"I'm glad you're both here," Father Renaldo said. "Rough day?" he asked, looking at Siobhan. She dropped her head to look at her hands in her lap. She absent-mindedly picked at a fingernail. Her mind reeled from her conversation with Adam yesterday.

"He talked to me," she said, not looking up.

"He? The demon?" Father Renaldo asked.

Siobhan shook her head. "Adam. He's fighting inside himself. He's in bad shape."

Father Renaldo nodded. "I know."

Siobhan snapped her eyes to the priest's. "He's hurting. He's emotionally unwell. His body is bloody and bruised!" She got more agitated and louder as she continued. "On top of that, I want you to help him and all we're doing is sitting around talking about some stupid rules for a ritual that might not even work permanently. *And* this is the *second time* he's been through this!"

"Siobhan," the priest said calmly, laying his glasses down on the book. "I know it's hard. But we have to do this the right way, or there will be a third time. I'm already beating myself up over not laying the rules down before. Had I made Rosemary agree…" He shook his head, clearing the thought. "I need to ensure this exorcism goes better. We need to work together. Anger, frustration, hatred, all these negative emotions feed the entity. We need to be on the same page. But your frustration is natural. And to be frank, I'm glad to see it finally. You've finally gotten a dose of real emotion to replace the fear."

A knock on the door frame broke the tension in the office. Siobhan kept looking down. She knew she needed to focus on Adam first, or she'd never be able to help anyone else.

"Am I late?" Dr. Hill asked as she entered the room. Her glasses were perfectly aligned on her face.

"No," the priest said. "Have a seat. Let's get started. First things first," he continued as Dr. Hill sat to Siobhan's right. "I need to make sure you all know that there isn't likely to be bishop approval for this exorcism, like the first time."

Siobhan kept picking at her fingernail, her gaze trained on her hands. She sat in silence as she pursed her lips in frustration.

The priest sighed heavily. "The assistant, a priest who looked at the video, recommended exorcism, but the bishop wants more evidence. I won't make any of you sign nondisclosure agreements because we all have the same goal, but I do need you to be discreet. That means we cannot mention the exorcism to anyone outside of this room. That also means that you all need to agree to follow my rules. I didn't lay these down the first time. Because of that, Rosemary is no longer with us, and I'm not going to let anything happen to any of you."

Father Renaldo paused for a moment.

"We are all here to save Adam from demonic possession. To do that, I need you all to let me have control of the exorcism."

Melina and Dr. Hill both nodded at the same time.

Siobhan sighed heavily and sat back abruptly, snapping her head up to look at Father Renaldo.

"I can do that, Father," she said resolutely, her blue eyes filled with a courage she'd never experienced before. The determination set in firmly, and she resolved to become a person who could stand and face evil.

The priest nodded once at Siobhan. "Okay, then. This is the first rule, and you all need to abide by this…" He leaned forward on his desk. "You cannot engage with Adam at all during the exorcism. You can restrain him," he said, looking at Melina and Siobhan. "And Dr. Hill, you can examine him when you need to. Under no circumstances am I to be interrupted while conducting the rite, nor are any of you to speak to the demon. During an exorcism, demons try to confuse. It will make you think you are talking to Adam. It is not Adam, and I cannot stress that enough. It will say horrible things, and it will try to deceive you. It will also bring up your biggest failures, fears, and sins. You have to be strong. You have to ignore it."

They were listening intently. "You may warn me if there is a danger," he added.

Dr. Hill crossed her legs and lifted her hand. "Father? I'm sorry, but I've never seen a… you know… exorcism before. I've only done the one other examination," she swallowed hard. "What can I bring to ensure the safety of everyone there? During this… ritual, that's what I'm doing, correct? I apologize for my ignorance," she said.

"No apology needed, Dr. Hill," Father Renaldo said, shaking his head and waving her off with his hand. "I appreciate the question and the seriousness with which you are handling things."

"Please, let's drop the formalities. We're fighting a demon. You all can call me Amanda," she said with a small smile.

Father Renaldo nodded.

"Okay then, Amanda," he said with a quick nod. "The same things you brought to examine him will be helpful during an exorcism. You may want to bring a simple first aid kit in a soft and small bag. Wear rubber gloves and a face mask even if you wish. There's likely to be blood, vomit, saliva, excrement, urine, pus, or any combination of those, especially when the demon is fighting to stay in.

"Melina," the priest said, turning toward her. "You need to

bring your book. I need you to find the demon's name if it gives us any clue as to who it could be. If it so much as mentions anything about itself, I need you to narrow it down and figure it out.

"Siobhan," he continued, looking at the blond woman. "I need you to hold a crucifix. The demon is likely to go after you the most intently because you are the closest to Adam. I need you not to question me if I ask you to touch him with it. It might hurt him. He may scream. I need you to understand that this is going to be the most difficult task. It will seem like you're inflicting pain on your husband, but you have to do it. Can you?" he asked, raising his bushy silver eyebrows and sitting back.

Siobhan nodded. "Other than that, you might be asked to try to keep Adam from further damaging himself or us. You may get injured, but that's why we'll have Amanda there," the priest said.

He sat back in his chair and took a deep breath. "This next rule is very important. Let me send it to hell. Do not make any deals with any entity that speaks to you in your mind. It might try. It will take a sacrifice, and if you do make a deal with the devil as Rosemary did, you are all but ensuring this thing comes back again. We cannot risk it. You must ignore it. It will try to tell you it's going to kill Adam. That's probably what it did to Rosemary. It tricked her. It was losing the battle, but because she engaged with it out of love for her grandson, we lost her."

Sadness painted the room. "You all have to be mentally strong in order for us to win this battle."

The priest continued speaking and laid down a few more straightforward ground rules, such as not eating in the two hours leading up to the exorcism. Demons can induce vomiting, and the less there is in a stomach, the lower the chance that someone not possessed will void the contents.

Father Renaldo also discussed the rite of exorcism and explained what would occur during the ritual. He would read from a book While Dr. Hill was to sit in a corner, ready to assist with a medical-related issue or concern.

"We will wait another twenty-four hours for the bishop to approve or deny the exorcism. If he approves it, we will begin Friday night at 9 p.m. If he denies it, we will begin Friday night at 9 p.m. If I do not hear from him, we will begin Friday night at 9 p.m. I have already decided this is what's best for Adam, and Amanda agrees," Father Renaldo continued. "So do I," Siobhan said.

Father Renaldo nodded. "The bishop's priest has also recommended an exorcism. I have informed him I will be doing it Friday night regardless. He has vowed to be discreet."

The priest wiped the sweat forming on his brow with the sleeve of his shirt. "I will be spending the next day going through my notes and rewatching Adam's video so I can get an idea of where I made mistakes before. I intend not to make the same mistakes twice. Let's send this demon back where it belongs."

"Thank you," Siobhan said nervously but with a strength that came from deep within.

Melina reached over and placed her hand on Siobhan's forearm. "We will do this together. And once it's done, we'll help others, sister," she said. Siobhan smiled at her, and they hugged each other.

"All right. So, to hell with this vile creature. Let's all get ready. There's a spiritual battle around the corner, and we should prepare," he said.

Father Renaldo blessed each of the women and anointed them with holy water before they left his office.

Once outside, the bright light slapped their eyes, and Dr. Hill's expensive glasses darkened automatically.

"I know this isn't normal circumstances," Amanda said. "But I am glad I met you two. You will both do a lot of good in this world. God bless you, and I'll see you in a few days." She pushed her glasses up her nose and took off toward her car, the black luxury sedan in the front row, leaving Melina and Siobhan in the bright parking lot.

"I'm sorry I am so…" Siobhan started.

"It's okay. I'm not married, so I don't know what it's like," Melina said, looking down at her feet.

"I know what I have to do," she said. "But I may end up in a mental institution first."

"Not if I have anything to say about it," Melina said in a crestfallen tone, tugging the door of her car open.

CHAPTER 26

"They are planning it, you disgusting worm," the demon mocked, using Adam's voice.

"Eat shit," Adam replied through the red-hot lava the demon poured into his eye sockets from inside.

"My, my. Such a potty mouth today," it said, making the clicking sound. "You could be a more hospitable host, you know," it snarled as the words melded with the growl.

Adam couldn't respond. He wanted to, but a molten metal had been poured from his eye sockets down his throat, choking his words off at the source.

"Can't talk?" the demon said cruelly. Then, it slung its snake-like three-foot-long tongue out of Adam's mouth to lick the wall behind the bed's headboard. The whipping tongue missed him this time, and he didn't add another lash to his welting body. "Count it down. Our victory awaits."

"My... victory," Adam said with difficulty. The demon responded with roaring laughter that shook the entire bed, jerking Adam around like a puppet being commanded.

"NEVERRRRRR!" the demon roared, shaking the house and the entire town with an earthquake.

*

"Oh. You have one, too," Helen said, admiring Jesus's bloodstone.

They were in his small, clean, and homely apartment. Helen had been looking around at all of the things he had on his shelves, comparing his aesthetic to an authentic Mexican adobe. The large bloodstone which sat on a flat bottom had caught her eye. The oblong stone held its beauty tightly and it reminded her of the crystal Siobhan had been wearing around her neck lately. Somehow, it suited Jesus, but she couldn't put her finger on why.

Jesus followed Helen's gaze.

"My mother gave it to me," he said. "Before she died."

He reached up on the shelf in his small living room apartment and took it down.

After rolling it around in his hands for a moment, he handed it to Helen. She eagerly grabbed a hold of it. The heavy and cool stone's smooth surface somehow had a mild vibration of warmth to it.

"She said she's in there, and she'll always be with me," Jesus said in a sad but soothing tone. "I hope she's up there, though," he said, looking upward as he pointed one finger to the ceiling.

"She's both, I'm sure," Helen said. Jesus looked into her blazing green eyes and knew he had fallen for the spunky little redhead. He pulled her in for a hug as she cradled the bloodstone to her chest like it was a kitten. "Thank you for showing me this," she said, looking at him.

She couldn't help but be drawn to his deeply empathetic and kind heart. But Jesus stood tall, dark, handsome, and kept himself in excellent shape, making him easy to be attracted to. Helen's heart raced as the magnetic and unavoidable pull she felt toward him had her leaning tighter against him.

Jesus leaned over and kissed Helen, long and deep. She tightened her grip on the bloodstone to keep from dropping it. His hand slid to the back of her neck as he deepened the kiss.

The entire apartment started shaking.

The tiger's eye crystal got warm right before the earthquake rattled Melina's house. It knocked three books off Melina's shelves.

"I think that was it," Melina said after the shaking subsided. "It's trying to scare us about the exorcism," she added.

"Maybe. If so, I'm glad that's all that thing's got. This," she said, lifting the necklace, "got warm. She knew."

Melina nodded. "We need to be ready. I'll study the book and try to narrow down which evil demon could be possessing Adam. If that earthquake was any indication, the priest is experiencing something crazy right now."

"It's going to work. He's going to be okay, isn't he?" Siobhan asked, looking at her hands.

"He will be. Then we can help others," she said, reaching out to touch Siobhan's hands.

"Thanks, Melina. I hope this creature rots in hell forever for what it's done to Adam."

Dr. Hill grabbed the sides of her desk as it started shaking. The expansive room that doubled as her and her husband's home office shook enough to hear the rattling. The large brand-new house had never known the warmth of children or pets. She hadn't gotten around to putting her career on hold to have a child or a dog.

Her large bookshelf, which held her textbooks, scientific journals, and a few small houseplants, had vibrated. Nothing fell off and the shaking died down. She paused for a moment, then pushed her glasses up her nose and got back to work, taking notes from the *Psychology of Demonic Possession* book she'd been studying.

"Amanda!" her husband called from the living room. "Did you feel that?"

"Yes. But I think it's done," she said, not completely understanding how it had happened. She sensed the air move around her and her mind tingled with the idea that the shaking had been a message from hell and not a mere coincidence or natural occurrence.

"Weird to get an earthquake here, isn't it?" he yelled back, his voice nearing. Amanda looked over at her doctoral plaque on the wall, hanging next to her husband's.

"Yep! Sure is!" she yelled back as the slender man appeared in the doorway. "I'll probably have a few injuries today from it," he said as he crossed his arms over his chest. He leaned against the doorway and crossed one foot over the other. "Working on something important?" he asked..

Amanda nodded. "It's an interesting case. House visits," she said, intentionally avoiding the word exorcism.

"Well, good luck," he said, crossing the room and sitting across from her, his spindly frame wrapping around the chair. "Need help?"

"No, but thanks," she said.

"Spoken like the best psychiatrist around," he said, smiling.

Father Renaldo paused the video of Adam's exorcism. The shaking broke his concentration, and he looked around his room.

The amethyst geode one of the altar boys had given him as a gift rattled against the bookshelf and then fell to the floor with a thud.

White noise showed on the TV for a moment, then returned to the paused screen as the priest looked back. Adam sat in a chair with his hands tied behind his back; each leg lashed to the leg of the same chair. His younger face contorted to the side as a long purple tongue snuck out and curled around his chin. His eyes were wide. The priest leaned forward, trying to get a better look at the older video recorded on a VHS tape nineteen years ago. He set the remote down and leaned in some more.

He remembered this like it happened yesterday, but the hairs on his arms prickled. He'd seen this video dozens of times, so he knew it had changed.

Adam's body jerked on the screen while the pause lines continued to run across it. The priest knew the remote wouldn't change what blasted across the screen. The nameless demon sent him a message. Hell itself taunted him.

Adam smiled in the video and twisted his head downward, close to completely upside down. He showed his stained teeth, then said: "I'm coming for you, priessssst." The low, growling voice diabolically mocked him. A slow sting of ice-cold air traveled up the back of Father Renaldo's legs and into his spine, mingling with his clammy skin. Goosebumps covered the priest's arms.

"It's warrrrrr," the demon roared as Adam's head twisted further down into an unnatural angle. "I will rip you from limb to limb!" It growled loudly as it sped up the cadence of its speech. "And will suck the flesh off your bones and toss them to the slaves of HELLLLL!" The hissing voice ran into a clicking sound of the demon's audible mark. The rumbling laughter sounded wet against a rough throat but overly dry at the same time. It started to surround the priest, tightening around him like a snake.

Everything stopped. The TV returned to the place where the priest had paused it.

"Prepare for war, demon," Father Renaldo said right before snatching the remote off the table and pressing play.

"Did you like that, worm?" the demon asked Adam of the earthquake. "Do you see how powerful I am? Not even God can save you," it continued as it tried to provoke its host's spirit into a response.

It laughed mockingly.

"Are we not in the mood to talk today, worm?" it said in response to Adam's silence.

"Fuck off," Adam said weakly. He had gotten better at retreating from agony, but violent strikes still came when he got defiant with the demon. The deep gash in his left arm throbbed where the demon had left its mark. Acid had poured itself in rivulets all over Adam's arm. The upside-down cross burned as it sizzled in a bright amber hue, but the darkness of the house snuffed out any color that tried to arise.

The raucous laughter filled the entire house, and Adam's

ear began to bleed. The demon tried to pop his eyeballs by grabbing them from inside his head and squeezing. The more he fought, the more confident he became that he would lose an eye. His mental fortitude diminished, and his energy waned. The evil being wore him down to the point that his essence took a whipping, along with his body.

"I command YOU, worm. And I will show you how to make humans squeal like the swine they are…" It trailed off into a growl before setting Adam's body down on the floor in the corner of the bedroom. "We should keep up our strength," it said in a quick cadence. Using Adam's hand, it fed itself a spider that had clung to its web in the corner.

The bug wiggled in Adam's mouth as the demon used its tongue to crush it into his gums, spreading the black legs all over his yellowed teeth.

The clicking sound started again, and it fused with the low-volume laughter of the demon as Adam rolled around, back and forth on the floor, with his mouth smiling much too wide. His torso cocked away from his lower half, and he contorted into a synthetic twisting, broken shape as he fought the pain flowing through his veins like razor blades.

"They can't stop me this time, and neither can you," it taunted Adam. "You let me in. You can't back out now," it said as its words descended into a deep, animalistic growl.

Adam stayed quiet. It had him eating bugs, and his bones were out of place. He hoped he could survive this.

CHAPTER 27

"I'm sorry, Siobhan," Father Renaldo said into the phone. She let out a deep sigh. "But you know we're proceeding anyway. Even if they dismiss me from the priesthood. I know this is the plan God has for me."

Siobhan put her hand over the mouthpiece so she could shout at Melina, who fed Scamper in the kitchen. Siobhan heard his meow as she said loudly, "The bishop denied the request, citing a lack of evidence."

"Shit," Melina muttered as Siobhan took her hand back off the phone.

"Okay. So, nine o'clock tomorrow, then?" Siobhan asked.

"Nine o'clock tomorrow. Be ready. Vile taunts are coming from the dirtiest and most evil thing imaginable. You'll have to be strong. I'll see you," the priest said.

"Be safe, Father. And thank you," Siobhan said as she hung up the phone.

Melina came back into the living room holding Scamper. The cat licked his jowls, trying to get all the food remnants out of his whiskers.

"So, nine then?" Melina said.

Siobhan nodded. "I wish we could do it sooner," Siobhan said.

"This will give us more time to study. Amanda needs to make sure she's ready for any possible psychological and physical damage after the demon leaves. I need to learn everything I can, and I need to know where to find information quickly if the demon slips up. Father Renaldo needs to look for clues from Adam's first possession. It is for the best. We have thirty-two hours or so to go," she said.

Siobhan rubbed her eyes. "I wish I was more help. Let me hold the cat. He's such a cutie," she said, reaching out her arms. Melina set Scamper in Siobhan's arms, and she embraced him and hugged him while the cat rubbed his head on her chin. She petted his back and looked up at Melina with tears in her eyes.

"It's going to be okay," she said for the thousandth time, but for the first time, understanding.

Melina nodded. "Yeah," she said.

Siobhan called Helen and made sure she and Jesus had everything under control at The Flex. Helen assured her friend they were doing everything they could to help and stay on top of things. Helen even relayed that nothing had been damaged in the earthquake, and Jesus had put things back in place that had bounced around.

"I need to run payroll," Siobhan said to Melina. "I want to grab my laptop from home, but I'm not sure I should go back there before the exorcism."

"No, the priest said not to. I'll go with you to the gym if you want. I can study there," Melina said.

Siobhan sighed. "No. I'll go," she said. "Text me if you need anything. I'll text if I hear from Father Renaldo or Dr. Hill," Siobhan added. "Bye, Scamper," she said, scratching the tuxedo cat's head as he rubbed around her ankles, purring.

When Siobhan arrived at The Flex, the hectic environment distracted her from the evil lurking inside her husband. People moved around banging equipment, and the smell of sweat hung in the air.

This gym belonged in her past life—an everyday, mundane life—a life before the tiger's eye necklace and ensuing evil conquered every cell in her body.

The horrific images stuck in her head had sealed her determination to come out on top and figure out a way to help others fight the demonic.

After scanning her key card, she flung open the door and sauntered into the gym like she owned the place for the first time. Helen sat behind the desk. She closed the fitness magazine she read when Siobhan entered.

"Hey, boss!" Helen said, standing. "Wow, you look great. Did you get a haircut?" she asked.

"No. But Adam's... How are things here?" Siobhan asked, setting her purse down under the counter. She blew out a breath and steadied her nerves.

"Great! The counter is still all staticky, but everything else seems fine," Helen said in her bubbly voice, radiating feisty energy.

"Thanks, Helen," Siobhan said, running her hands through her hair. "I need to process payroll, then head back out and…" She paused and swallowed. "Check on Adam. I need to make sure you and Jesus are paid for helping me this week."

The mindless accounting and tedious paperwork took Siobhan's focus off her husband's condition. How close was she to getting back to her normal life, which included processing payroll and washing towels?

When she'd finished, she logged out, scanned her gym one last time, and left quickly, the door thudding behind her. She headed back to Melina's house to study and prepare for her last night's sleep before they exorcised a demon.

The next morning, Melina and Siobhan made bacon and eggs together, vowing to stay hydrated and calm before the exorcism. The priest had called once, already verifying that they would both be there on time.

The day flew by in a blur of preparations. Siobhan's body jolted often at the unknown while Melina stayed steady and calm.

The apprehension rolling through Siobhan's mind related to all the possibilities, even the ones she couldn't describe. She had no idea what the priest would read from his book or what he would say. She had no idea what the demon would say and how it would insult or try to offend and confuse her.

Siobhan steeled her resolve as she let Melina drive her to her house. They arrived at eight o'clock so they could get ready with the priest and Dr. Hill. They had things to do before the exorcism began, and they had agreed to let the priest bless them all before it began.

Melina pulled her red Ford Explorer into Siobhan's driveway and parked in the Jeep's spot. She switched the key off, and the hum of the engine silenced.

The black, smoky haze covering the front of the house in a colorless smear over the upstairs window loitered. The shadow figure with glowing orange eyes probed at Siobhan and Melina as they gathered the books from the backseat and cradled them against their bodies.

"You ready?" Melina asked.

Siobhan shook her head. "I am. You?" Siobhan replied. They looked at each other for a moment, Melina's brown eyes locked on Siobhan's icy blue gaze.

Melina nodded slowly. "Let's reduce this son of a bitch to ash."

"That's more than it deserves," Siobhan said.

"They are here, worm," the demon said as it poked one of its claws into Adam's liver. The pain radiated into his chest under the three deep gouges. "I am Hell...." The demon trailed off, his words mingling with the all too familiar clicking sound that had become an announcement of its manifestation.

Adam's body jerked with extreme pain, and he attempted to hold off cringing as long as he could. But the demon had been consistently upping the ante and causing brutal and agonizing fits of torture to try to push him out. If Adam left his body, the demon would be strong enough to keep him out, and the battle would be lost.

Adam's consciousness now centered in the middle of his chest, which made it difficult to see and hear. But when the demon wanted to hear, it cranked the dial, and it heard.

In a much more susceptible spot, Adam found the dull and consistent pain the demon inflicted increasingly taxing. But he stayed, being closer to where he needed to be. He had to trust Siobhan and wait for the priest.

The demon's ears perked up to listen as Siobhan and Melina talked outside. Adam would have smiled if he could have because he knew she had shown up. As his body lay twisted in the corner of the bedroom, his thoughts drifted to how much he needed her. Beaten and broken, his very soul had been smashed against the rocks of despotism and washed with the salty waters of hell itself.

The demon had ripped the mattress on one side and flung it against the far wall of the room in a fit of rage several hours ago. Thanks to the entity's claws, the carpet had been shredded in several places, but it had not tried to leave the bedroom.

Adam had survived by eating the wriggling red worms crawling out of the walls and carpet. He refrained from engaging with the demon. He weakened and the demon felt it; but he couldn't let it know that his idea might not work.

CHAPTER 28

As Siobhan opened the front door of her house, an eerily familiar pungent odor of diabolical resentment coupled with the blast of icy air smacked her in the nose. The heavy and oppressive energy pushed hard against Melina and Siobhan as they made their way into the house.

A smell of dust, death, and something rotten wafted into their nostrils and tingled the back of their throats. The stench was so potent that it traveled down into their stomachs and forced them to taste it. It hung all around.

Melina set her books down on the coffee table, then rifled through the stack to find the one she wanted: *Demonology and Exorcism Success*. The book explained the importance of expelling the demon using its name, the real name that Lucifer himself gave it.

Click click click click click click
Click click click click click click

Siobhan steeled herself against the sound, trying to ignore it but to no avail. It morphed around her body into terrifying loops of negative energy she couldn't escape from.

"At least we'll know next time," Siobhan said, nodding and referencing the horrific clicking.

Melina nodded, looking around. "I hate that it's

everywhere, and we can't find it because it's also nowhere. I hate that it's touching my skin, even though it isn't there," she said.

"Yeah. I know. And it'll get worse," Siobhan said, looking at her drab and putrid house. Bathed in a dull, monochromatic gray color reminiscent of her dreams, her home looked devoid of any light. The black-and-white painting she'd stepped into materialized as a sinister tapestry. The artist had chosen to forego white for black. There were shades of black and another darker black that made her house look like it belonged to a nightmare. Even in the light gray, the darkness stung her as palpable.

The priest arrived with Dr. Hill, and they all sat together in the living room, discussing the steps they'd need to take to perform the exorcism successfully. Adam would need to be tied to the bed, which should not be a problem if they could get him while the demon stayed latent.

Father Renaldo explained the first step of the exorcism, and they headed toward the bedroom. Adam remained silent as they plodded upward.

The sound of the consistent clicking of scratchy claws on concrete in the thick-as-molasses air held them hostage as they trekked forward.

All four made their way to the bedroom, and the priest slowly cracked open the door. He looked at the bed, or where it should have been. The frame stood firm, but it had been pulled two feet away from the wall on one side and pushed into the smashed drywall on the other. The yellow ropes were still attached at all four corners.

The priest pushed the door open all the way to see Adam twisted in the corner, eyes open and all white, looking straight ahead. Adam moved his mouth as if he whispered words, but no sounds were made. The mattress had been flung against the far wall, cutting off the closet and bathroom entry. It had three long cuts right across the middle at an angle.

"You both get the mattress," the priest said to Siobhan and Melina, pointing to it. "Doctor, help me with Adam."

Melina and Siobhan worked to return the mattress to the bed frame and put it slashed side down.

Father Renaldo and Dr. Hill slowly pulled Adam to his feet and struggled under his dead weight. They were able to drag his body to the bed and drop him on it. Melina and Siobhan helped roll him over and adjust him. Then, they each took a corner and tied Adam to the bed with the rope. The yellow clashed harshly against the darkness of the room.

Other than the bloody crimson cross carved deep into Adam's arm, no other perceptible colors surfaced.

The pungent odor once again hit her like a slap in the face as it radiated off everything, including itself. Steeped with a sour stench, the air swirled around her, sickening her stomach. The scent of decaying flesh and bone flowed in all crevices of the house.

Adam hadn't showered in a long time, and his dirty human body odor mixed with the putrid stench created a fetid headache-inducing odor so vile that Siobhan retched.

Brown stains speckled the carpet, and the slashes ran in groups of three in several areas. Sharp implements had shredded it in several places, making gouges so deep that they sunk into the base floor below. They were very similar to the deep cuts on Adam's chest.

"Now we prepare ourselves," the priest said as they filed out of the room. Back downstairs, Father Renaldo opened his briefcase, took out the rosary, and handed it to Melina. He gave Siobhan two crucifixes and two candles. He took his book out and set it on the coffee table, noticing for the first time the dark oil-like stain spewed in splatters on the front of the couch.

Dr. Hill shifted her papers, put her stethoscope around her neck, and checked in her bag for first aid supplies and her blood pressure cuff. She tested her watch to make sure it would work correctly.

The priest handed Melina a box of matches. She shifted the book in her hands to accept them. He worked quietly, but the blood rushing in Siobhan's ears killed the silence

Father Renaldo grabbed the purple stole from his briefcase.

He held up the scarf-like item in both hands as if offering it to someone and closed his eyes. He silently mouthed a prayer, kissed the stole, and then put it around his neck to hang down in two long strips on each side of his chest. He stood and said: "Please, come closer."

Click click click

Click click click click click click

The vibrating and slow staccato pierced the quiet and evolved into a clunk rather than a click, drowning them in its density. Siobhan tried to follow the sound with her eyes as if she could pinpoint where it came from for the first time.

The priest raised his arms above his head. He made the sign of the cross, then with outstretched hands, said: "Father, protect these servants of yours as they battle the evil that lives here today. Help guide us as we free your child Adam from the bonds of oppression and return Satan's minion to hell."

The clicking got louder and started to come much faster. The priest raised his voice to continue his prayer over the increasing volume. "In the name of your son, Jesus Christ, as we rely on your holy authority, cover us in your protection as we undertake this task of expelling a diabolical infestation. In Jesus' name, we pray. Amen," he said, raising his voice.

"Amen," said Dr. Hill as she and the priest made the sign of the cross. Siobhan glanced around the room, her eyes darting from one wall to the next, unable to find the epicenter of the intensifying clicking sound that created visible waves in vibrational patterns around the living room.

A blackness that had little to do with night had descended over the house, and a haze of hatred filled the atmosphere, sinking it into a colorless realm of desolation.

"And now, we start," the priest said. Melina and Siobhan shared a terrified look, and every hair on Siobhan's body stood at attention as her skin crawled.

Father Peter Paul Renaldo began the second exorcism of Adam Keller right after nine o'clock on Friday, July 23rd.

Siobhan entered the bedroom second, following the priest. Melina trailed Siobhan, setting the candles down on the table. She lit them as Siobhan laid a crucifix down between the wax pillars, which were casting an orange glow in the dank room. The light from a lamppost outside created a mild glow as its light fell through a blackened fog into the window.

Dr. Hill took Adam's blood pressure as he lay on the bare mattress, still moving his mouth but not saying anything. She took his pulse, made a note on a page of paper, and nodded to the priest before stepping back into the shadows to remain out of the way. She took a small video camera out of her lab coat and pushed record.

Melina clutched her book to her chest and shivered visibly as she tangled the rosary around her fingers.

Siobhan gripped the crucifix tightly. The same level of discomfort she felt the first time she'd laid eyes on one came rushing back. Her blood pulsated in her temples, and her neck heated against the sting of the icy air.

Father Renaldo set his aspergillum down and opened his rite of exorcism book, the gold cross flinging a scattered glint of hope into the heavy atmosphere.

He lifted the end of his stole and placed it on Adam's head. Adam's body jerked, and he hissed like a snake at the priest. Father Renaldo remained steadfast and started reading the rite.

His voice rang out over the consistent thrashing and hissing as the snake-like tongue came out to whip the priest in the face. A red welt appeared across his left cheek, and without wincing, he continued reading.

Siobhan and Melina remained perfectly still. Petrified, they stared as the demon surfaced. It started to speak, using its voice instead of Adam's. It made unintelligible sounds that were not actual words but which nevertheless felt like they were mocking those in the room.

The priest removed the stole, and a red hot patch burned in its place on Adam's forehead. Sounds came out of his mouth as several blisters snapped and popped on his neck.

The growling laughter started low, then curled around the room, threatening to suffocate anything living.

"Ten and one and one and ten and ten and one and one and ten," Adam repeated over and over again, drowning out the priest's voice. His chapped lips never rested; they were always moving.

The priest again increased his volume and read the rite louder, trying to speak over and cover the demonic. He lifted one hand, palm toward Adam, and read in the limited light coming from the lamppost outside the window behind him. He took a small step backward so he could see better, but the demon took it as a retreat.

Adam jerked against the ropes holding him down. "I will win, and you will lose, priest," a voice hissed as the clicking sped up. It came so fast now it slurred into a dull hum.

"You cannot confuse a servant of the Lord, vile serpent," the priest said as he picked up his aspergillum and flung holy water at Adam. He recoiled and hissed violently as the water contacted his bruised and scratched face.

A tear slid down Siobhan's cheek, and she reached over to put an arm around Melina. The two steadied each other. Adam's body lay mangled, in much worse shape than the last time Siobhan had seen him. His festering wounds were leaking liquid, pus, and blood and smelled of decaying flesh. His arm lit up like a bonfire from within, illuminating his flesh's deeply etched upside-down cross.

The priest took several steps toward Adam. He stood close enough to touch him. He sent holy water flying toward Adam once again, and the drops smacked Adam in the face as he snapped his head to the side and grimaced in pain. An animalistic growl came from low in his chest. The deep scratches were heaving with his breath.

A stench so vile that it burned Siobhan's eyes lingered in the room, permeating everything.

A sinister laughter arose as Adam sneered at Father Renaldo, curling his heavily chapped and bleeding lips into that too–large-to-be-human smile. Steam bubbled up from his skin in every spot where a drop of holy water had landed as it stretched across the bones of his skull.

Green foam frothed at the corner of Adam's mouth. He grinned and, using his tongue, licked some of it off before it cascaded down the front of his shirt and rolled onto the destroyed mattress.

Adam let out a hiss and lunged at the priest. The ropes held him back as he strained against them, pulling on his wrists. He cocked his head to the side as the priest continued to recite the prayers.

"You know…" Adam said, twisting his head on his neck.

"You're not stopping me, liar," the demon said. "Lies, lies, lies, and whores. Priests are liars and whores," it continued as it mocked and taunted, singing the line. "Siobhan is a whore. Melina too. I remember. The little whore is too weak to help her brother. What a JOKE!" Adam yelled and spat at Melina. A spray of green foam landed on the ripped carpet in front of her feet. She flinched.

"And you," the demon said, its eyes going white as it looked at Siobhan and grinned. "Never good enough. You never will be. You'll always be at the mercy of others like a little slave. La la la… going about doing what others want. What a weak little cunt."

Although its words stung, Siobhan stood firm, fighting the urge to run.

Adam tried to fight through the exhaustion and pain. He had a migraine, and his eyes were becoming inflamed. He caught a glimpse of Siobhan through the sinister haze of the demon as it mocked her. She held a crucifix and sobbed, but she did so quietly and without changing her facial expression. She shook so violently that she struggled to hold onto the crucifix with one hand as she clutched Melina with the other.

Siobhan dipped her head as Melina pushed away long enough to put the rosary around Siobhan's neck for extra protection. The rosary and crucifix were on fire from the perspective Adam looked through.

He glanced at Siobhan one last time and jumped, putting his plan into motion. He had to try at least to weaken the demon from the inside. Siobhan's strength showed more than he'd ever seen, and he had to do the same for her. Her necklace glowed and cast an orange hue in the darkness of the room. He wouldn't be able to see her for much longer.

"He's not coming back, bitch. He's mineeee!" a low, deep, growling voice said as it came from Adam's mouth. He threw his head back to carry out the last syllable. Siobhan narrowed her eyes and sealed herself in a box of steadfast determination.

Adam mustered up the remainder of his energy in advance of trying to travel toward his cut arm. He loathed that mark, but as the source of the demon's power, he needed to get inside it and stir the crux of what kept the demon glued to him.

The priest raised his black leather book in his hands and resumed reading.

Melina made her way to Adam's left side as he thrashed about on the bed. He pulled so hard on the ropes that they were cutting into his skin, and he had started to bleed.

"God the Father commands you," the priest said, resting his thumb on Adam's forehead and making the sign of the cross with it. Melina held Adam down by his upper arm on the other side of the bed.

"Siobhan!" she said. "I need your help."

Adam sat up and down repeatedly and violently flung himself from side to side. Siobhan made her way to Melina's side and set down the crucifix. She held Adam's arm below where Melina gripped his upper bicep tightly, trying to avoid his mark.

"Vile cum filled cunts," a voice boomed. It wasn't masculine or feminine and it wasn't human. Siobhan tightened her grip on Adam's arm. He opened his mouth, and a green gas that smelled of vomit and anemic blood flew out into their faces. Siobhan turned her face away but kept the pressure on Adam's arm.

"You are losing your husband today. He's a piece of shit anyway. My little wormmmm…" the voice said in utter evil as the whipping tongue wagged toward Siobhan.

The word *worm* ran into an atrocious laughing roar that came from everywhere and nowhere at the same time. A stab of pain shot from inside Adam's head and dug its way outward into his eardrums. But the priest continued, his wrinkled face and crystal-clear gray eyes filled with determination as evil reverberated all around him.

The demon stayed busy taunting Siobhan and mocking the priest. Adam took advantage of that, hoping it wouldn't notice him. He stole one last glance at his wife, then made his way through the pain and wedged his consciousness into the gaping wound on his left arm, allowing his life force to fill it. The demon held on to Adam, but the priest now had its full attention.

"God the Son commands you," Father Renaldo said, making another cross on Adam's forehead, still reading from the book he held in his left hand.

"God the Father, God the Son, God the this and that and this and that. Spit and shit and disease God the Father, God the Son, and the priest and his shit-filled pants," Adam said in the same sing-song voice that shot shivers of ice down spines. Adam sent a hiss toward the ceiling as the bed started to vibrate and lift off the floor.

"God the Holy Spirit commands you!" the priest said, making another sign of the cross on Adam's forehead. The bed slammed down, and Melina and Siobhan let go of Adam during the impact. They grabbed Adam once more, and the demon focused its attention on Siobhan. Adam's head twisted on his neck to look her right in the eyes. The crucifix lifted off the floor next to Siobhan, but she couldn't reach it in time.

"Look out!" Siobhan yelled as the demon sent it flying toward the priest like a spear. Father Renaldo ducked in time, but the edge of the cross caught his left cheek, leaving a cut next to the welt that had bubbled up on his face from the forked tongue lashing he'd already sustained.

"Had enough yet, priest?" Adam's mouth said as the inhuman smile opened from ear to ear. Blackness filled the space between the chapped lips. "Time to payyyy!"

It let out a roar as it sent a blast of energy toward Father Renaldo. The priest lifted off the ground and flew into the wall by Dr. Hill. A loud crack boomed throughout the room as he slammed into the wall behind him, then slid down it, collapsing to the floor. Chunks of chalky drywall fell on top of him.

It was impossible to know if the crack had been the wall or the priest's bones. Amanda reached down to help him.

"Are you okay, Father?" she asked quietly, concern etched across her face. He stood slowly, nodding through the agony that shot through his right hip. He grimaced and grabbed his midsection momentarily as he leaned on Amanda for support. On his way up, he grabbed the crucifix off the floor and lifted it over his head, standing with weight on his right side.

"You're weak, priest. Old washed-up pig. Piss and shit and blood and shit and cum filled shit…" the demon said, singing in a childlike voice of disgusting convoluted hysterics.

But Father Renaldo swayed, his eyes glassed over. He had to work through the agony that spread through his body. He made careful movements and tried to shake off the pain in his hip. He limped and staggered, but Amanda caught him and held onto him, keeping him upright.

With a small drop of blood hanging on to the fresh cut on his cheek, he raised the crucifix higher.

"You let Rosemary die," Adam said, as the demon mentally struck at the heart of the priest's mistake. His hip throbbed with pain, but his heart hurt worse as he once again registered the sting of her loss. "My grandmother," the demon said in Adam's fourteen-year-old voice. It rolled its words into the horrible clicking that started to send a violent throbbing stab into the priest's side, radiating through his pelvis.

"She could have lived," the demon snarled, trying to instigate a reaction from the priest. Rosemary's voice pierced through the demon's raucous clicking. It's your fault, Father," she said, her voice generated by the demon. Father Renaldo braced himself, pushing off Amanda. She backed into the shadows and checked the video camera.

Father Renaldo knew who spoke, and yet the twinge of emotional pain still registered in his chest. As the demon pretended to be Rosemary mocked in full force, the priest struck a massive blow.

"Tell me what to call you, evil serpent!" the priest yelled over the voice and its raspy breathing that mingled with the clicking, causing a deafening roar that came from hell itself.

The demon clicked its tongue and ran it over Adam's chin.

"I am the alchemist!" Adam shouted in an animalist growl,

then spat in the priest's face. Adam smiled and pulled the skin up on the sides of his nose as the grin opened from ear to ear showing his teeth, with green foam and dead bugs wedged between each one. One side of his mouth curled up past his ear in a crooked, demonic twist.

The priest looked at Melina as the green-tinted saliva traveled down his silver beard. Some of the pain abated as the priest smiled and nodded.

Melina's eyes shot up, and she made eye contact with the injured priest. He heavily favored his right side. Steadfast gray eyes locked with brown ones in a deep understanding. Father Renaldo nodded at her again, smiling through the pain.

"I'll find it," she said, letting go of Adam to pick up her book, which she'd set on the floor.

"Hold him!" Melina said to Siobhan.

Adam pushed himself harder against the wound on his arm, embedding himself in the mark, taking as much of the demon's power as he could. He couldn't hear the priest any more. He had drifted so far from his own ears. The demon's control loosened. He had to somehow muster more strength through the agonizing whipping he took at the hands of the sinister entity. Adam tensed up and stayed put, taking the lashes. Each one lit him up in a painful blow. He knew he couldn't take very many more strikes and he hoped he could hold out.

The priest grinned as he looked at Adam. Keeping his eyes trained on Adam, he handed the crucifix back to Siobhan over the bed, falling forward in progress.

Adam's face followed the transfer, then snapped back to the priest.

"Smile away, but he's dying in here," the voice said as Adam's body thrashed. A cross-shaped cut on his arm started oozing black blood, staining the bare mattress beneath him.

Melina had crouched down and voraciously flipped through the aged pages of her book. She stopped for a moment when she knew she'd found it. "Berith!" she yelled, pointing at her book but not showing the pages to anyone. Siobhan looked down and saw the words "Berith, the Alchemist" scrawled across the top of the page.

Adam's head snapped to Melina. He slowly pulled against the ropes that were tethering him to the bed. "Cuuuuuunt!" the demon screamed at Melina with enough force to blow her black hair behind her.

Siobhan's tear-stained face recoiled; her eyes were filled with complete fear and ultimate strength. Her hair fell out of the bun she had it in, and she had a smear of blood on her shirt that had come from his mark as she strained to hold him down.

"Leave this servant of God, Berith! Comply with the commands of the most high Jesus Christ! Berith, be gone!" the priest yelled. He nodded to Siobhan. She lifted the crucifix and pressed it to Adam's chest over the three deep scratches. Adam's skin hissed on contact as the crucifix burned through his flesh all the way to the bone.

He arched up on the bed, screaming with a mix of humanity and demonic agony. His scream lasted for over a minute, but it slowly became more human and less evil and animalistic. Smoke billowed up where the crucifix had contacted his chest. He flopped down on the bed, and his head lulled to the side. He had fallen asleep.

Siobhan stayed still holding the crucifix to Adam's chest even though it burned his cut up flesh.

The lashing stopped. The pain subsided. Adam forced his way toward his own brain once again and settled his consciousness in its rightful place where the demon Berith had previously presided. He had space, and he had peace.

His body lay still, beaten and sore, but it had left the grip of the spiritual pain that melded with the physical pain of the possession. He looked around inside himself for any lingering evil and couldn't find any. The pressure of having two consciousnesses in the same body had alleviated. His eyes were closed, the exhaustion too much for him to open them. He fell asleep, hoping Siobhan would be the first thing he saw when he awoke.

Dr. Hill made her way out of the dark corner, a look of terror plastered across her face. She remained quiet as she waved Siobhan and the crucifix away. She took Adam's vitals and looked at Siobhan, smiling. "The instruments are working," Amanda said.

Siobhan held the crucifix tightly in both hands, afraid to let it go. She stared at Adam's welted and bleeding body.

"Normal. He's back," Amanda said to Siobhan. She smiled at the priest. Father Renaldo had crumpled to the floor and lay on his side, grimacing in pain. "You did it, Father," she said as she knelt to offer him medical assistance.

Siobhan dropped the crucifix and fell to her knees by the bed. She aggressively grabbed Melina and hugged her tightly. They cradled each other. The tiger's eye crystal warmed on their skin as it pressed against them. Its warmth diminished. Siobhan pushed away from Melina to look at it. Its glow decreased, and she knew this would be the last time she'd see the necklace light her face from underneath.

No one heard it, but everyone knew Rosemary had spoken the unspoken into the room from beyond the grave as the crystal's final light flickered out. A simple necklace devoid of life remained.

The two candles in the corner were still casting their dancing light on the scene, but the air in the room had cleared. The gray and smokey haze that had covered everything had dispersed. It all looked normal—destroyed, but normal.

Melina flipped on the light in the bedroom and sat by the priest, who Amanda had helped lean against the same wall the demon had flung him into.

"He's going to need to sleep," Amanda said, nodding toward Adam. "I'll bandage up all of his wounds. Some of these are going to scar, though." She nodded toward Father Renaldo. "We need to get him to the ER as soon as possible. I'm pretty sure he broke something," she said.

"Help Adam first," Father Renaldo said, wincing. The priest had aged, and dark circles had formed under his wrinkled eyes.

Siobhan stood to get a better look at Adam.

His face held a dozen cuts and even more welts and his lips were still chapped and bleeding. But he finally looked like himself, like the man she'd married and not the twisted distortion he'd become. She lifted his marked arm. On it, a simple scratch which had scabbed over and looked relatively insignificant.

She ripped his t-shirt away from his chest to reveal the three long gouges still seeping with blood. Those were brutal and needed attention.

"Will these need stitches, Doctor... I mean, Amanda," Siobhan asked. She put on rubber gloves but looked over.

Amanda nodded. "Yeah. I'll check them out, but his arm was my biggest concern," she said.

"It's a scratch," Siobhan said, lifting his arm to show the doctor.

CHAPTER 29

After they cleaned what they could in the room, Amanda started to stitch up and bandage Adam's wounds. Siobhan had helped untie him while Melina offered water and emotional support to Father Renaldo.

Before leaving her bedroom, Siobhan put three blankets on Adam and followed Melina and Amanda as they helped the priest down the stairs. His hip had been seriously injured during the exorcism.

While the exorcism had succeeded, the priest and Adam both paid a heavy price. Adam would be riddled with permanent scars from the demon's claws, and the priest's injuries would take months to heal.

The remnants of demonic possession lingered in the living room—the dark stain on the front of the couch where Adam had spewed black vomit after the infestation took hold, and the splatters of blood that riddled the carpet where his ears had bled. But it was the bedroom upstairs that bore the worst of the destruction.

"I need to take him to the hospital," Amanda said, nodding to the priest. "Call me if you need anything. I will come back, or I can bring my husband with me. He's an ER doctor if anything gets serious. I'm glad this all worked." Amanda gently raised Father

Renaldo's arm over her shoulder.

"I will be okay," Father Renaldo said. "If I'm not, it'll be okay. I fear it is worse than a broken hip." He seemed to have aged ten years since he'd arrived at the house earlier. "I'll leave you two to do… whatever it is that you're called to do," he said to Melina and Siobhan. He made the sign of the cross as a blessing and let Amanda carry him out and to the emergency room.

"Wait, are you saying…?" Siobhan started.

"I don't know, my dear," Father Renaldo said. "I will have Amanda call you when we know. Rest, and help Adam heal."

Amanda helped the priest out of the house. "I'll call you," she said, to which Siobhan replied with a nod.

At just before six in the morning, Siobhan flopped onto the couch, and Melina sat next to her.

"It's just us," said Siobhan.

Melina nodded.

"Wanna stay? We could sleep on the couch. I'm exhausted," Siobhan said.

"I would love to. I should go home and feed Scamper, though," Melina said, standing. "That took all night. If you need anything, call me, sister." She reached her arms out.

The women hugged, and Siobhan whispered, "Thank you," into Melina's hair before she left. Siobhan grabbed a blanket and fell asleep on her couch.

Adam rolled over. He looked around through his own eyes.

Dear God. She did it.

He pushed himself up on the bed. There were no sheets on the stained and stench-filled mattress he laid on. He wrinkled his nose, noticing the horrific smell for the first time.

The carpet had been shredded, and pieces of drywall were missing and hanging in spots. He winced in pain.

His chest burned, and he looked down to see three long gashes running from his chest plate to his navel. They had been bleeding at one time but were now scabbed, stitched, and healing.

His head snapped. He remembered. He remembered it all. The demon. He remembered the mark. The black cloud forced its way into his body, pushing his own consciousness aside. The torture. And the exorcism.

Adam lifted his left arm to look at the mark. It amounted to nothing more than a scabbed-over scratch, mild and insignificant.

He stood and stretched as his mind drifted to Siobhan. He wanted to see her, but the smell coming off him stopped him from going downstairs. Instead, he jumped in the shower to wash off the remnants of evil and bodily fluids that still clung to the outside of his heavily taxed body.

Siobhan heard the shower start and woke up.

ADAM!

She tossed the blanket off and ran upstairs, flinging open the door to their bedroom. She sat at the end of their destroyed and smelly mattress, looking around at the room that they had no choice but to remodel now.

For the first time, she could rely on herself and not need Adam's advice. She could finally handle this and whatever else came her way.

The shower turned off, and Adam moved around in the bathroom, creating shadows that played in the light under the door. He took extra time brushing his teeth, and she started to get impatient while waiting for him.

He opened the bathroom door, and they locked eyes. Both stayed frozen in time for a few moments. Siobhan smiled wide and slowly stood. Adam's wet hair cascaded around his bruised face in black waves. He had a towel wrapped around his waist, exposing the three long gashes on his chest.

"Siobhan," he started. "Listen, I'm so sorry, I didn't…" She strode over to him and pressed onto her toes to kiss him, silencing the words. He kissed her back, his hands moving up and down her spine.

She pulled away and grabbed his hand, leading him to the shredded mattress that used to be their bed. Smiling, she said,

"Welcome back, stranger." He leaned his forehead against hers. His wet hair tickled the skin near her temples. Adam smelt of general cleanliness and the mint of the toothpaste, but the odor of what had happened last night still clung to the air.

The deep scratches on Adam's chest were swollen and raw. Amanda had said that they would likely scar badly, leaving that reminder of the demon's wrath. He would have to wear those marks forever as a memento from Hell for the pain he'd gone through.

"Thanks to you," he said. She wanted to give all the credit to Melina, the priest, and even Dr. Hill. But she had blossomed into a strong and independent person, capable of fighting the forces of Hell. She faced her discomfort with the crucifixes and even used one to force an evil entity to evacuate its residence. And she did it all without needing reassurance or approval from her husband.

"I had to. I was so used to doing what was expected and deferring to others, especially you when I needed advice or help. When I didn't have you," she said, looking at her hands. She put them in his, then looked into his deep brown eyes, the eyes she married. She let out a breath and continued. "I figured out I needed to trust myself and be strong so that I could get you back. I'm sorry for what I did." She put her hand over the cross-shaped welt on his chest. It had been embossed right over the three long gashes, but it would heal.

"I'm proud of you. I've always been proud of you. And I love you more now than I ever have," Adam told her. "You were the reason I even wanted to fight the torture I was going through."

She winced. "Torture. It sounds so... harsh," she said. He nodded.

"It wasn't pleasant. But I remember it, and I don't think I would remember if you hadn't been here. I would have suppressed it like it did before," he said with a dry voice through his chapped lips.

"Why don't we get some food? It's been a long time since you've eaten."

"Unless you count bugs and birds."

. Siobhan cringed.

"Too soon?" he asked.

She shook her head and offered a slight smile. "You're still funny. I like it," she said, heading toward the door.

CHAPTER 30

The Night of the Exorcism of Adam Keller

"You can't set that up like that, you imbecile," the priestess yelled. "If you botch that Pentagram, I'll slit your throat from ear to ear," she added. She considered slicing him up anyway to disable Taylor's incompetence permanently.

"Sorry, priestess," he said nervously as he shifted his cloak and knelt to realign the Pentagram's southern point.

Taylor shuffled around the Pentagram, attempting to smooth the lines as much as he could.

The priestess lifted the sleeves of her robe to look at her watch. It was already past eleven, and the Blood Pope hadn't arrived yet. She started to worry that he had gotten caught up with other affairs on his way. He said he'd be traveling across the state so he could make it to the ritual.

"And work faster. There's an exorcism tonight," she said as she lowered the hood of her cloak to cover more of her face.

None of these little Satanic minions knew her identity, and she liked it that way. It made the blood rituals easier to do. Offerings to Lucifer had to be done precisely right, and she wasn't in the mood for any errors.

Her connections made her privy to information that most of the other Satanists were unaware of, and once the Blood Pope arrived, she would be ready.

However, she also had to be the most discreet. Flinging her billowing black cloak around her ankles, she stared at the clear night sky. Lifting the red satin-lined hood, she glanced at the stars. Closing her eyes, she mouthed a prayer.

Lucifer, Lord of Light and generator of evil, please find it within your authority to send any released demons to me to aid me in my quest to serve you in all that I do.

She put her hand in her pocket and fingered the switchblade's cold steel as it pressed against her palm. She smiled. *I will be successful tonight.* She glared at Taylor.

Everything had to be perfect.

"Well, look at you," the deep voice behind her said.

The priestess spun around and came face to face with the Blood Pope. A sinister smile pulled her lips up as she tipped her head and kissed his forehead.

Now, everything would be as it should.

THE END

To be continued in POSSESSED: Blood Sacrifice Book II
The Priest's Amethyst

www.ingramcontent.com/pod-product-compliance
Lightning Source LLC
Chambersburg PA
CBHW071247250626
47163CB00002B/360